Anne Allen lives daughter and meant a number of moves, the longest stay being in Guernsey for fourteen years after falling in love with the island and the people. She contrived to leave one son behind to ensure a valid reason for frequent returns. Another son is based in London, ideal for her city breaks. A retired psychotherapist, Anne has now published six novels. Find her website at www.anneallen.co.uk

Praise for Anne Allen

Dangerous Waters - 'A wonderfully crafted story with a perfect balance of intrigue and romance.' *The Wishing Shelf Awards, 22 July 2013 – Dangerous Waters*

Finding Mother - 'A sensitive, heart-felt novel about family relationships, identity, adoption, second chances at love… With romance, weddings, boat trips, lovely gardens and more, Finding Mother is a dazzle of a book, a perfect holiday read.' *Lindsay Townsend, author of The Snow Bride*

Guernsey Retreat- 'I enjoyed the descriptive tour while following the lives of strangers as their worlds collide, when the discovery of a body and the death of a relative draw them into links with the past. A most pleasurable, intriguing read.' *Glynis Smy, author of Maggie's Child.*

The Family Divided -'A poignant and heart-warming love story.' *Gilli Allan, author of Fly or Fall*

Echoes of Time - 'Not only is the plot packed full of twists and turns, but the setting – and the characters – are lovingly described.' *Wishing Shelf Review*

The Betrayal – 'All in all, totally unputdownable!' *thewsa.co.uk*

Anne Allen

The Betrayal

The Guernsey Novels – Book 6

Sarnia Press
London

Sarnia Press
London

A CIP catalogue record for this book is available
From the British Library
ISBN 978 0 992711252

Typeset by Sarnia Press
This book is a work of fiction. Names, characters,
businesses, organisations, places and events are
either the product of the author's imagination
or are used fictitiously. Any resemblance to
actual persons, living or dead, events or
locales is entirely coincidental

To my mother, Janet Williams, with love

"To me, the thing that is worse than death is betrayal. You see, I could conceive death, but I could not conceive betrayal."

Malcolm X

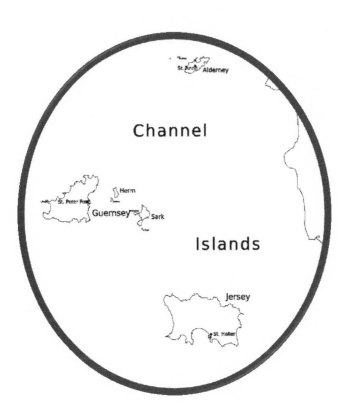

Chapter 1

Guernsey – June 1940

'I won't go! I won't!'

Tears streamed down Teresa's face as she sat slumped in a chair, her hands twisted together, as if in supplication. His heart lurched, hating to see her like this. Before he could say anything she went on, 'I can't leave you here on your own, Leo. Anything might happen to you if...if the Germans do come.'

He fought to stay calm, not wanting his beloved wife to see how much it hurt him to let her go. But what choice did he have?

'Darling, it's precisely *because* the Germans are more or less expected to invade us, that you and the baby must go. I need to know you're safe, and you will be with your parents in Suffolk. With a bit of luck, it won't be for long, and we'll all be together again.' Leo bit his lip. The omens were not good for a swift end to hostilities, in spite of the early optimism displayed by the British politicians. And the news from the mainland received that morning, that Guernsey was to be demilitarised, meant all the islands were vulnerable to attack and invasion. The Germans were edging closer now, at Cherbourg...

'But why don't you come with us? You could leave Ernest in charge of the business and surely someone would keep a watch on the house?' She raised her head, a sudden flicker of hope in her eyes.

He shook his head.

'I can't risk us losing everything. How would we live if that happened? There's no opportunity to send the most valuable items to England and,' he shrugged, 'it doesn't seem right to run away and leave other men to defend my birthright. I may be too old to go and fight, but at least I might be of some use here. Guernsey is my home. It's in my blood, just as England is in yours.'

Leo pulled Teresa to her feet and held her tightly, letting her sob on his shoulder. His shirt was soon soaked, and he had a lump in his throat as he soothed her. After a few moments, he pushed her gently away. Red blotches marred his wife's lovely cream complexion, and her eyes were swollen. He couldn't remember ever seeing her cry like this.

Handing her his handkerchief, Leo smoothed her thick, wavy hair off her face and kissed her forehead. She sniffed, and her shoulders sagged. Defeated.

'When...when does the evacuation start?'

He sucked in his breath. It was all too soon.

'Tomorrow.' Her eyes widened in horror, and he hastened to add, 'But that's when the ship arrives for the schoolchildren and teachers. Other ships will carry on departing until Saturday for anyone else, including mothers with babies and toddlers. I will arrange for you and Judith to be on one of them. You'll only be able to take one case–'

Teresa pulled away and began pacing around the sitting room, touching the backs of chairs and stroking the bureau, her face turned away from him. He'd failed her, should have made better provision for her and their child. Leo thrust his hands in his pockets, cursing himself for leaving it so late. Once the Germans had invaded France, the Channel Islands looked vulnerable, lying as they did a few miles off the French coast. He should have shipped their valuables over to England as a precaution, only following themselves if it became necessary.

A cry from upstairs made Teresa stop, and she gazed upwards as if waiting to see if it would be prolonged. It was.

'She's hungry; I'll go and fetch her–'

'Let me go, and you can feed her in the kitchen while I make you a cup of tea.'

Leo caught the look of surprise on Teresa's face before he left. He knew what she was thinking, 'Why's he offering to help when he's never done it before?' As he shot up the stairs, Judith's cries growing more insistent, he was painfully aware of how little he'd been involved with his daughter, leaving her care to Teresa. That was, after all, the role of the mother. But now, the thought of her going to England within the next forty-eight hours and not seeing her for what might be years, made him want to make up for his lack.

Judith, a sturdy nine months old, was gripping the bars of her cot and she opened her mouth to release yet another heart-rending cry when she caught sight of her father and stopped. Leo smiled reassuringly, but she was about to cry out when he reached over and lifted her into his arms, kissing her wet cheek.

'Hush, now, darling, Daddy's taking you to Mummy for your feed. Won't be long.' Her mouth trembled, but she remained quiet as he hugged her close, taking his time on the stairs. Leo drew in the smell of her skin and the soft, fair hair. Like her mother's. He had to push down the thought of saying goodbye to the child he never thought he'd have. A bachelor until his forties, he'd given up hope of being a father. And then Teresa entered his life...

'Here she is, ready for her tea, aren't you, Judith?' He handed the baby to his wife, saying, 'I'll put the kettle on.' Teresa settled Judith in her high chair, ready to spoon the rice into her daughter before she could start crying again.

Leo set the teapot, with matching milk jug and sugar bowl, on the table alongside two cups and saucers. A beautiful French porcelain, the set had been his maternal grandmother's, and a family favourite. He glanced up to find Teresa's gaze on him, her eyes puffy. She inclined her head as if acknowledging what he was about and he relaxed. For the moment they had to behave as if nothing had happened. That the family wasn't about to be torn apart. He forced a smile as he poured the tea, determined to maintain a level of normality for as long as possible, for Judith's sake, at least.

Chapter 2

Guernsey 2011

Something was wrong. The alarm didn't blast out as he pushed open the back door of the shop. Standing still, he heard a noise. Someone was in the shop. Or more accurately, the basement. Nigel paused as he closed the door quietly behind him, his heart hammering against his ribs as he debated what to do. Whoever was in there knew how to disable a burglar alarm otherwise lights would be flashing and a discordant wail would be piercing the air. Best to shut them in the basement and call the police. Following the thought, he crept into the main shop, guided by the dim light coming through the rear window. His eyes adjusting to the dimness, Nigel tried to pick out the area where a rug should cover the trapdoor. For a moment he wondered who could have known about the basement, only discovered a few weeks before when they completed the renovations and replaced the flooring. Odd. And why the basement when the shop was full of valuable antiques?

Crouched at the edge of the hole, light from a torch casting shadows below, he was about to push the open door downwards when a hand snaked up and grabbed his arm. Before he could pull free another hand came up, and he found himself pinned down, struggling to breathe.

'Don't make a sound, or you're a goner,' a voice hissed. 'I've got a knife and I ain't afraid to use it.'

Nigel was in no state to shout, his throat bone dry and the air in his lungs squeezed out of him. Gasping, he found himself dragged back towards to the office. The door was kicked shut behind them, and the light flicked on. For a split second, Nigel caught a glimpse of his attacker. A large, heavy man with a lined face and muscled arms. His heart sank. He couldn't possibly overcome him, not as he was now. A few years ago, yes, but...something was thrown over his head, it felt rough with an oily smell, and he wanted to retch but couldn't, fighting to breathe. He found himself thrust onto a chair and muscles screamed in angry protest as his arms were pulled back behind him. His breath came in short bursts as they were secured with what felt like tape. Tight. Then his feet. He couldn't move. Oh God, what the hell is he going to do to me?

'You must be the owner of this place, yes?' The rough voice had an odd accent, a hint of Guern but something else, too. Nigel strived to recognise it. He hadn't known the face either, so not someone he knew. Strong hands grabbed his head, pulling it back so hard, the pain in his scalp and neck was unbearable. Perspiration trickled into his eyes.

'Answer me! You the owner?'

'Yes,' he whispered, the effort of replying almost too much.

'Right, so where's the painting? The Renoir? The one stored with the others in that basement.'

Nigel's mind reeled. How could he know about the Renoir? They'd only found it after discovering the basement. Was probably there years...

Another rough yanking of his hair made him yelp with pain. Should he tell the truth? Or pretend ignorance? By now every muscle in his body hurt, the pain worse than anything he'd ever endured and his brain was turning to mush. He couldn't cope. The violence had triggered an attack, and he knew, from experience, it would get worse. But he couldn't endanger Fiona.

Sucking in what air he could, Nigel said, 'I don't know anything about a Renoir. Haven't seen it. You must be mistaken–'

'Don't mess with me! I know what was down there. You must have moved it. Tell me, or it'll be the worse for you.'

His assailant's hands moved to his waist and tugged at his belt. The next thing he knew it was round his throat, being pulled tighter and tighter as the man urged him to tell the truth. He struggled to draw breath as the blackness descended.

Chapter 3

Guernsey 2011

Fiona was ecstatic. The tests had proved positive, and it looked as if she and Nigel would be celebrating. Once outside the professor's office, she hit the button on her mobile, tapping her feet as she waited for him to pick up.

'Come on, Nigel. Where are you?' she muttered when the call went to voicemail. Leaving a message for him to get back asap, she clicked off, feeling deflated. Typical, you have something wonderful to tell someone, and they're not there. Glancing at her watch, she saw it was time to head to Gatwick. Damn. If the signal was poor on the train, Nigel might not get through. Trying not to feel too disappointed, she headed for the station, hugging the news to herself as she relived their discovery on that fateful day.

'Hey, let's take a look, shall we?' Nigel said, his eyes bright with excitement as he studied the trapdoor. It had been well hidden, only the faintest of gaps around the floorboards marked it out. 'Give us a moment, would you, mate?' He turned to the builder hovering in the background, who nodded as he moved away, looking as if he'd like to have stayed. Nigel grabbed a torch, its light illuminating wooden steps and a handrail.

'I'll go first.' He went backwards on the steep steps.

Fiona peered down, trying to see what the torch illuminated. It looked deep, certainly more than head height. A musty smell caught her nostrils as dust motes floated upwards.

Nigel reached the bottom and splayed the torch, catching shelves displaying wrapped packages. Her pulse began to race at the thought of treasures they might find.

'Okay, come on. Looks like someone's stored spare stock – which we didn't pay for!' He chuckled.

Fiona joined him, watching as Nigel focussed the torch on the ceiling. A single bulb hung down, and he looked for the switch, finding it situated at the bottom of the steps. By some miracle, it worked, and a dim light offered relief from the darkness.

'Wow! This is some space. Must be nearly the size of the shop floor.' Fiona moved away slightly, and Nigel joined her as she took in the rows of shelving fixed to all the walls. Empty shelves bore marks in the dust where objects had once been stored. Only those nearest the steps were still in use.

'I suppose it made sense to store smaller, more valuable items out of sight before burglar alarms were invented,' Nigel mused. 'But it's odd Mrs Domaille didn't say anything when we bought the business.' He lifted up a rectangular package.

'Perhaps she didn't know. After all, it was her husband's business, and women of her generation probably didn't get involved.' Fiona watched as Nigel started to unwrap layers of oilcloth. 'Judging by their house and the business accounts they didn't need her to work.'

'Mmm.' Nigel unwrapped the last layer, revealing a small painting. 'Interesting. I wonder why this is down here? Looks like a Naftel or possibly a Toplis. I need better light to be sure. But why wasn't it in the shop for sale?' He lifted up another package of a similar size, again wrapped in dusty oilcloth. 'Another local watercolour. Odd.'

Fiona pointed to other packages.

'They seem to be mainly paintings, and you're right, we need better lighting to see them properly. Why don't we wait until the builders have left and take them upstairs to study them more closely? I think we're talking a few thou each if they're Naftel or Toplis, aren't we?'

'For sure. Valuable, but not too valuable to display if you have a decent burglar alarm. Though Ernest's system wasn't as good as ours, he'd have been covered by insurance. All rather odd. Right,' he said, replacing the picture on the shelf, 'let's do as you suggest and bring them up later. Exciting, isn't it?' He rubbed his hands together and grinned.

'It's like Christmas, but instead of a stack of presents at the bottom of the tree, our pressies are left in the basement.' She laughed.

A couple of hours later they carried all the wrapped packages upstairs. There were over a dozen of various sizes. They split the pile between them, carefully peeling off the layers of oilcloth.

'I think these must have been down there donkey's years. The cloth's so old it's become stiff and cracked. More and more mysterious.' Nigel shook his head as he unwrapped yet another local landscape.

'Seems like a private collector's hoard, doesn't it? Perhaps old Ernest bought it, but for some reason didn't sell it on. Wanting to see if the values rose.' Fiona peered at the signature of a painting. A Naftel. She started unwrapping one of the larger paintings, wrapped with even more sheets of oilcloth. As the last cloth fell away, a dazzle of bright colours met her eyes, and she gasped. 'Oh, my God! It can't be. Can it?' She turned to Nigel and saw his eyes widen in shock.

They both stared at the scene of a family group painted against the unmistakable backdrop of Moulin Huet Bay, in Guernsey.

'Well, it might not be genuine, but it certainly looks uncannily like others he painted on the island. Could it be a genuine Renoir?'

'Is it signed?' Fiona asked, her art historian's pulse quickening at the idea of discovering a new Renoir, possibly worth millions.

'Hard to see, it's a bit dark in the corner where he usually signs.' Nigel switched on the desk light and peered closely, Fiona's head touching his.

'Yes! It's signed!' Nigel punched the air, and Fiona squeezed his shoulder as she let out a whoop.

'We'll need to have it authenticated and find out its provenance. But how on earth did it end up here in the basement and who's the owner?' Fiona stood back, torn between professional detachment and the excitement of a potentially rare find.

Nigel pursed his lips. 'Yes, it's pretty odd. Legally, I doubt if we're likely to have a claim. Although there's always finders keepers.' He grinned mischievously.

She laughed. 'Not a hope in hell, brother. But there might be some reward. Anyway, imagine the kudos of finding an unknown Renoir?' Scratching her head, Fiona added, 'The obvious owner would be Ernest Domaille, but wouldn't he have had the painting hung in his home, not buried under layers of dust in the basement? Doesn't make sense. And surely his widow would have known if they owned such a valuable painting?'

'Yep. So perhaps it's not the real McCoy. Pity.' Nigel sighed.

'Hey, don't give up yet. I'll run it past my old professor, Sam. He's an expert on the Impressionist artists, and I'm sure he'd be happy to take a look.'

'Sounds good. In the meantime, we'd better put everything back in the basement. Should be safe enough.'

Ecstasy turned to worry. Fiona heard the answering machine at the house kick in once more and threw the mobile into her bag with an exasperated sigh. She heard the flight called, and she'd be home in less than two hours. Joining the queue, her earlier feelings of jubilation had completely dissipated to be replaced by the overriding fear that something was wrong. More than wrong.

The previous night she had stayed with a friend in London, and they were chatting after supper over a bottle of wine, when Fiona had choked on her drink, unable to swallow. At the time she dismissed it as one of those things, but once in bed, a sense of unease crept over her. Too late to phone, she sent Nigel a text, asking him to phone her in the morning, but he hadn't. She knew he hated her fussing but wished he understood how hard it was for her. The whole reason for her moving to Guernsey with him was to provide much-needed support since his diagnosis. And when he didn't answer her calls, she was bound to be worried. She chewed her lip while waiting to board, wishing he hadn't been too stubborn to let their cleaner stay over.

'For God's sake, Fi, I can manage for one night on my own! I'm not a complete invalid, you know. Or at least, not yet.' His face darkened with anger at the idea, and she backed off.

'Sorry, I...I've been on edge since you ended up in hospital the other month. You gave me such a scare, and you don't seem to be completely well yet.' Fiona squeezed his arm and Nigel's face softened.

'I know, I know. Trouble with us being twins, eh? We're wired to each other.' He patted her hand, saying, 'I'll be okay, not planning on doing very much except a spot of paperwork. Not exactly rushed off my feet in the shop these days.' He grinned. 'Must be the gorgeous weather keeping everyone out of doors. No-one thinks about buying antiques when the beach beckons.'

Nigel's car was in the drive when Fiona arrived home. She hadn't expected anything else on a Sunday, as he usually pottered about at home or went for a brief walk if in the mood. But still, she felt uneasy as she grabbed her overnight bag and headed for the front door.

'Nigel! I'm back. Where are you?'

Silence.

Leaving the bag in the hall, Fiona raced up the stairs, her heart skittering in her chest. Please God, don't let him be unconscious like before...But when she pushed open his bedroom door, the bed was made up, and there was no sign of Nigel. Not sure whether to be relieved or more worried, Fiona searched all the rooms before ending in the empty kitchen. Filling a glass with water, she drank greedily, her throat dry from rising fear. Once more she tried Nigel's mobile, but it went straight to voicemail. Fiona rang the shop, but the answering machine kicked in. She would need to check for herself. Back in the car, she reversed out of the drive into Colborne Road and headed towards La Charotterie and Trinity Square. Lucky to find a parking space, she locked the car and ran the few yards to Contrée Mansell and their shop, 'N & F Antiques'. Casting a quick glance at the bright gold lettering, she noted the shop was in darkness and walked around to the back. Her hands shook, and she dropped the keys. Scrabbling about on the stones to retrieve them, Fiona was glad of the still-present daylight. Gritting her teeth, she unlocked the door and stepped inside the dimly-lit room. As she switched on the light, she saw her brother hanging with a belt from a hook on the door.

Chapter 4

Guernsey 2011

T he shop was filled with police and paramedics, and all Fiona could do was sit huddled in a proffered blanket and watch as if in a trance. Even though she could see his body from where she sat in the main shop her mind wanted to deny it. Surely it was impossible? Someone thrust a glass of water in her hand, and she took a gulp, hoping the image would somehow disappear, a figment of her imagination. But it remained, burned forever in her brain. It was clear nothing could be done for Nigel, his body had felt cold to her touch. Through blurred eyes, she watched as photos were taken and his body carefully removed from the hook and placed on a stretcher, then enshrouded in a black body bag. The memory of his purple lips and bulging eyes made Fiona feel sick, and she rushed to the toilet.

'You all right, Miss Torode?' the inspector called out.

After bringing up her lunch, she managed to croak, 'Yes', before rinsing her mouth and splashing water on her face. Taking a deep breath, Fiona returned to find only the policemen remained. Nigel had been taken to the ambulance. With his body gone, she wondered again if she'd dreamt it. She would wake up, and Nigel would be there, in his battered chair, moaning about the paperwork. But the sight of the policemen in the office told her a different story. Her knees buckled and the inspector took her arm and led her gently back to the stuffed armchair at the back of the shop.

'Are you sure you don't want the doctor to check you out? You've had a nasty shock–'

'No, thank you. I'm just...' Tears slid down her cheeks as Nigel's face floated into her mind. Oh, God! Nigel, what happened?

'I don't want to distress you further, Miss Torode, but can you think of a reason why your brother might have taken his own life?'

Fiona's head shot up.

'Nigel didn't kill himself! He would never have done that to me and had no reason to. He had...everything to live for.'

The inspector coughed.

'We haven't found any signs of a break-in or a struggle, and at first sight, this does look more like a suicide, I'm afraid. Naturally, we'll be looking at all avenues, but as nothing appears to have been stolen,' his gaze swept across the room full of antiques and art, 'there's no apparent motive for, for murder.' His voice dropped to little more than a whisper, for her ears only.

Fiona remembered Nigel's anguish when he told her about his illness almost two years ago, but at no time had he said he didn't want to live.

'Please, check to see if anyone else was here. I know it doesn't look like it, but–'

The inspector sat in an adjoining chair and took her hand.

'We will. I'll get forensics round, and we'll keep an open mind until after the autopsy and what, if anything, turns up here.' He turned to ask a sergeant to call the forensics team. 'I'm afraid we'll have to search your brother's stuff at the house, to make sure we don't miss anything.'

Fiona nodded, too numb to argue. She absolutely *knew* Nigel hadn't killed himself, but what else could have happened? It couldn't be real; it was all a nightmare...

Fiona woke the next day and for a wonderful moment didn't remember what had happened, looking forward to telling Nigel about her meeting with Sam. Then it hit her like a physical blow, and she gasped. Her wonderful brother, her rock, was dead. And it looked as if by his own hand. But no! Couldn't be. Was he murdered? Oh, God. She buried her head in her hands as wild thoughts filled her mind. Whatever had happened, she could no longer talk to him, hold him. For the first time in her life, she felt completely alone. They had always been there for each other, connected as only twins are. When their parents died in a pile-up on the M1 years before, Nigel had supported her as she grieved.

Pulling herself up in bed, Fiona hugged her knees to her chest, allowing the tears to fall unchecked.

'Nigel, how will I manage without you? And what happened? I wish you could tell me!' She rocked back and forth, Nigel's distorted face filling her mind. The harsh ring of the telephone cut into her grief, and she had to grab a tissue before answering it.

'Miss Torode? Inspector Woods. Sorry to trouble you, but I wondered if forensics could come round this morning to check your brother's room? We'll be as quick as we can.'

She agreed to let them come in an hour and dragged herself into the bathroom for the hottest shower she could stand. Tears mingled with the stream of water as she washed her hair and body in a futile attempt to feel normal. Through the veil of numbness, she was somehow aware her life had changed. Part of her had died with Nigel, and she felt lost. She went through the motions of towelling her body, letting her hair dry into its natural curls.

Fiona pulled on black jeans and a T-shirt, and as she tugged a comb through her damp hair, she glanced at the mirror, taken aback by her pale face with black-shadowed eyes. For once she didn't care what she looked like and shuffled downstairs to the silent kitchen. Normally Radio Guernsey would be blasting out from the stereo on the worktop, switched on by Nigel as he made their early morning coffee. Fiona's stomach clenched as she pressed the on switch to be greeted by a cheery Jenny Kendal-Tobias announcing the next song. She switched the radio off, not able to cope with such normality. Even making her own coffee proved challenging; taking over her brother's task of setting up the espresso machine felt like a betrayal. As she sipped the coffee, her stomach rumbled, reminding her she hadn't eaten since lunchtime the previous day, and that hadn't stayed down. Fiona popped a couple of slices of bread in the toaster and set out butter and marmalade. It was like chewing cardboard, and she found it hard to swallow, but persisted, knowing she would need sustenance for the long, painful day ahead.

Before the police arrived, Fiona rang her friend, Louisa. Through her tears, she managed to tell her about Nigel.

'Oh my God! That's awful! I can't believe it. Why on earth didn't you phone us last night? You shouldn't be on your own. Look, I'm coming round now. I'll tell Paul. Stay strong.' Louisa's voice broke as she said goodbye and Fiona was left sobbing. Telling her friend had brought it home to her. It *was* real. Nigel *was* dead.

Louisa arrived moments before the police. Fiona fell into her arms, desperate for the feel of a loving embrace.

'Oh, Louisa, am I glad to see you. I should have phoned last night, but I was...numb...the shock...crawled into bed...'

'I understand, but I'm here now.' Louisa hugged her tight and Fiona saw the tears in her friend's eyes. She wasn't the only one to mourn her brother. The sound of a car pulling into the drive made them pull apart, and Fiona ushered in two policemen and took them upstairs to Nigel's room. In the kitchen, Louisa was making two mugs of tea, and she sat down at the breakfast bar.

'Do you feel up to telling me more about what happened?' Louisa gripped her hand before pushing across a steaming mug. Fiona saw the mix of pain and sympathy in Louisa's blue eyes and took a deep breath. By the time she'd told her friend everything, they were both crying.

'So the police are saying it's suicide? And surely you don't agree with them, do you?'

'No, definitely not. Oh, I know Nigel had low moments since his diagnosis, but at no time did he so much as hint he...he didn't want to carry on. I think they're expecting to find a note or something.' Fiona raised her eyes to the ceiling from where could be heard the sound of opening drawers and cupboards. 'But they're not confirming anything yet, at least not until the...autopsy, later today.' She brushed away the last tears, determined to stop giving into her emotions. She had to be strong; there would be so much to arrange.

Louisa frowned, pushing her hair behind her ear.

'I don't believe Nigel would have taken his life either. He was a fighter and was in his element with the business. But I must admit it's odd that nothing seems to have been taken. Surely Nigel didn't have any enemies?'

'Not that I can think of.' Fiona hesitated, wondering whether or not to share what had just occurred to her. Oh, sod it! She had to tell someone. Clearing her throat, she went on, 'There's a chance an intruder was looking for something which was stored there, but we'd moved it, and Nigel was unlucky enough to disturb him.'

Louisa's eyes widened.

'No! What was it? Something valuable? You've never said anything–'

Fiona twisted a used tissue to pieces before facing her friend's shocked and somewhat hurt expression.

'It's virtually certain to be confirmed as a painting by Renoir. And worth millions.'

Chapter 5

Guernsey 2011

'What! But how on earth–?' Louisa gasped.
Before Fiona could answer, one of the policemen tapped on the kitchen door to say they were ready to leave. She escorted them to the door, asking if they'd found anything relevant and they said they couldn't comment, but were taking Nigel's laptop for checking. She returned to the kitchen and her bemused friend.

'Long story. And I don't have all the answers yet, in fact, I was in London to meet up with my old professor and ask his opinion. But that's jumping the gun. You know we renovated the shop a few weeks ago?' Louisa nodded. 'Well, when we came to replace the old flooring we found a concealed trapdoor which led to a basement we didn't know existed. We were in the shop when the builder discovered it.'

Fiona told Louisa about what they found, struggling to stay composed as she described their initial excitement.

Louisa sat speechless, her eyes widening as the story unfolded.

'Do you have any idea who the paintings belong to?'

'No, not yet, we...I, wanted to see if it was a genuine Renoir first. Whole different ball-game if it is. And...and my professor came over for a brief visit a couple of weeks ago and was pretty sure then, in fact, he got quite excited but wanted to carry out tests, which meant having it sent to London.' Fiona chewed her lip, remembering how upbeat Nigel had been about the news.

'Just think about the great publicity for the business if it turns out to be genuine! We'll be all over the internet.'

His eyes had shone with a brightness which had rarely been present since his illness.

'So, did he do the tests?'

'Yes. I went over at the weekend and met with Sam in London. He said there's no doubt it's genuine. I...I tried to phone Nigel with the news, but...but it was too late. He must have been dead for hours.' She could hold back no longer and let the tears fall. Louisa came round the table and hugged her tight. It was a while before either of them could speak, and Louisa suggested she might want something stronger than tea. Fiona nodded, saying there was wine in the fridge.

After pouring a large glass for Fiona and filling a glass of water for herself, Louisa asked, 'What happens now? About the painting?'

'We have to try and find the original owner. Sam suggested checking out lists of reported stolen Renoirs to start.' She sniffed. 'Which reminds me, I must phone him and tell him what's happened. See if he'll hold onto the painting for a while. At least it should be safe in the university vault.'

They sipped their drinks in silence, lost in thought.

'I don't like to think of you here on your own, Fiona. Why not come and stay with us for a few days? You know we'd love to have you, and we've plenty of room.' Louisa squeezed her hand.

'Oh, that's kind of you, but I've got a lot to organise, what with the business and...and the funeral. I might be better here for the moment. Perhaps when things are more settled?' Fiona was touched. They'd been friends since she'd come back to live in Guernsey, and had soon become close. And her husband, Paul, was delightful. She was tempted to accept the offer, knowing she would be cossetted, but thought it would be unfair for the couple, busy as they were at La Folie, Guernsey's popular health centre.

Louisa frowned. 'Well, if you're sure. But I insist you must at least come round for a meal sometimes, starting tonight.' She glanced at her watch. 'Look, I'm sorry, but I have to go, or I'll be late for an appointment I couldn't change. I can come back afterwards if you like?'

'No, don't worry. I've calls to make, but if you could phone our friends and tell them, I'd be grateful.'

'Of course. Do say you'll come round tonight? About seven? Get a taxi, and one of us will run you back.' Taking a last swallow of water, she added, 'Is there anything I can do to help? Shopping?'

'I'm all right at the moment, and I'd love to come tonight. You'd best get off, don't want you to be falling out with the boss.' Fiona managed a grin, the 'boss' being Paul, who managed the centre for Malcolm, Louisa's father and the owner.

Her friend smiled and stood, flinging her arms around her.

'Hang on in there, girl. I've been there, as you have too, with your parents. It's tough, but you'll come through. And never think you're alone, cos you're not. You have us and Charlotte and Andy and the others in the gang. Call, and one of us will come running. Okay?'

'Thanks. Now go, and I'll see you later.'

Once she had closed the door on the departing Louisa, Fiona returned to the kitchen and made a cup of coffee. Tempting as it was to continue on the wine, she needed a clear head for the phone calls she had to make.

Chapter 6

Guernsey 1940

The night before Teresa and Judith were due to leave, Leo lay in bed with his arms wrapped around his wife's sleeping body. He found it odd she could sleep peacefully at such a time, but was also glad of it. Her lovely blue eyes had lost their sparkle, and she was prone to bouts of crying when their child was asleep, only putting on a brave face when Judith was awake.

Watching Teresa pack for the two of them, choosing the largest suitcase they possessed, had hurt as much as a physical blow to his chest and Leo had been forced to leave their bedroom and escape to his study, saying he had letters to write. This had been true; he needed to get letters to his business associates and bankers in London before the Germans arrived and cut communications.

Leo thanked God his father had never been an 'all his eggs in one basket' businessman and had set up an account with a private London bank some years previously. Each quarter, any profits over and above any income required by the family, had been transferred to London, and would now provide a source of money for Teresa. Essential, as Leo had been horrified to learn evacuees were only allowed to withdraw £20 from the bank before leaving.

Her parents were well off, but his pride baulked at the idea of them supporting his family. Teresa was taking her jewellery, but he sincerely hoped she wouldn't need to sell it. It had been such a pleasure to buy her the exquisite pieces to enhance her beauty. As he lay, wide awake, he recalled how happy he had been these past three years. But now, as he listened to Teresa's even breathing, he was afraid their life together was over, that he might never again hear her laugh, see her smile or hold her tight.

The next morning dawned bright and clear, promising to be hot later. Leo was glad the journey to England would take place in fine weather but concerned the clear skies would make the boats vulnerable to attack from the air. Teresa clung to him on waking and, without a word spoken, they made love with more passion than usual. A cry from Judith next door broke them apart, and Teresa kissed him before sliding out of bed and reaching for her dressing gown.

Leo, with the scent of her skin in his nostrils, jumped out of bed and hugged her tight.

'I shall miss you more than you can ever know, my darling. I…I don't say much, I know, but you have brought me so much pleasure, so much love these past few years, I can't thank you enough.' He kissed the top of her tousled head, drawing in the smell of her hair, capturing it for future reference.

Teresa's eyes were bright.

'And I'll miss you. You've made me very happy, Leo, and I'll be counting the days until I can return.' Judith's cries grew louder, and with a quick moue, Teresa released herself from his grasp, calling, 'Mummy's coming, darling!'

Two hours later Leo parked the car at White Rock, and his small family joined the queue of the hundreds of men, women and children waiting to embark on the ship alongside. Glancing around, Leo saw a mixture of fear, anticipation and sorrow on the faces of his fellow islanders. Not many men appeared to be leaving; like him, they were sending their families away to safety. A few children jumped up and down in excitement at the prospect of going on a ship, but many clung to their mothers, as if afraid to let go. Women were embracing the men they were leaving behind, their faces damp with tears as they said their goodbyes. For some, it was too much to bear, and Leo watched as a woman with a babe in her arms left the queue, handing back their tickets to a waiting sailor, who nodded, silently. Although he hated the thought of his family leaving, Leo held his breath, praying Teresa wouldn't copy her.

She must have read his mind as, squeezing his hand, she murmured, 'Don't worry, I won't change my mind. I want Judith to be safe.'

They both looked down at their sleeping daughter, snug in a lightweight TanSad canvas pram. Teresa had exchanged it for the coach built Silver Cross they'd bought when she was born. A reluctant swap, but necessary thanks to the space restrictions on the small ship. Leo, his heart heavy with dread now the parting was so close, bent his head to kiss Judith's downy cheek. She stirred, opening her eyes to stare at him and then smiled. He smiled back, and she sighed and went back to sleep. By now they were near the gangplank, and Leo turned to his wife and hugged her. A sailor lifted up the pram with ease and passed it to another waiting on the deck.

'Goodbye, my darling. Ring me if you can or...write.' The words choked in his throat. They'd agreed on no long goodbye in public, but it was hard not to hold on a little longer.

Teresa's eyes were moist as she said, 'I will. And you take care of yourself and...and everything until our return. I love you.' He was about to say 'I love you, too' when the sailor took Teresa's hand and helped her onto the gangplank. Leo stepped back to let another passenger through and watched as his wife turned to wave before being ushered aside. He raised his hand in return, but she was already out of sight in the crowd.

The uppermost thought in his whirling head was, would he ever see his family again? A small, insistent voice assured him the chances were slim.

Chapter 7

Guernsey 2011

After phoning their advocate and arranging to meet him the following morning, Fiona called a few distant relatives scattered across the globe, becoming more upset in the process, and explaining Nigel's death as a burglary gone wrong. She then rang Sam Wright. Shocked by Nigel's death, he offered his condolences. Telling him she didn't think he'd killed himself; she mentioned a possible connection to the painting.

'It does appear to be one hell of a coincidence. But without the provenance, it's hard to see the link.' She heard a deep sigh. 'Do you feel up to doing some research? Tracing the legal owner? It'll be needed before the painting can be properly verified, anyway.'

'I think so. Getting my teeth stuck into something might even help. Take my mind off...what's happened. In the meantime, could you hold onto the painting, please? It's obviously not safe to bring it back here.'

'Sure, no problem. But if someone is looking for it, isn't there a chance they'll try again? Perhaps break into your house?'

'Oh my God! You're right; I hadn't thought of that.' Fiona's hand shook as she gripped the phone. Assuming Nigel hadn't told the burglar where the painting was, then there was every chance they'd search the house.

'Sorry, didn't mean to frighten you.' Sam sounded contrite.

'It's okay, better to be forewarned. I'll sort something out, don't worry. There are friends I can go to.'

'That's good. Stay in touch, Fiona, and do let me know if there's anything I can do to help. Take care.'

They signed off and Fiona, feeling dizzy, immediately grabbed a glass of water. It looked as if she should accept Louisa's offer after all.

Later that afternoon she received a call from Inspector Woods.

'Thought I'd better let you know the results of the autopsy, Miss Torode.' He broke off to cough. 'We found no signs of violence and there's no trace of a third party's DNA on the body. We're waiting on the toxicology results, but if there's nothing suspicious there, we'll treat the death as a suspected suicide, and advise the coroner accordingly. An inquest was opened and adjourned until the results are through, usually within about three weeks. I'm sorry, I know it's not what you wanted to hear.'

Although not entirely surprised by the news, Fiona experienced a hot surge of anger on her brother's behalf. She took a deep breath before replying.

'I think you're wrong, Inspector, but I understand your reasoning. Will – will I be able to organise a funeral now?'

'No, I'm afraid not. We need the toxicology results before a death certificate can be issued prior to burial. You can make initial arrangements with a funeral director now, however. But the good news is the shop's no longer a crime scene, so you can reopen tomorrow if you wish.' Another bout of coughing. Definitely a smoker, she decided, thanking him for the call.

Fiona experienced mixed feelings about the delayed funeral. Part of her wanted it out of the way as quickly as possible, and another part dreaded all that it involved. The memory of her parents' funeral came unbidden into her mind, and the pain made her catch her breath. Only the feelings of anger stopped her spiralling down into grief. She wouldn't give in. Had to prove the police were wrong and she was right. Heeding the inspector's words, she phoned the firm who'd arranged the funeral for her parents. They said they'd take care of a notice in the paper and she was to contact them when the death certificate was issued when further details could be finalised.

Scared of the potential threat of being burgled, Fiona had phoned Louisa earlier, admitting she'd changed her mind about staying with her. She was now glad she'd done this, as the reality of what lay ahead hit home. Packing a case, Fiona wondered about the business. There was no way she could run it herself; facing customers or worse, time-wasters with a prurient interest in Nigel's death. No, not an option. But neither was leaving the shop closed longer than was decent after a death. Closing for a few days should be enough, but then what?

A vague memory stirred. There was a guy who'd worked for old Mr Domaille when he became too frail. Now, what was his name? Ken Turner, that was it. Nigel mentioned he was an experienced antiques dealer, now retired. Perhaps she could coax him out of retirement, for a while anyway. Grabbing the phone book she searched for his number. Luckily there was only one K. Turner registered, and he lived in St Peter Port, which might help persuade him to return to work. No having to cope with the awful traffic jams. He answered the phone on the first ring, and Fiona explained about Nigel and the need for someone with experience to run the shop for a few weeks.

'I'm so sorry about your brother, Miss Torode. I met him briefly when he took over the business. Lovely man.' He sighed. 'And of course, you wouldn't want to be in the shop for a while. Totally understandable. As it happens, time does hang heavy on my hands these days, and I was only telling the wife the other day I needed something to get me out of the house. She seemed to agree, probably glad to see the back of me.' He chuckled, before seeming to realise levity wasn't appropriate. 'Not that I would have wished anything to happen to your brother, you understand. But it could be most opportune.'

Fiona sighed inwardly. If he did take the offer, she wouldn't want to spend too much time in conversation with him. She suggested they met at the shop the following afternoon and he agreed on three o'clock. Relieved to have ticked another item off the list, she finished her packing and drove off to St Martins and Louisa's house at Icart.

Driving through the gate, Fiona felt the unworthy pang of envy she experienced each time she visited. It was the setting. Perched on the cliff overlooking Saints Bay and surrounded by lawns and a mature garden bursting with colourful spring flowers, it was idyllic. From the front, it appeared an ordinary, white painted single storey house, but looks were deceiving. The inside had been brought into the twenty-first century by their architect friend, Andy, and was full of light and open spaces. A haven of calm, which is what you'd expect from a home owned by a yoga master and physiotherapist, Fiona acknowledged, feeling her shoulders ease as she rang the bell.

Louisa welcomed her with a hug, saying, 'Paul's working late, as usual.' She searched Fiona's face and said, 'You look as if you need a drink. Come on through; we can sit outside, it's warm enough.' Louisa led the way through the living area, full of comfy sofas and chairs, and out onto the terrace. The early evening sun was sliding downwards, casting shadows over the garden. Fiona took a deep breath of the pure sea air. She'd made the right decision to come.

Moments later they were cradling glasses of chilled white wine and gazing over the bay to the far cliffs of Jerbourg.

'How's your day been? Any news?'

Fiona frowned as the day's events returned full tilt. She told Louisa about the call from the inspector and how angry she felt.

'I'm not surprised. So would I be.' Louisa squeezed her shoulder. 'But is there anything to prove the police are wrong?'

'That's the problem; there isn't. I haven't told them about the painting and I'm not sure if I should. It provides a reason for a break-in, but there's still no proof. I'm not keen to publicise the discovery yet. We need to trace the owner first.' She rubbed her forehead. 'What do you think?'

'I don't know. Tricky. Let's run it past Paul later, three heads being better than two.' She sipped her wine, looking thoughtful. 'On the phone you said you were afraid of being burgled. Is the house secure?'

'There's a burglar alarm, but that didn't stop the guy getting in the shop, did it? I might have to consider other security measures, but am hoping he won't try again just yet. Let the dust settle after...what happened.' She swallowed her wine, determined not to cry. A sudden chill in the air made her shiver.

Louisa must have noticed. 'Let's go in, no point in being cold.' Collecting their glasses they headed into the sun lounge, settling into squashy armchairs which swallowed them in feathered comfort. From here the view was direct south, towards Jersey, now invisible against the darkening horizon.

'You two were incredibly lucky to buy this place. It must be one of the best spots on the island. Not that I'm jealous.'

'We were lucky, thanks to Dad knowing the owner. In a way it reminds me of La Folie, having similar views and such a calm ambience. But smaller and without the Gothic towers, thank goodness!'

Fiona managed a smile. La Folie wasn't exactly beautiful from the front, a granite mansion built as a Victorian gentleman's 'folly'. But now gorgeous inside and with fab gardens, it was popular with those looking for a retreat from the world. Something Fiona would love at the moment.

'Hi, girls! Sorry to be late.' Paul strode in and pulled Fiona to her feet, enfolding her in his arms. She loved his hugs; it was like being wrapped in the softest, air-spun blanket, offering warmth and comfort. Clinging to him she felt safe for the first time since she found her brother.

'I can't begin to say how sorry I am about Nigel. It's hard to believe he's gone. How are you coping?' He kept one hand around her waist, brushing her hair back from her face with the other.

'Not great. There's the police and...and everything.' Sitting together on a sofa, she relayed the events of the day while Louisa disappeared to the kitchen. Paul's face creased in concern as he held her hands.

'You're right about Nigel. No way would he have killed himself; he knew the pain it would cause you. And when I saw him last week he was full of life, telling me about an important discovery which he couldn't share at the time, but would make headlines.' His mesmerising blue eyes seemed to emit a kind of energy, and Fiona experienced a flow of warmth spreading through her. Healing. Just as Nigel had described to her after his sessions with him at La Folie. Paul had offered to help with managing his debilitating symptoms, and her brother was convinced the treatments were working. Another reason why he wouldn't have given up on himself.

'But what can I do to change the police's mind? We're only speculating what happened–'

'Dinner's ready, you two,' Louisa called from the dining room.

'We'll talk about it later. I'm sure there's something we could do.' Paul hooked his arm with hers, and they joined Louisa at the table, set with a mixed salad, a dish of potatoes, herby scented chicken pieces and a bottle of wine.

Fiona sniffed the air. 'Smells delicious, Louisa. I'm absolutely starving.'

An air of awkwardness descended on them as they ate as if no-one knew a safe topic of conversation. Fiona hadn't exaggerated when she said she was starving – she'd barely eaten since Sunday lunchtime, and her stomach was rumbling at the delicious smell of cooked chicken. It wasn't long before all plates were clear and a collective sigh went around the table.

Paul smiled at his wife. 'That was great, darling. Should I warn Chef he has competition?'

'I hardly think so. But thanks for the compliment. I do wheedle a few tips out of him, though,' Louisa said, standing to collect the plates. 'Anyone for strawberries? Served with crème fraiche as a healthy option.'

'Lovely. Let me help.' Fiona grabbed a couple of dishes and walked with Louisa to the kitchen.

'I'll load up the dishwasher later.' Louisa piled everything by the sink and turned to face Fiona. 'I've thought about what you can do to challenge the likely verdict on Nigel's death. I'll explain after we've had dessert.

Settled on the sofas later, Louisa leaned towards Fiona, saying, 'I think it might be worth talking to an ex-policeman I know, John Ferguson, who's now a private investigator. He was hired by my father and helped us uncover the truth behind my mother's death and...other things. He's totally discreet, and you could tell him what you suspect has happened.'

Fiona sipped her coffee, letting the idea take hold. She could certainly do with someone onside.

'That's a great idea, darling. I liked John, and he'd be perfect. What do you say, Fiona?' Paul smiled at her.

'Well, if you both think it's a good idea, then I'm all for talking to him. What have I got to lose?'

'I can call him for you. Pave the way.' Louisa patted her hand, encouragingly.

Buoyed by the thought of action, she agreed and waited while Louisa made the call. After chatting to him for a few minutes, she passed her the phone.

'Hello, Mr Ferguson, I'm Fiona Torode.' She gave him the basic facts, saying there were sensitive issues involved, unknown to the police, and would be glad of his advice.

'If I can help in any way, I'd be glad to. Shall we meet and you can tell me more?'

They arranged a time for the following day, between her appointments with the advocate and Ken Turner. She released a deep sigh at the thought of what promised to be a full-on day.

Chapter 8

Guernsey 2011

The sound of squabbling seagulls dragged Fiona out of a dream in which she was chased by a man dressed in the caricature style of a burglar – striped sweater and a black mask. Opening her eyes, she saw the sunlight pouring through the chinks in the blinds and heaved a sigh of relief. She was safe. Tucked up in Louisa's guest room and with the sounds and smells of the clifftop filtering through the open window, a far cry from the dark tunnel in the dream.

Giving herself a shake, she crossed to the window and opened the blinds. The view over the garden and out to the sea was beguiling, the only sign of life the birds circling overhead as they kept beady eyes open for a morning snack. Resting her head against the window frame, she wished for the moment to be frozen in time, not wanting to face what needed to be faced. All the ugliness. A knock on the door destroyed that wish.

'Fiona, are you awake? It's eight o'clock, and we're leaving for work soon.'

'Yes, give me a minute.' Pulling on a cotton kimono-style wrap, she opened the door to Louisa, dressed in her white therapist's uniform. 'I'd just woken up and was admiring the view. It was weird to be roused from sleep by the sound of gulls rather than heavy traffic.'

'I bet. Want to join me for a quick coffee? I've already eaten.' Louisa hugged her briefly before leading the way to the kitchen. 'There's the usual bread, cereals, yoghurts, etc. Just help yourself to anything you fancy,' Louisa said, pouring two mugs of fresh coffee and sitting beside her. 'Feeling any better?'

'A bit, thanks. Though I'm not looking forward to today. I need to go back to the shop for the meeting with Mr Turner. It's going to be difficult seeing where…' She bit her lip.

Louisa squeezed her hand. 'Yes it will, but I'm sure you'll cope.'

'I have to.' She managed a weak smile before taking a sip of coffee. She would get through this day regardless. And, with luck, the detective might help her nail the bastard who killed Nigel.

By eleven o'clock Fiona was flagging, after an hour spent in intense discussion with the advocate. She and Nigel had made wills when they bought the business together, and she'd known she was the sole beneficiary of his estate, which included his half of the family home. It was still painful to go over the details with the advocate and to learn there would be a delay in applying for probate until the death certificate was issued. Fortunately, she was able to access the business bank account, the only bright spot in the meeting.

Needing to be revived, she left Le Marchant Street and headed down to a coffee shop in Le Pollet. The buzz of chatter and the occasional laugh added to her sense of unreality, of not being a part of the world around her. Fiona had experienced similar feelings when their parents died, wanting to hide from the world, not wanting to be pitied for her loss. An orphan at twenty-five. And now…now she had lost her only close family member, her other half, the person she'd loved best.

Desperate to lift her mood, she picked up the cup of coffee and spotted a copy of *The Guernsey Evening Press* left on a nearby table. A headline jumped out, *'Local antiques dealer found dead'*. Her hand shook, dropping the cup and spilling coffee over the table. A waitress rushed up.

'Oh dear, let me clear this up for you. Are you okay? You're a bit pale.' She began mopping up the liquid, her glance sympathetic.

'Sorry, I...I've just had a shock. Can I have another cup, please? I'll pay...'

'No, it's okay. Back in a moment.' The girl bustled off to the counter, and Fiona gripped her hands together to stop them shaking. Glancing at the paper, she was relieved to see there were few details and no mention of how Nigel had died. The phrase, 'the police are investigating the circumstances around the sudden death' gave little away.

Fiona pushed the paper away. She shouldn't have been surprised the news had got out, but seeing it in print jolted her. No doubt the press would be after her for more details and a photo of Nigel, and her stomach clenched at the thought. As she drank her replacement coffee, she hoped she wouldn't bump into anyone she knew while in town; she couldn't face awkward questions if they'd seen the paper. Louisa had already contacted their close friends, for which she was grateful, but she knew she couldn't put off speaking to people for much longer.

Her appointment with John was for twelve and Fiona left the café, keeping her head down as she made for his office above a shop a few doors away. A sign pointed her towards the first floor where she found a half-glazed door opening onto a tiny waiting area. Taking a deep breath, she forced herself to regain some semblance of calm as she took a seat opposite a closed door.

'Miss Torode? John Ferguson, please come on through.'

In her head, Fiona had imagined someone like Detective Columbo, slightly scruffy and wearing old clothes, but the well-groomed man in his fifties holding out his hand was a world apart. She followed him into an office not much larger than the waiting area, filled with a polished wood desk and a couple of filing cabinets. A notepad, phone and computer adorned the desk. Ushering her into a chair, the detective sat down facing her.

She cleared her throat. 'Thanks for seeing me so promptly, Mr Ferguson. I do appreciate it.'

His warm smile was reassuring.

'Not at all. Let's see if I can be of help. Perhaps you could start by telling me why you think your brother didn't take his own life?'

Fiona explained about the recent find of the paintings, in particular, the suspected Renoir, and Nigel's excitement. And that, being twins, they were extremely close, and he would be unlikely to do anything to give her pain.

Ferguson steepled his fingers, as if in prayer, as he digested what she told him.

'I understand where you're coming from. It does seem too much of a coincidence so soon after your discovery. The difficulty lies, from what you say, with the lack of any forensic evidence showing the presence of a third party. Whoever killed your brother was no amateur burglar. Which begs the question: how did they know about the painting?' He lifted an eyebrow.

'That's what's been bugging me, Mr Ferguson. Hardly anyone knew about the discovery. We didn't even tell our friends. The only person I spoke to was Sam Wright, the art expert in London, and he's the last person to go blabbing about something like this.' Something struck her. 'Are you saying you believe me? That Nigel was murdered?' She leaned forward over the desk, her heart lifting at the prospect.

'Please, call me John. Given what you've told me, I think your brother was unlucky enough to be in the wrong place at the wrong time. But there are still a lot of questions remaining unanswered. I take it you haven't told the police about the paintings?' She shook her head. 'May I ask why not? It would provide a motive for the killing.'

Fiona bit her lip. 'I know, but I felt it could leak out about the Renoir, and that would bring worldwide attention even before we know who the owner is. Not something I could deal with at the moment. And we need the provenance to be able to confirm absolutely that it's genuine.'

'Fair point. Although, if they knew, the police might look more closely at the bigger picture.' John tapped his fingers on the desk, lost in thought. After a few minutes, he looked up and smiled. 'How would you feel if I had a word with the chap in charge of the case? We worked together for years, and I trust him completely. I could drop a hint about something valuable being searched for, but it has to be kept secret at this stage, for various reasons, including your safety. Which is a big priority, in my book. We do need to look at the security on your house. Would you let me have a set of keys so I can take a recce?'

'Sure. I've got a spare set with me.' She handed them over.

'Thanks. Right, if I were to drop a hint about a reason for burglary, it might lead to an open verdict at the inquest, which could be revisited when the killer's arrested. What do you say?'

'I can see the advantage in having the police onside, but do you think they'll take our word for it? Inspector Woods seemed pretty convinced it was suicide.' She liked the idea of an open verdict; it would help quash any suicide rumours.

'In his shoes, I'd probably have thought the same. But he doesn't know the whole story and if I can offer a reason for doubt, then...' he spread his hands.

'Okay, please talk to him for me. Assuming I can afford your fees,' she said, flushing, 'would you be happy to take on the case, John? You might end up treading on your old colleague's toes, but I'd feel happier knowing there was someone working undercover, someone I could trust.' She shifted on the hard seat of the chair, overcome by the ramifications of what lay ahead. Police. Detectives. Prying into people's lives. Including her own and Nigel's.

'Yes, I would. And my fees are reasonable, as I take on cases to keep the old grey cells working more than to make pots of money.' He smiled, and she found herself returning the smile. 'The police will only be interested in the immediate past, and it looks to me as if there's a long-buried story here. The mysterious owner of a valuable painting for a start. And someone out there knows who it is. Or was.' He made some notes. 'Louisa said you're an art historian. Could be useful. Can you gain access to lists of missing or stolen paintings?'

'Normally no, but as an associate of Sam's I could gain clearance. Interpol holds a database of stolen art, and there's the Art Loss Register in London which focuses on art stolen or missing after WWII.' It was if a light had been switched on. 'Hey, that could be the answer! Perhaps it's connected to the German Occupation. The Nazi's commandeered loads of artworks wherever they went, particularly from the Jews.' She felt her face flush with excitement.

'Not being a local, I'm afraid to admit I know little of the Occupation, but I understood it had been fairly peaceful. Would private property have been stolen?' John's eyebrows shot up in surprise.

'Worse than that. Locals were sent to prison camps in France and Germany for comparatively minor offences, and the few Jews on the island were rounded up and sent to concentration camps and didn't return. So it's quite possible there's a link to the painting, although I wouldn't have thought any local would have owned a Renoir, even though this one's a Guernsey scene. You see, Renoir spent some weeks here in 1883 and produced a number of paintings and drawings. As I understand it, all his work was sent to France and sold there. But it's definitely worth checking.'

'Right.' John made a note. 'Is the previous owner of the shop still alive? They'd be a good place to start.'

'No, but his widow is. Mrs Domaille sold us the business after Ernest's death, but I hear she's now quite frail and in a nursing home.' She paused. 'She told us Ernest had owned the business since the war, so it's possible she knew the person who owned it beforehand.'

'Great. I'll start with her. Do you know which home she's in?'

Fiona gave him the name, and he made a note. 'Right, once I've spoken to Woods, I'll focus on Mrs Domaille if you're happy to check out the stolen art lists?' John tilted his head, and she nodded her agreement. 'My gut feeling is, if we find out who originally owned the painting, we're well on the way to finding the killer. And obtaining justice for your brother.'

Chapter 9

Guernsey 2011

Fiona's hands shook as she unlocked the back door to the shop. It was less than forty-eight hours since she'd found Nigel and the image still burned brightly in her brain. Taking a deep breath, she pushed the door open, triggering the alarm. Fumbling with the key code, it was a while before the strident noise stopped. Turning around she eyed the office last seen full of police. Although in a mess, with drawers and cupboards left open, there was nothing to indicate the horror of what had happened.

Sinking into the battered chair, Fiona hugged herself, trying to stop the shakes taking over her body. As they slowly subsided, she began to tidy up, closing drawers and cupboards. Reaching down to close the last one, she spotted a business card caught under the desk. Picking it up, she saw the name and address were that of an Australian lawyer. Puzzled, she was about to bin it when she heard a whisper so soft she couldn't make out the word or words. Jerking her head up she looked around. No-one. But she could have sworn...It came again, and this time it was clearer – 'Fiona'. She gasped. 'Nigel, is that you? Oh! Can you hear me?' Her heart pumped fast as she strained to hear while looking for any sign of his presence. The temperature dropped, and she felt a feathery touch on her cheek. Lifting up her hand she found nothing. 'It is you, isn't it? Oh, how I miss you! Please, talk to me, Nigel.' Tears pricked at Fiona's eyes as she willed Nigel to show himself. Unconsciously, she held her breath. Then the doorbell sounded, and she let go. Ken. Great timing. Shoving the card into a drawer, she went to the front door.

'Miss Torode, how do you do? Ken Turner.'

A large man in his early sixties, dressed in a tweed suit and bow tie and sporting a bushy moustache, he smiled as held out his hand.

'Please, come in.' She ushered him inside, feeling dwarfed by his presence.

'Thank you.' He looked around the shop, and she tried to see it through his eyes. Large desks and tables, either oak or mahogany, jostled for space with upholstered chairs and sofas, making it difficult to weave a path towards the back and the office. Every available surface held ornaments, glassware and the occasional leather-bound book. She saw it as organised clutter. Nigel had been the buyer for most of the stock, although odd pieces remained from the original stock. For the most part, it wasn't to Fiona's taste, but it sold. Her own love was the array of paintings on the walls, predominantly local oils and watercolours.

Ken's eyes swivelled back to her. They shone with a passion she recognised. Nigel's eyes had had the same look. She bit her lip to stop herself crying out.

'How strange to be back here. And only eighteen months after old Ernest died. I see you've updated the stock and spruced the place up a bit. Excellent.' He rubbed his hands together. 'I told Ernest it needed doing, but he was what you might call careful with his money and refused to consider it.'

'Indeed. Well, Mr Turner, shall I show you round properly before I explain the sales and purchase systems? We record everything on computer spreadsheets, but if you're not used to computers–'

'Ah, I might be a bit of a dinosaur in some ways, Miss Torode, and Ernest loathed computers, but I've embraced them. I have a PC at home, you see, and put all the household expenditure on Excel. So it shouldn't be a problem.' He twirled his moustache.

'Oh, that's a relief. Right, let's make a start.'

Fiona was keen to get through the necessary explanations speedily, hoping Nigel would make his presence felt again. Fortunately, Ken was quick to learn, and they returned to the shop to discuss the stock. He proved his knowledge by accurately dating and valuing items without reading their sale tickets. They agreed he would start that Saturday and close on Mondays to give him a day off.

'I'm looking forward to coming back, though naturally, I'm sorry it's under such sad circumstances.' He frowned. 'I now realise how much I've missed being in the shop among these beautiful *objets*,' Ken said, waving his arms perilously close to an original art nouveau vase.

She managed a brief smile as she handed over a set of keys and reminded him of the alarm code.

After locking the front door, Fiona headed for the office, her heart hammering in her chest.

'Nigel? Are you there? Ken's gone. Please, please show me you're here.' Standing in the middle of the office, she held her breath, wanting Nigel to speak. Or to feel his touch again. But there was nothing.

Her brother was gone.

As they sat around the dinner table that evening, Fiona described her meeting with John and their proposed plan of action.

'I thought you'd get on well with him, he's lovely, isn't he?' Louisa said, and Fiona agreed.

'He's made me feel more positive about discovering the truth.' She paused, wondering how much to tell them. 'Something odd happened in the shop. I...thought I heard someone call my name. I think it was Nigel. And I felt something touch my face.' Her hand went up instinctively to her cheek as she waited for her friends' reaction. Would they think she'd lost it?

'How did it make you feel?' Paul's expression was gentle, caring. Louisa's gaze was calm.

'Scared, at first. Then I got goosebumps, hoping it *was* Nigel, and we could communicate.' Her throat tightened as she relived the wonderful moment when her beloved brother seemed so close. Able to touch. 'I suppose you think I imagined it.' A touch of defiance in her voice.

'Not at all. I think it's quite possible Nigel wants to make contact. You two were especially close, and his spirit will be in torment, both from leaving you and dying so violently.' Paul held her hand in his and, once again, she experienced a warmth, a sense of peace, flow through her.

'I agree with Paul. Although I haven't personally experienced anything like this, Jeanne and Natalie have, so I think you should be open to it.'

'Yes, I remember Natalie saying how her house was haunted, although it's clear now. Guess I'd never given it much thought before. What happens after death, I mean.' Which was true. When their parents died, Fiona assumed that was it, end of their lives and then – nothing. But if she had sensed Nigel's presence, then perhaps there was an afterlife.

'Will you go back to the shop? See if his spirit's still around? I'd be happy to go with you if you'd rather not be alone.'

'Thanks for the offer, Paul, but it's better if I go on my own. I won't be scared, in fact, the opposite. I'm desperate to have some contact with Nigel. Perhaps even hear his voice once more.'

Fiona's first task the next morning was to contact Sam and ask about being granted access to the lost art registers. By adding her as a research student, she was provided with the necessary log-in details to begin her search. They both agreed the best starting point was the Art Loss Register set up specifically to trace art lost during WWII. Scrolling through the files provided a welcome distraction from the heaviness engulfing her, taking her back to her previous life working at London's V&A museum, a job she'd adored. As a curator in the Fine Art department, Fiona had been ideally placed to undertake research and had contributed to several courses run by the museum. The decision to leave and return to Guernsey had been the hardest of her life.

'You're buying an antiques business in Guernsey? But why? I thought you loved living in London as much as I do.' Fiona stared in shock at her brother. He'd managed a small antiques shop in Bloomsbury for years and seemed happy, only returning, like her, to Guernsey for holidays.

'Ah, well, there's something I need to tell you, Sis,' he said, as they sat in a quiet corner of a trendy wine bar in Soho. He'd phoned her at work, saying he needed to see her. Soon as.

She cradled the large glass of Pinot Grigio he'd thrust into her hand as she arrived. 'Okay, I'm listening.'

For once Nigel looked unsure of himself, shifting in his seat and avoiding her eye. After taking a large swallow of his beer, he said, 'I've got MS.'

'What! Oh, no! I can't believe it, you...you look so well.' She grabbed his hand and felt it tremble in hers. Moving closer Fiona leaned in for a hug, and they clung together until some wag walking past called out, 'You two should get a room!' Nigel released her gently, dropping a kiss on her cheek.

'And before you ask, I've had a second opinion and loads of tests, so there's no doubt, I'm afraid. To be honest, I've known for a couple of months, but didn't know how to tell you.' He sat back and took another sip of beer.

'Two months! Oh, Nigel, you should have told me. We tell each other everything, remember?' Which they had, from childhood. No secrets, that was the rule. Except now. Her initial shock gave way to fear, fear for her brother and what he faced, and fear for herself if the worst was to happen. She had to grip her glass to stop her hands shaking.

'You were busy at work with that course you'd set up, and I wanted time to think it through, look at my options. Assuming I had any.' For a moment his face clouded and her heart ached for him.

'What exactly have you been told? What about treatments?' Surely there was something to be done. Was there a cure? Her mind raced.

'I've got what's called Relapsing Remitting MS and can experience relapses months or even years apart. So far I've not been too bad. I'd been having balance problems, had pain in my legs, was clumsy and my hands shook,' he said, clutching his glass. 'My doctor referred me for tests and,' he grimaced, 'I was told it was MS.'

'And the treatment?' Fiona felt sick as she imagined her brother ending up in a wheelchair, like a distant aunt of theirs had. Although she had been much older.

'Oh, there are drugs to control the symptoms, and it's best if I avoid stress and rest as much as possible, but no cure. I could carry on for years, living a reasonably active life, or…' He shrugged.

'And going to Guernsey will help? How?'

'Yes, for sure. The pace of life is so much slower than here, less pollution and I can live in our family home instead of paying out huge rents for a tiny flat here. But, I'm not sure I can do it alone, Sis.' He stroked her cheek, a habit he had when he needed a favour.

The penny dropped.

'You want me to come with you? Leave my job?' For a moment her instinct was to say no, no way. But then she looked at Nigel's drawn face and knew there was no choice.

'Of course I'll come. Now tell me more about this antiques business.'

Continuing to scroll through the lists, Fiona wished they'd never bought the bloody business from old Mrs Domaille. It had seemed the perfect solution at the time, but if they hadn't bought it, then Nigel would still be alive. Struggling with his MS, yes, but alive. Her vision blurred and she had to wipe her eyes before continuing her search. Life was full of 'if only'. If only their parents had been driving ten minutes earlier on that section of the motorway, they'd still be alive, too. Taking a deep breath, Fiona forced herself to focus on the screen where an image jumped out at her, accompanied by the description 'Tissaud Family at Moulin Huet – Renoir'. She'd found it!

Chapter 10

Guernsey 2011

Fiona was still on a high from her discovery when John Ferguson called.

'I popped in to see Inspector Woods and mentioned a possible reason for a burglary and he's agreed to think about it. He was a bit miffed I wouldn't share all the facts, but seemed to accept the issue of your safety. For the moment he'll hold back on suggesting suicide to the coroner unless toxicology results suggest otherwise. So, that's a result, I think.'

'Thanks, it is. And I've had a result, too.' Excitedly, she told him about the painting on the Art Loss Register. 'I've emailed the listing to Sam for confirmation, but I'm convinced it's the one we found.'

'Well done. And does it mention who the painting belonged to?'

'It was reported as stolen from a Guernsey home by the Germans during the Occupation.'

'Blimey! You'd suspected that, hadn't you? Do you have a name?' John's voice rose.

Fiona smiled, feeling pleased with herself.

'A Mrs Bichard, who made the claim after the war, saying it belonged to her husband–'

'Don't tell me he'd been deported and didn't return?' John interrupted.

'Yes. His property was commandeered, but she had evacuated before the Occupation. The Germans denied the claim, saying they had no record of it and it's been an open case since. I'd guess her claim wasn't taken seriously, as until then all Renoir's Guernsey paintings were accounted for. Perhaps they thought she was trying it on. Otherwise, investigators would have dug deeper. You don't let a Renoir just disappear!'

'Guess not. So, we need to find this Mrs Bichard, assuming she's still alive. Is there an address for her?'

'No, and we don't know if she returned to live here after the war. I had a quick look in the phone book, and there are about two columns of Bichards.' She sighed. How would they trace someone after more than sixty years?

'What puzzles me is how did the painting end up in the basement of your shop? There must be a connection between whoever owned the business during the war, Mr Bichard and possibly Mr Domaille. Which reminds me, I phoned the nursing home and was told the old lady is ill with a chest infection and can't receive visitors until next week. Pity, as I think she could know something.'

'Mmm. I could try the archives to see who owned the business during the war. Should be a record somewhere. And why was Bichard deported? He doesn't sound Jewish. It should be in the records.'

'Are you sure you're happy to do that? If you tell me where to look, I could do it. After all, you're paying me to investigate.' He sounded dubious.

'I know, but I'd rather be busy, John. Otherwise, I'll dwell too much on Nigel.' She didn't tell him what had happened in the shop, thinking an ex-policeman wouldn't hold with such 'ghostly' happenings.

'Fair enough. Then I'll start going through the Bichards on the island and, if necessary, check for the mainland. Oh, and I went to your house and noted where we could improve security. I'll email you the suggestions, and you can let me know what you think.'

'Thanks. Looks like we're both going to be busy. Catch you later. Bye.'

Fiona stood and stretched. She'd been glued to the computer for long enough, and the spring sun was luring her outside. A few minutes later she'd locked up and was heading for the cliff path running alongside the garden's boundary. With a shock, she realised she couldn't remember the last time she had been out for a walk.

The warm sunshine felt good and deep breaths of salty air soon had her striding out towards Moulin Huet Bay. The yellow flowers of the gorse, shading pink campion and yellow celandine, made a bright contrast against the deep green of the grass and Fiona felt her spirits lift a little. Cliff walks had played a large part in her childhood and youth. Her parents considered them an integral part of the weekends and school holidays. They always started from Soldiers Bay, within easy reach of their home in Colborne Road. The path led them close to Bluebell Wood, a delightful sea of blue in spring and one of Fiona's favourite places.

A bit too far to walk now, she thought but determined to make an effort another day while the bluebells were at their glorious best. There were times as a child, and even more so as a teenager, when neither she nor Nigel wanted to accompany their parents on the walks, preferring to stay slumped in front of the television. But their father would virtually drag them out, bribing them with the promise of a cream tea at Fermain Bay.

Bittersweet memories flitted in and out of her brain as Fiona kept going, determined to make it as far as Moulin Huet. It seemed appropriate to follow in Renoir's footsteps, and with few people out and about mid-week, she would be able to imagine herself back in Victorian times when the fashion of bathing in the sea was gaining in popularity.

The route took her down and up the cliffs around Saint's Bay and then high along those surrounding Moulin Huet. She let out a sigh of satisfaction as, eventually, she made her way down to the beach facing Cradle Rock, one of the rocks featured in Renoir's paintings.

The beach was almost deserted as she'd hoped, and Fiona chose a spot to sit down, propped against one of the many rocks scattered around the bay. The view was not quite what Renoir had painted; he'd used a little artistic licence by including rocks from adjoining bays. But the essence was there, and Fiona closed her eyes to recall the painting found in the basement. The bright colours of the clothes, rocks and sea were in sharp contrast with what lay before her.

Opening her eyes again, she liked the softer tones of the reality. Although undeniably beautiful, Fiona wondered what had prompted Renoir to produce fifteen versions of the bay and not record other beautiful parts of the island. His life and work had featured in her degree studies, and the Guernsey connection had made him a special attraction for her. Added to which, his lodgings in St Peter Port were a short walk from her family home. So, perhaps, she now mused, there was some weird but indefinable reason why his painting ended up in her hands. Just then, Nigel's distorted face floated into her mind, and her stomach clenched at the terrible price attached to their find.

The following day Fiona drove into Town and was lucky to park at the Mignon Plateau adjoining the archive building, saving herself a steep walk up the hill from a town centre car park. Her legs still ached from her cliff walk. A couple of hours later she left, happy to have achieved success in one of the searches, if not the other. And it slipped another piece into the jigsaw puzzle. It seemed a Leo Bichard had been the owner of the antiques shop throughout the war, having taken over from his father, Henry. Fiona hadn't as yet found a reference to Leo's deportation among the huge stack of documents kept by the States Administration during the Occupation, and planned to return another day.

She phoned John with the news.

'I knew there had to be a connection! It's beginning to make sense, isn't it? If Ernest knew Leo, then he had the opportunity to get his hands on the Renoir.' Fiona heard the excitement in his voice. She'd had the same thought.

'Hopefully, Mrs Domaille will be able to throw more light on their association. In the meantime, I'll try to find out why Leo was deported. Any joy with the local Bichards?'

'Not so far. It's going to take me a while to get through them all. If I were still in the force I'd rope in a constable or two,' he chuckled. 'To save my sanity, I'm taking time out to fix the security issues at your house, as you agreed in your email. Will give you an update later.'

After dinner that evening Fiona drove into Town and parked yards from the shop. Dusk cast a soft light over the old buildings and cobbled street, and for a moment she hesitated. Was it wise to be on her own with a murderous burglar on the loose? She knew John wouldn't have approved, would have insisted on accompanying her. Which would have defeated the object, as she was sure Nigel wouldn't make contact if a stranger were present. Telling herself it was unlikely the burglar would try again so soon, she unlocked the back door and switched off the alarm.

An almost eerie silence enfolded her as she reached for the light switch. Changing her mind, Fiona left the light off. Wouldn't a ghost or spirit prefer the dark? Light filtered in through the windows and her eyes adjusted to the dimness.

'Nigel? It's me. I'd...I'd really like to talk to you. See you. It's been so awful since...' Her voice caught on a sob. The gnawing pain in her gut threatened to overwhelm her. She forced herself to breathe deeply and focus on her love for her brother. He wouldn't want to have a weeping Minnie on his hands. An image of the wailing girl in the toilets in a Harry Potter film flashed into her mind. The girl had managed to tell Harry what had happened to her, how she died. It wasn't real life, of course, just a story, but it helped her to focus. Fiona perched on the edge of the desk, Nigel's desk, and concentrated on the last time she'd seen him alive. His big smile as he'd waved her off to the airport.

'Nigel. Can you hear me?'

In response, she felt the same delicate, feather-like touch on her cheek, as the air around her cooled.

'Fiona.' The merest whisper. 'Hear...you. Want to tell...But tired. So tired...'

Her heart pounded against her ribs. She tried to speak, but her throat was tight. She coughed.

'Darling Nigel. I'm listening. Stay with me.' Her eyes strained as she focused on where the voice had emerged. As she watched, the hazy outline of a man appeared.

Chapter 11

Guernsey 1940

Leo was in his study searching for anything incriminating in his papers when the phone rang. Absorbed in his task, he jumped. Much to his relief, it was Teresa calling to say they had arrived safely at her parents' house, Oak Tree Farm, in Suffolk after a long, tiring journey.

'The ship was so crammed I was afraid we'd sink, and the captain had to change tack in case German planes were spying on us.' He heard the exhaustion in her voice and, not for the first time since she'd left, Leo regretted not accompanying her. He was her husband, for God's sake! It was his job to take care of his wife and child. Guilt lay heavy within his breast.

Teresa went on to describe the rest of the journey by train via London to Sudbury, where her father collected them in his car.

'Judith's teething again so I'm not getting much sleep. How are you faring? Any news on the Germans?'

'I'm coping, thanks to Elsie who's kept me well fed, as usual. Although we've been warned to be careful as supplies might be cut off soon. The Germans haven't arrived yet, but the word is it could be any day.' His grip on the phone tightened. Only days left of freedom...Leo took a deep breath before asking after Judith, who had screamed through most of the journey, Teresa told him. They talked for a while longer until a loud wail echoed down the line and his wife had to go and calm the baby. She promised to telephone the following day.

Leo sat staring at the now silent phone, feeling bereft. Instead of being cheered by hearing his wife's voice and knowing she was safe, he now felt his vulnerability as the

Germans drew ever closer. Only the thought of the family valuables – and heaven knew what else – falling into the enemy's grasping hands, kept him resolved to stick it out. Boats continued to leave with passengers, but a good proportion of the men were staying. Leo, leaving the papers scattered on his desk, headed for the drawing room. Time to hide the paintings.

'Bichard & Son Antiques' sprawled over two floors of the old building at Contree Mansell, yards from Trinity Square in St Peter Port. As Leo unlocked the door on Monday morning, he paused, wondering how long the business would keep going if the island were invaded. Who would be interested in antiques and fine art when food and household goods would be in limited supply? He sighed, turning the closed sign to read open. He had only taken a step when the door pushed open behind him, and he turned to see his manager, Ernest, a surprised look on his face.

'Good morning, sir. Wasn't sure if you'd be opening up today.' Ernest limped in, his thinness emphasised by the over-large suit he wore, a hand-me-down from his fisherman father.

Leo smiled. The lad, never cheerful at the best of times, looked even more downhearted today. And with good reason.

'I didn't see why not, at least not until things change.' Leo let his eyes wander over the shop, admiring the craftsmanship of the wooden furniture, most of it made locally, and the collection of assorted upholstered chairs. China, glassware and silver covered every surface, and the walls hidden behind paintings and mirrors of every size. Many of the best families on the island had looked to fill their homes with his stock and Leo had to admit it did seem unrealistic to stay open now. People would be wanting to sell, not buy.

'Let's see what happens, shall we, Ernest? I can afford to keep you on if the shop stays open, even if we sell only the merest trinket,' he said, picking up a glass ashtray.

Ernest's mouth turned up in a glimmer of a smile.

'Thank you, sir. I was so worried.'

Leo waved his hand.

'As I said, we'll see how things develop. With a bit of luck, this dreadful war will be over soon, and it will be business as usual. If it drags on,' he added, shrugging his shoulders, 'or the Germans arrive and impose severe restrictions, I might have to reconsider. In the meantime, I need your help in hiding my family's more valuable items in our safe place.'

His father had created the safe place years before, now only known to Leo and Ernest, who had worked for the firm since leaving school. 'We'll wait until it's dark tonight if you don't mind me collecting you after nine? And not a word to anyone, mind.'

'Not at all, sir. And you know you can trust me.' Ernest grinned and disappeared into the tiny kitchen area at the back to make tea for them both. Always the first task of the day.

Chapter 12

Guernsey 2011

'Oh, I can see you!' She reached out towards his insubstantial body, and he mirrored her, their fingers seeming to touch, but there was only air. Tears of joy pricked at her eyes, blurring the image further.

His expression was a mix of sorrow and – what? – frustration? He seemed to draw up all his energy before saying, 'Big man...basement...grabbed me...chair...office. ' His voice was faint, kept fading in and out, as if on the end of a long-distance telephone call.

Her pulse quickened at his words.

'What happened next, my love?' Fiona's voice sank to a whisper, matching Nigel's. She could see his strength waning, his body fading in front of her.

'He...know...Renoir...' Nigel's body disappeared, and Fiona crumpled into a heap on the floor, hugging herself as the held-back tears fell freely. She cried out, 'We'll get him, Nigel, we'll get him, I promise. May he rot in hell for what he did.'

Slowly she calmed down, conscious that time was marching on and Louisa and Paul would be anxious about her. Dragging herself upright, Fiona switched on the light to drive away any remaining shadows. Drained, she reset the alarm before leaving. She needed to be with her friends.

When Fiona arrived back at Icart, Paul took one look at her face and wordlessly poured her a small brandy and pushed her gently into a seat.

'Take your time. Looks like you and Nigel made contact?'

She nodded and took a sip of the burning liquid. It still felt unreal. Could she really have been having a conversation with a ghost? Her dead brother? But he told her something of what happened! It must have been real. After a few more sips she told Paul and Louisa everything.

Paul's face remained calm, but Louisa's mouth fell open.

'Oh my God! That's…that's incredible! No wonder you looked so pale. As if you'd…' she stopped, her hand covering her mouth.

'Seen a ghost? Yes, well I had.' Fiona gave a short laugh, hysteria threatening to take over. 'I'm glad I did, but it, it hurt.' She gripped the glass tighter, determined not to fall apart. At least not in front of her friends.

They sat facing her and now Paul moved to kneel in front of her, placing his hands on her shoulders. Gently he released her grip on the glass, handing it to Louisa. He took Fiona's hands in his and held them as his eyes locked onto hers. Something like a current of electricity flowed into her arms and through her body. In its wake, it left a sense of calm, of relaxation and her eyes grew heavy and slowly closed. Colours swirled in her brain, like her childhood kaleidoscope, and she found herself mesmerised by the ebb and flow of patterns. Gradually, the colours dissolved and all she could see was a bright golden light, and the feeling of calmness grew stronger. She wanted it to last forever, to lose herself in the light's comfort.

'Fiona, are you okay?'

She opened her eyes reluctantly and saw Paul's face close to hers, his eyes searching hers. She smiled. 'Fine, thanks. Whatever you just did, was wonderful. Nigel said you were a healer.'

'Whether I am or not, I'm glad you feel better.'

Louisa asked if she needed any more brandy, but she shook her head.

'You know, it might help if you spoke to Natalie. She went through quite a full-on experience with her ghost and may be able to offer some reassurance,' Louisa said.

'I might do that. It would be good to catch up, anyway. Everyone's been very kind, leaving messages for me, and I should make an effort to reply.' She sighed, suddenly overwhelmed with feelings of guilt.

'Hey! Don't beat yourself up! Everyone understands you're going through a tough time and want you to know they're there for you once you're ready.' Louisa squeezed her.

'Thanks, I guess you're right.' She yawned. 'Time for bed, it's been quite a day. Night, night, you two.'

Fiona looked forward to a good night's sleep. As her head hit the pillow, all she could see was the ghostly image of her brother in the office. Tears slid silently down her cheeks.

Feeling calmer the following morning, Fiona phoned Natalie, and they arranged to meet at Natalie's cottage on Saturday morning. She also contacted other friends who'd tried to get in touch and expressed her thanks for their condolences. By the time she'd finished, she felt both humbled and strengthened by their support. She wasn't alone after all.

The archives beckoned, and Fiona once again found herself immersed in the harrowing events of the German Occupation. Her grandparents had died when she and Nigel were young children, so she'd not had a chance to ask them about their wartime experiences and had only a patchy knowledge of what it had been like for the locals left on the island. Ploughing through the transcripts of documents left behind by the then States Controlling Committee and the local police was a tedious and, at times, sobering, experience and she was beginning to wonder how much longer she could go on when the name

'Leo Bichard' appeared on the page. She jotted down all the relevant details. At last, she was beginning to understand what had happened all those years ago. And it didn't make for good reading.

John was waiting for her at the house in Colborne Road. He had been supervising the installation of the extra security devices when she had called to tell him about her research. After showing her the security improvements, they sat in the garden while she gave him more details.

'It's such a sad story, John. It seems poor Leo was betrayed by an anonymous informer, who told the Germans that Leo's French, maternal grandmother had been a Jew. Can you imagine anything so mean? So vile?' She stood up and paced about, filled with rising anger on behalf of the unfortunate Leo.

'It does sound a horrible thing to do, I agree. Perhaps Leo had made an enemy of "anonymous" in some way. Did many locals act as informers in the war?'

'There were some who did, yes. Probably earned some brownie points from the Germans for their trouble.' Fiona continued pacing, hating to admit any of her fellow islanders could have behaved in such a way. She knew her grandparents would have been more honourable. Distracted, she started dead-heading nearby flowers in the abundant herbaceous border, once her mother's pride and joy.

'So, what else did you find out?' John asked, bringing her back.

She smiled. 'Sorry, I was miles away. Well, after Leo was arrested, he was sent with other Jews to a concentration camp in Germany in 1942. None came back,' she sighed. 'All his property was confiscated, except the family business, which somehow slipped under the radar as it had been closed down at the time the Germans arrived. Someone must have taken over after the war, but the name isn't recorded. I guess it must have been

Domaille. I'm hoping his widow will be able to throw some light on that when you eventually get to see her.' She sat down on the garden chair next to John, flicking an errant flower head off her jeans.

'You've done well, Fiona. We've a good place to start, and I'll press on with searching for any surviving Bichards on the island. Even a distant relation might know something about Leo's widow.' John beamed at her, and a thought struck her.

'I might be clutching at straws, but how about if Leo's French grandparents had met Renoir, which is feasible time-wise, and bought the painting from him? It could explain how it came to be on the island.' She leaned forward, excited at the prospect.

'Yes, that makes sense. Leo, not wanting the Germans to commandeer his art collection, hides it in the basement of his shop. Smart move. Except that someone must have found out. And surely Leo wouldn't have left such valuable stuff there without telling someone? And why didn't they tell the widow when she turned up after the war? That's what any decent person would have done, surely?'

'Except not everyone is decent, as we said earlier.' She sat back, pushing a hand through her curls.

'No, that's true. But whatever did happen, it's becoming clear the Renoir did belong to Leo, and his widow would, understandably, have accused the Germans of theft. The poor woman seems to have lost so much!' He shook his head in sorrow. 'What a can of worms we've opened! Did they have any children?'

'Oh, I don't know. As the wife left before the occupation, it's likely she went with children. Thousands of children were evacuated, and many mothers went with them. What a horrible choice to make!' She bit her lip.

'Once we find out what happened to Mrs Bichard, we'll have more pieces of the jigsaw. If they had a child or children, there's a good chance an heir's kicking about somewhere. About to inherit a bloody valuable painting!' John rubbed his hands together as if he were the one due to inherit something worth millions.

'Hoping for a reward, John?' Fiona grinned.

'Not really, but it always feels good to return property to its rightful owner. Mind you, it's usually something more mundane, like a phone or a wallet. I've never been involved with anything worth millions before.'

'Nor me, except for my work. And I want to find the rightful owner of this painting. It might make Nigel's death seem a bit less pointless. Something that's hard to believe at the moment.'

Chapter 13

Guernsey 2011

'Fiona! It's good to see you, come in.' Stuart hugged her before ushering her inside. 'I'm so sorry about Nigel, what an awful thing to happen. We're all gutted.'

She nodded, hardly trusting herself to respond. When people said how sorry they were, it made it more real, reminded her of her loss. Stuart was a nice guy, though, and Fiona sensed he felt awkward, too.

'Natalie's in the kitchen, and I'm leaving you girls in peace. I've been given a huge shopping list and told not to come back until I've bought everything or I'm in trouble.' He rolled his eyes in mock fear before dashing out of the door.

Natalie's head appeared round the kitchen door.

'Thought I heard you arrive. How are you?' She flung her arms around her and Fiona succumbed to the warm embrace of her friend.

'Coping. Being well looked after by Louisa and Paul, as you can imagine.'

Natalie released her, and Fiona saw the compassion in her huge blue eyes.

'Lovely couple, aren't they? And so well matched,' Natalie said, switching on the kettle. 'Coffee okay? Or something stronger?' She tilted her head towards a bottle of wine on the counter.

'Coffee's fine, thanks.' Fiona looked around the smart, streamlined kitchen. 'It was in here, wasn't it? Where your ghost appeared.'

Spooning coffee into the cafetiére, Natalie hesitated. 'Sort of. I didn't see him until much later on when Reverend Ayres was here, but before that objects got moved or thrown about and I heard his voice.' She shuddered. 'Really creepy. And sometimes my kitchen "disappeared", replaced with one from the war.' Natalie poured in hot water before turning, with a grin, to Fiona. 'It's history now but wasn't a great experience at the time. And it blew Stuart away! He couldn't get a handle on it initially, but now he's cool about it, and I think it's brought us closer. Moving here meant I became caught up in his family's history, creating a bond.'

Fiona nodded. 'I can understand that.'

Natalie handed her a mug of coffee.

'Let's go into the garden, get some sun on our faces. And you can tell me all about your own experience.'

Once settled on the patio, Fiona told her about seeing Nigel and even having a brief conversation.

'Must have been so weird for you. Are you going to try and connect again?' Natalie asked, sipping her coffee.

'Yes. I want to learn more about what happened to him. But talking, and taking a...form seem to drain his energy.'

'Well, I don't know if this will work for you, but my other "ghost", Olive, somehow got into my head and I learnt her story through my dreams. It was as if I was *her* somehow.' Natalie grimaced. 'Pretty awful, some of it. But she was desperate for me to know what happened and managed to connect with me, even though we weren't related. We just shared this house. But with you and Nigel being twins, perhaps he could "talk" to you silently, like a voice in your head.'

'You're right. We were almost telepathic at times, in fact, I sensed something was wrong at about the time he must have died. But didn't realise how...how bad it was.' A lump formed in her throat as she wondered, again, if Nigel had been trying to reach her. There was nothing she could have done from England, but it didn't stop the guilt.

Natalie squeezed her arm. 'You see what I mean? I didn't ask Olive to get inside my head, but you hardly need to ask Nigel. When you're in bed, ready to sleep, try focusing on him. Less traumatic for you both than him trying to appear in spirit.'

'You're right, it would be, but something is comforting in actually seeing him again. Though I know it can't last.' Her hands gripped the mug in her frustration. She would make one more attempt to connect with Nigel in the shop, and if it didn't happen, she'd follow Natalie's advice, she decided. Glancing up at her friend, she forced a smile. 'Enough of me, you can show me around your super garden. The spring flowers look fab.'

That evening Fiona drove to the shop, ostensibly to check on Ken's first day, but mainly to see if Nigel would make an appearance. She was pleased to see Ken had dusted and rearranged some of the smaller items in the window. Always a good idea to refresh the display, Nigel used to say.

In the office all was tidy, and she found a note addressed to herself – Ken had presumably expected her to check up on him. He said, apart from some obvious curiosity seekers, keen to see if Fiona would be present, there had also been genuine buyers, and he'd made some good sales, as per his list. It seemed that a tragedy brought out the best as well as the worst in people, she thought grimly. Many had wanted him to pass on their condolences to her.

Once she was satisfied all looked in order, Fiona settled in the office chair and called Nigel's name. Nothing. She tried twice more and gave up. Maybe Nigel sensed that someone else had been manning the shop that day and this had put him off. Disappointed, she went back to Icart.

A slight breeze blew along the cliffs the next morning, and Paul and Louisa suggested they went for a brisk walk before lunch. This suited Fiona, needing to escape her obsession with contacting Nigel. They struck out towards Petit Bot Bay with the plan to return for lunch at Saint's Bay Hotel, handily situated opposite their house. The scent of wild garlic hung in the air as they walked and gulls dived from the cliffs, constantly looking for food. Fiona gulped in the heady sea air.

'Natalie had a point when she suggested I tried to contact Nigel when I'm relaxed or about to sleep. But I can't relax! My head's constantly buzzing and I can't let go. Would you help me, Paul? You have a magic touch.'

He fell into step beside her as Louisa led the way.

'Of course, pleased to help. I do sense a huge amount of tension in you, not surprising. Perhaps later, just before bedtime. But you will have to let him go sometime, Fiona. He needs to move on, just like you.' His voice was gentle, but the words hit her hard. She knew he was right, but that didn't mean she was happy about severing the link between them. Nodding mutely, she increased her pace to join Louisa, as if by doing so she was delaying the inevitable.

Paul was as good as his word and later that evening eased her into a meditative state, simply by holding her hands as he talked to her. It was as if he was drawing all the tension and upset from her, leaving behind a calmness Fiona rarely felt. She went to bed keen to focus on Nigel, silently seeking a connection. She had an awareness of him, but it was through a fog, and if he spoke she couldn't hear the words. She must have drifted asleep as the next thing she knew, Louisa was knocking on the door with a cup of tea. Disappointed, she resolved to keep trying.

Chapter 14

Guernsey 2011

John replaced the phone with a satisfied sigh. At last, some progress. He'd finally tracked down a surviving member of Leo's family, the grandson of his uncle. Too young to have ever met Leo, Andre Bichard had told John his father had talked about him, had met him. After arranging to meet at Andre's home early Monday evening, John phoned the nursing home to check on Mrs Domaille. He drummed his fingers on the desk impatiently as the phone continued to ring.

'Pine Forest Nursing Home. Can I help you?' A rather breathless voice answered.

'I'm enquiring after one of your residents, Mrs Domaille. Has she recovered enough to receive visitors, please?'

'Sorry, I'm new. Hang on a moment while I check.'

John heard the sound of retreating feet and voices murmuring in the background. He sighed. So much of his time was spent hanging on the end of phones waiting to talk to people. It had been different when he was in the police. He wasn't kept waiting then.

'Hello? Sorry to keep you waiting. Mrs Domaille is much better and can have visitors from tomorrow. Who shall I say called?'

'Mr Ferguson. Thank you, I'll call round tomorrow afternoon.'

Good, more progress, he told himself, continuing to beat out a tattoo on the desk. In his line of work, you learnt to be patient, but it wasn't always easy. The pressure was off now he was his own boss, but he liked to deliver for his clients. And this case had got under his skin.

Since moving to Guernsey thirty years ago, he hadn't had to deal much with murders. They had usually turned out to be domestics gone too far. But this one...he sucked in through his teeth. Fiona's obvious pain and distress had touched him, and he was determined to find her brother's killer. And sooner rather than later.

Andre Bichard's cottage was barely visible above the surrounding overgrown garden in the narrow lane off Landes Du Marche. At first glance, it looked to be an uninhabited wreck, and John double-checked the address before pulling into a nearby gateway. Pushing open the rickety gate hanging off its hinges, John battled through a mass of long grass, weeds and the few spring flowers trying to survive. The granite walls were covered in ivy, forcing itself into the mortar cracks, and the weathered window frames held dirty pieces of material masquerading as curtains.

Hoping his stomach would survive any sights or smells waiting inside, John knocked on the old wooden door. He heard the sounds of heavy feet making their way along a passage. The door inched open a crack.

'Mr Bichard? John Ferguson, I phoned earlier.'

A heavy-set man in his fifties, John guessed, dressed in dirty jeans and T-shirt, pulled the door fully open.

'Yeh, come in. I don't use the front room so we'll go in the kitchen, shall we.' Andre led the way down a dark, unlit hall and past the front room with its door ajar, exposing a room full to the ceiling with what looked like rubbish collected over many years. John caught a whiff of unwashed body and clothes as he followed him. Even the narrow hall had piles of papers and boxes stacked against the walls, making it difficult to find a way through without knocking anything over.

The back door lay open and John wondered if he could suggest they sat outside, but as he drew closer, he saw the back garden was as impenetrable as the front. Taking a deep breath of fresh air while he could, he followed the man into the kitchen. Oddly enough, this wasn't quite as bad as he'd expected. The kitchen units had seen better days, but the worktops looked clean and not too cluttered, with a kettle and toaster, in a matching shade of green, near a sink only half-full of dirty dishes. An old cooker and fridge sat among the units and in the middle of the room were an old Formica-topped table and plastic chairs.

Andre waved him to a chair. 'Sit down, please. Want some tea?' He stood near the kettle, poised to switch it on.

John decided not to risk it. How clean were the mugs?

'No thanks, I'm good.'

He nodded and sat down.

'So, why the sudden interest in my grandfather's brother, Leo? He's been dead many a year now.' He scratched the back of his head; his eyes screwed up. John's attention was caught by a selection of colourful tattoos on Andre's arms and didn't reply immediately.

'Mr Ferguson?' He sounded annoyed.

'Oh, sorry, Mr Bichard. It's to do with the antiques business Leo owned, in Contrée Mansell. Did you know he owned it before the war?'

He grimaced. 'For sure. Dad used to go on about it, like. How his father, Nathaniel, had struggled all his life as a fisherman, while his bloody brother had married a French heiress. Pah!' He grimaced. 'Gave him the money to pour into the antiques business and buy a fancy house in the Talbot Valley.' He paused to flick a crumb onto the floor. 'When he died he didn't leave nothing to Nathaniel; bloody Leo copped the lot. Did very well, he did, by the sound of it.' Andre spat on the floor.

Ah, so there's been a family split, John thought. And it's about money. Nothing new there, then.

'Was there a falling-out between your grandfather and Leo over the will?'

Andre scratched his head.

'They were never close, not from what Dad said. Not sure if Leo even acknowledged Nathaniel as his uncle. He was beneath him, see. They wouldn't have mixed in the same circles. Dad reckoned as Leo saw himself as superior to him; his father having bagged himself a wealthy wife. Huh!' He spat again.

John edged his chair out of range.

'How did your father and Leo get on?'

'They didn't. Dad was a fisherman like his father, and Leo would sometimes buy lobster and crab from him if he was having some posh dinner-party, but otherwise, they had no contact, as he told me. Dad said 'ol Leo wasn't much of a social man, kept himself to himself before he got married. Softened up a bit then, he did.'

'I understand Leo's wife evacuated before the Germans arrived. Did your father see anything of Leo after that?'

'No, he'd already joined up. But afore that, he and me ma were invited to their daughter's christening. Dad reckoned it was the wife who insisted on it. Dad liked her, although she was from a posh family, she was friendly like.' Andre suddenly sat forward, scowling. 'You're asking an awful lot of questions, you are. What's this all got to do with the antiques shop, anyway?'

'Something was found recently which may have belonged to Leo, and the finder's anxious to trace his family. And if you can help us, it would be much appreciated.' John smiled encouragingly. This man would likely sell his mother for money.

Andre looked deflated.

'Not sure as I can help. Is there a reward?' His eyes gleamed.

'Could be. Do you know what happened to Leo in the occupation?'

'When Dad came back after the war, Leo was gone. He heard as how the Germans had arrested him for being a Jew, but no-one knew nothing about that. If he was, had to be from the French side.'

'What about Leo's wife?'

'Ah, now then, Dad did see her briefly.' Andre brightened, the pound signs beckoning. 'She contacted Dad to tell him about Leo, not that Dad was much upset like, but it was thoughtful of her, being family. Said she was quite shaken. He felt sorry for her, he told me. Didn't stay long, went back to England and he never heard from her again.'

'I see. You wouldn't know where Mrs Bichard went, would you? If we can trace her or her daughter...' he spread his hands.

Andre rubbed his nose, his eyes screwed in concentration.

'Somewhere east, Dad said. North of London, I think.'

'Norfolk? Cambridge? Suffolk–'

'Suffolk! That was it. Where her folks came from.' He sank back into his chair and grinned.

'Brilliant. Thanks, you've been a great help. I'll get back to you if we trace Mrs Bichard or her family.' John stood, pleased to stretch his legs. 'Was this your parents' house? Looks old.'

'Yes, I inherited it a few years back. Lucky to have a roof over my head, I am. Not working, you see.' Andre lifted his bulk and John stepped back towards the door and fresh air.

'Oh, that's a shame. Thought it was easy to get a job here. You didn't take up fishing, like your father?

'I did, for a few years, anyway. But I got sick, see, found it hard to work. Depression, and something else I can't remember the name of, the docs said. Been on benefits for some time now. Find it hard to make ends meet, I do.' He gave John a hard stare.

'Right, well let me see.' He took out his wallet and placed a £20 note on the table. 'Hope that helps, Mr Bichard. And there could be more later.'

'Appreciate that, Mr Ferguson. I'll see you out.'

John headed back to the front door, pulling it open before Andre reached it, and took a deep breath of fresh air. That was better.

'Goodbye, and thanks again for your time.' Wanting to avoid a handshake, John nodded and turned away. As he pushed his way through the mass of old shrubs and weeds, he heard Andre call, 'Bye for now,' before closing the front door. Slipping into his car, he switched on the engine and drove off, a big smile plastered on his face. The jigsaw had gained another piece.

Chapter 15

Guernsey, June 1940

The family's valuables now safely hidden, Leo was marginally more sanguine. Whatever might happen to him, at least Teresa would inherit most of his family's wealth, to be passed to little Judith in the future. The rumours flying around since the mass evacuation of nearly half the islanders were not encouraging since most predicted an early invasion by the Germans.

On the evening of Tuesday 26th June Leo arrived home from work after a mind-numbingly quiet day. Until a few days ago, he would have been looking forward to an evening with Teresa and spending some time with Judith. Now all that awaited him was the meal prepared by the housekeeper, Elsie, and an evening with only the wireless for company. As he parked his beloved MG sports car around the side of the house, he wondered how long he'd have petrol to drive it. Sighing, he stood for a moment looking over the garden Teresa had spent so much time on, making it her special project. Flowers and shrubs flourished alongside an area devoted to vegetables and fruit. At least he wouldn't starve if he were to take good care of it.

Inside, the entrance hall was cool and welcoming, the flagstone floor covered with a bright Turkey runner, chosen by Teresa in place of the old faded brown rug his father hadn't bothered to change. Her influence was everywhere; from vases filled with flowers from the garden, now courtesy of Elsie, to bowls of potpourri on the hall table. He threw down his briefcase and perched his hat on the hall stand before walking along the corridor to the back and the kitchen.

'There you are, Master Leo. You're looking a bit peaky, if I may say so. Not going down with something, are you?' Elsie's round face creased in concern as she studied him, wiping her hands on her apron. Behind her dirty pots were soaking in the sink while the aroma of baked fish filled the air.

'No, I'm fine, Elsie. Just worried about what's going to happen. Like all of us.' The silence was broken by the sound of the old grandfather clock ticking away at the bottom of the stairs. Leo shrugged off his jacket and loosened his tie, placing it carefully on the back of a chair. Since Teresa had left, he'd taken to eating in the kitchen instead of the formal dining-room and didn't feel the need for formal attire.

'Shall I pour you a glass of nice cold beer, Master Leo? It's been a hot day today, hasn't it?' Elsie pointed to the jug of beer she'd placed ready for him, and he nodded his thanks. While he took a welcome swallow, Elsie served up his supper of baked fish, fresh carrots and beans and boiled potatoes. Although plain, it was well cooked, and Leo appreciated Elsie's efforts. She'd been with the family for years, and her stiff movements as she shuffled around the kitchen reminded him she was well into her seventies.

'This looks wonderful, Elsie, thank you.' He cleared his throat, 'You are sure about carrying on here? After all, you have your Bert to look after.' Leo took a bite of the fish, which melted in his mouth. He knew he was selfish, and he didn't want to lose her but was conscious of how much she had to do.

Elsie looked shocked.

'Why, of course, I'm sure! As long as I've breath in my body, I'll be round every day as I've been these past forty years or more. I've heard tell as we may have to ration our food soon, particularly if them Germans arrive, but I'll still cook and clean for you.'

She held herself straighter as she went back to the washing-up and Leo smiled to himself. Elsie was the one constant in his life, looking after him since his mother died in childbirth and taking on the role of housekeeper with the help of a maid or two and a man for the hard work. Thanks to the war, now there was only Elsie.

'Right then, I'll be off. There's an apple crumble warming in the oven for your pudding, Master Leo. You make sure you eat everything up, now. I'll be back tomorrow as usual.' She gave him a nod before shuffling out of the kitchen. Her cottage was five minutes up the lane, shared with her husband, Bert, known by all as a lazy man who had scraped a living as a farm labourer until old age had given him an excuse to stop. Leo finished his meal and poured another glass of beer from the jug, before leaving the plates to soak.

He decided to take a turn in the garden while there was enough light, settling on a bench overlooking the view down the valley. To him, it was one of the most magical spots on the island, hidden away from passing traffic, with only birdsong breaking the silence. Not that many vehicles used the nearby road, with the local farmers preferring their horse and carts. Leo was sipping his beer when he was overwhelmed with a sense of foreboding. As if on cue, a black cloud appeared out of nowhere, obliterating the sun. Leo shivered and went inside to make a phone call.

'Good evening, Mr Spall.'

'Leo, my boy, how are you? The Jerries haven't landed yet, have they?' His father-in- law's gruff voice echoed down the line.

'No, sir. In fact, I was hoping you might have heard something from your brother at the War Office.'

'Afraid not. Personally, I think it's a damn disgrace we've left your wonderful islands unprotected. To think of part of Britain being occupied! Damned disgrace, I call it. Now I expect you want to talk to Teresa, hmm? I'll call her. You take care of yourself, my boy.'

Leo was fond of Teresa's father, a gentleman farmer with sprawling acres in Suffolk. At least his little family would be safe and well cared for.

'Leo! Lovely to hear from you. I keep expecting to learn the lines have been cut.' Teresa sounded out of breath as if she'd been running.

'Not yet. How are you both?' They spent several minutes talking about not very much, just wanting to hear the other's voice and he finished by saying he'd call the following evening. Unsettled by the call, Leo sifted through his gramophone records to find something uplifting, choosing a D'Oyly Carte production of *HMS Pinafore* and settled down in his armchair with the remains of the beer. As he listened to the music, his mind drifted back to the first time he met Teresa, three years before.

'May I introduce you to Mr and Mrs Spall and their daughter, Teresa? They're here for the summer, and I've offered to show them around.' Clem, an old friend of Leo's, smiled as he introduced them at the dinner party. Leo, cudgelled into attending, was well known for being unsociable and not a fan of small talk. But Clem had insisted, saying he needed to make up an even number. Leo shook hands with the pleasant enough couple, before turning to their daughter, partially hidden behind her rotund father. As he caught sight of her sparkling blue eyes and wide smile, something extraordinary happened. He opened his mouth to say something, and nothing came out. Embarrassment curled up inside him as he stared, open-mouthed at the young woman in front of him.

'Good evening, Mr Bichard. I'm so pleased to meet you and must say how beautiful your island is. You are so lucky to live here.' She tilted her head as their fingers met in a firm clasp. Leo found her grip firm and cool and managed to find his voice.

'Pleased to meet you too, Miss Spall. And yes, I am fortunate to live here. Where are you staying?'

As she told him about their rented home on the west coast, Leo found his attention straying from her words as he admired both her looks and intelligence. He guessed she must only be in her early twenties and as he was approaching forty, felt at a distinct disadvantage.

Clem's wife had arranged the seating such that Leo was next to Miss Spall – or Teresa as she asked him to call her. The evening passed quickly, and Leo couldn't remember having enjoyed himself as much for years. He even found himself offering to take Teresa out for a drive that Sunday and she accepted with a warm smile.

A year later they were married in her local church in Suffolk before returning to make their home in Guernsey, moving in with his widowed father, now too ill to leave the house. Leo had never been close to him, a Victorian by birth and manner, and when he died a few months later, found it hard to mourn him. Leo suspected his father blamed him for his mother's death. In a way it was a relief to be his own man, running the business and enjoying the graceful home nestling in the lanes of the Talbot Valley.

Teresa happily took over the running of the household, aided by Elsie and their other staff, and hosting dinner parties which once Leo would have hated, but now enjoyed. He took pride in his beautiful wife as she laughed and conversed with their guests, throwing him a smile when he caught her eye. He never ceased to be amazed at how much his life had changed in little more than a year, enjoying for the first time in his life a woman's love and companionship. When Judith, the image of her mother, was born in 1939, he surprised himself by how much love he felt for her, how much he wanted to protect her, this tiny scrap in his arms. Although happy to leave her care to Teresa, he was proud to be a father as well as a husband.

Leo was taking a stroll towards the market on Thursday morning when a German bomber flew low over Town and harbour, causing everyone around him to stop and stare in horror. He was equally stunned. Did this mean they were about to be invaded? The plane didn't drop any bombs and flew off towards France. For the moment they were reprieved, but for how long? After making his purchases, he returned to his shop in a sombre mood.

Chapter 16

Guernsey 2011

Fiona was chatting to Paul and Louisa in their sitting room when John called round.

'Sorry to come without warning, but I thought you'd be keen to hear how I got on with Andre Bichard.' He was grinning broadly as Louisa ushered him in.

'No problem. Go ahead. I'm sure we're all agog,' Fiona said, making room for him on the sofa.

They listened intently as John described their meeting.

'Fascinating stuff. Fills some of the gaps in what I've found in the archives.' Fiona couldn't help but smile. 'Sounds quite a character, this Andre. Do you think he's told you the truth?'

'I don't think he's bright enough to make it up. And why bother? He knows there might be some kind of reward if we find Leo's family, thanks to him, but otherwise, he's nothing to gain.' John sighed. 'I felt sorry for him. He's obviously picked up on the bitterness between his side of the family and Leo's, and feels hard done by.'

Louisa chipped in.

'You don't think he could be the burglar? It's possible he knew about the Renoir through the family connection.'

John shook his head.

'No, it doesn't fit the facts. I'd bet good money it was a professional job, someone who knew how to disable alarms and had the sense to wear gloves. This guy didn't have any tech in the place that I could see and, if anything, lives trapped in the past, surrounded by rubbish. But I agree he could, in theory, know about the Renoir. Which means he could have told someone else.' He looked thoughtful, tapping his fingers on the arm of the sofa.

Paul had disappeared to bring John a beer and now passed it over. The others were drinking wine, and for a moment no-one spoke as they sipped their drinks.

'You know, if Andre's right and Leo wasn't a mixer, saw himself as superior to others, this might explain why someone shopped him to the Germans. Bit extreme, but times weren't exactly normal, were they?' Paul said.

'The problem is, who knew he had a Jewish grandmother? Even Andre's family didn't know! With anti-Semitism spreading in Europe, it may have been kept private.' John sipped his beer, his brow furrowed in thought.

'And there were only a handful of Jews living in Guernsey at the beginning of the war, mainly foreign-born women. Leo's background must have been almost unique. And, of course, in his mind, he wasn't a Jew. His parents were Christians, and he was baptised as such. Poor man.' Fiona shook her head.

'Guess we'll have to forget that question for the moment and focus on who knew about the Renoir. My gut tells me there's a connection, so we may end up solving the two mysteries in one go.' John finished his beer and stood. 'Thanks for the drink, Paul. I'd better get off, or the wife will think I'm up to no good,' he chuckled.

Paul and Louisa said their goodbyes and Fiona walked with him to the hall.

'What's next on the agenda?' She held the door open.

'I'm going to see Mrs Domaille tomorrow, which I hope will give us some more clues. Then the focus is on tracking down Leo's family. By my reckoning, his widow could still be alive and then there's the daughter, although if she's married her name will be different, so...' he shrugged.

'I've every confidence in you, John. Look forward to your update.' Fiona rubbed her forehead, suddenly overwhelmed by tiredness and buried emotions.

About to leave, John turned and studied her.

'How are you coping? You look all in.'

'It's hard. One minute I'm excited about all the stuff we're finding out, the next I'm remembering why we're doing it. Then...then the pain returns,' she gulped and found herself embraced in a gentle hug. Surprised, she held herself stiffly for a moment, then relaxed.

'Not all policemen are as hard as nails, you know. Some of us have soft centres, and I have a daughter about your age. I wouldn't want her to go through what you're going through. I think you're very brave.' He let go, nodded and left.

Fiona closed the door, touched by John's concern. It hit her that, in some ways, he reminded her of her father. A doctor, he was all bluff on the outside, but soft underneath. The thought made her wish he was still around, ready to comfort her when needed. She had been closer to him than her mother, who'd been pretty wrapped up in her work as a lawyer, and hard to talk to. Get close to. Whereas her father would stop whatever he was doing and listen, glasses pushed up on his head.

The memories began to force their way in, and Fiona fought to keep control. She called a quick goodnight to her friends and made for her room. Once the tears had dried up, she took deep, calming breaths as Paul had taught her and focused on Nigel. Lying in bed, she clutched his photo to her chest, willing him to connect. Closing her eyes, she became aware of his face, as if in a dream, and he was trying to talk to her.

'Be...careful that...man wanted to know...where Renoir. Said didn't know...what he meant. Don't want him...coming after...you. Big, strong. Hurt me. Sorry, Sis. Love you...' His face and voice faded, and Fiona was alone once more.

◆◆◆

John Ferguson wasn't sure what to expect. In his experience, frail old ladies tended to be profoundly deaf and short-sighted and possessed butterfly memories. And if Mrs Domaille was one of these, then he wasn't likely to learn much of value. Still, nothing ventured, he thought, as he stood in the hallway of the nursing home, admiring the display of spring flowers on the side-table.

'Mr Ferguson? I understand you'd like to speak to Mrs Domaille?' A woman wearing a smart blue nurse's uniform bustled towards him, conveying a sense of having been interrupted from more important matters. He straightened up and offered a placatory smile.

'Thank you, yes, er Sister,' he said, catching sight of her badge. 'Is she able to receive visitors?'

Her eyes bored into his.

'She is, although only for short periods of time. May I ask what your relationship is to Mrs Domaille?'

'Quite truthfully, none. But I'm…involved in the inquiry into the death of a man who purchased her late husband's business from her, and hope she can help with some background information. I promise not to stay too long, Sister.' He smiled again.

The nurse frowned.

'Yes, I'd heard something about a sudden death, but had no idea about a connection with Mrs Domaille. I'm not sure she'll be able to help you much, Mr Ferguson, but I can't see any harm in letting you see her. She has good days and bad days, and today is one of the better ones.' Turning on her heel, she added, 'Follow me please,' and marched down the corridor.

She stopped at a closed door and after a brief knock, went inside, signalling John to follow. A white-haired lady, muffled in blankets in spite of the heat blasting from the radiator, was propped up in a chair by the window. She turned her head towards the nurse and smiled.

'Hello, Sister. Is it dinnertime already?'

'No, Mrs Domaille, there's someone here to see you, a Mr Ferguson. He'd like to talk to you about your husband's antiques business if you're feeling up to it.'

The old lady's eyes, a watery blue behind thick lenses, swivelled towards him. A puzzled look crossed her pale, lined face. 'Ferguson? Do I know you? The name isn't familiar.' Her voice wavered and John, worried she might refuse to speak to him, answered quickly, 'We haven't met before, Mrs Domaille, and there's no reason to be concerned. I'd be glad of your help solving a mystery concerning your late husband's business, that's all. It won't take long.' He proffered his warmest smile and reached for a thin hand.

'Oh. I suppose that's all right. What do you think, Sister? Is it safe for me to talk to this man?' She twisted her hands together, looking from John to the nurse.

'Yes, perfectly safe. But you can always press your button if you need me.' The nurse's voice was gentle, so different to her brisk manner towards him and John breathed a sigh of relief.

'Bring the chair close then; I'm a bit deaf.' Mrs Domaille waved a hand towards a chair a few feet away, and he positioned it right next to hers. The nurse left, reminding him not to stay too long.

'What does Ernest's business have to do with you, Mr Ferguson? I sold it over a year ago to a nice young man and his sister. It's them you need to talk to.' She pulled her blanket tight around her thin body.

'Yes, I know. And that's where the problem lies, Mrs Domaille. The young man, Nigel, was found dead in the shop a few days ago and I'm helping in the investigation into his death.' He hoped his old mate Woods never found out he'd said that, but still, it was the truth.

She gasped. 'Oh, how awful! I'm sorry to hear that, he was so young and keen. But I still don't see what it has to do with Ernest. He's been dead near two years.' Her hands pulled frantically at the blanket and John was concerned she'd start to panic.

'We're trying to trace whoever owned the business before Ernest as we think he may have left something in the shop. Do you know who that might be?'

Her face relaxed. 'Oh, that's before my time, I'm afraid. I didn't meet Ernest until after the war; I was much younger, you see. He'd owned the business some years by then.' Her gaze went off into the distance as if remembering the past.

'And he never mentioned anything about the previous owner?'

'I vaguely remember him saying he'd bought it for a song. Those were his very words.' She said, pursing her lips. 'Something about the owner having to leave suddenly. I was only a child when the Germans came, and I remember thousands of islanders leaving before the soldiers arrived. Always scared of them, I was. With their rifles and noisy boots. I was one of the few children left. My parents couldn't bear to send me away, you see.'

At least she remembers the Occupation. That's something, John thought.

'So, you think the owner left with the other evacuees?'

'No, that doesn't sound right.' She twisted the blanket, a puzzled look on her face. 'I remember, I think Ernest said he was working for the owner when war broke out, but he was forced to leave later. Something to do with the Germans.' She nodded. 'Yes, that's it. The Germans took him away.'

'Did he mention his name?'

She shook her head.

'No, or if he did, I've forgotten it. Ernest never talked about that time, said it was best left in the past. Can't say I blame him. I was only too glad to put it behind me too.'

'Thank you, you've been most helpful, Mrs Domaille. One last question before I leave you in peace. Did you know about the basement in the shop?'

'Basement? I don't know anything about a basement. But then, I hardly stepped foot in the business. Ernest never encouraged me neither, saw it as his domain, he did.' Her voice trailed off, and he saw she was falling asleep.

'I'll be off then. I can see you're tired. Thanks again, Mrs Domaille.'

She didn't seem to hear him, and he crept from the room and closed the door. As he neared the main entrance, the sister emerged from another room.

'Mr Ferguson, was Mrs Domaille able to help you?'

'Yes, a little thanks. But she was tired, and I left her sleeping.'

John was about to move on when she continued, 'Well, she's not used to visitors. She's been with us nine months, and you're only her second visitor. And the first one, her son, has only been the once.' She sniffed. 'And he didn't stay long. Poor woman.'

John stood still.

'Mrs Domaille has a son? She never mentioned him. Odd. And he lives in Guernsey? I might need to contact him.'

'I don't think they're close and she hadn't said anything to us about him until he turned up here. I'm afraid I don't have an address for him, but I got the impression he'd not lived here for some years.'

'Thank you, Sister. I might want to call on Mrs Domaille another time, if I may.'

'She may not remember you, Mr Ferguson. Early stages of dementia, you see. Today was a good day, but...' she shrugged.

'Understood. Well, thanks again and goodbye for now.'

John couldn't help smiling as he left. His well-honed instincts told him he'd just learnt something important. Extremely important.

Chapter 17

Guernsey 2011

Fiona woke to feel rotten after a night spent tossing and turning as she relived memories from her childhood. Flashbacks of her and Nigel playing on the beach in Fermain Bay, their parents recumbent on towels nearby, before they'd all troop up to the café for sandwiches or snacks. It had been their favourite beach, and Fiona remembered hot, sunny days laughing with her brother as they competed to build the best sandcastle ever. Even her mother had loosened up and joined in, siding with Fiona while her father partnered Nigel. Weekends and school holidays had been magical. Not that she'd realised it at the time, just took them for granted as children do.

Each time she'd surfaced from a dream memory, Fiona felt the full force of her loss. Her aloneness. The only one left of four. Her inward cry of, 'It's not fair!' did nothing to assuage the pain ripping her apart. By the time the early morning sun beckoned she would have given anything for temporary oblivion. Knowing her father wouldn't have approved of sleeping pills or antidepressants for grief, Fiona had resisted asking her doctor for help. She had to face it and go through to the other side, an attitude encouraged by Paul and Louisa with their much-needed support.

After a long drench in the shower, she felt marginally better, but with no real purpose for the day. Louisa was in the kitchen alone and, after quick good mornings, poured her a mug of coffee.

'Bad night?' she asked, frowning.

'Yep. Lots of memories floating around. But I did make contact with Nigel if you can call it that.' She explained about the voice in her head, how Nigel wanted to warn her.

Louisa's eyes widened.

'Wow! Are you going to tell John? It might help with identifying the killer.'

'I'm not sure. It does sound a bit off the wall to say my dead brother has sent me a warning. Don't want him thinking I'm a bit, you know,' she said, twirling a finger at her head.

'Tricky. Perhaps if you leave it for now and see what potential suspects turn up. That Andre was a big guy, wasn't he? Though John didn't think he was very bright.' Louisa munched on her toast.

'Yes, I wondered about him, too.' Fiona pushed a hand through her hair, feeling unsure what to do. She didn't want John giving up the case thinking she was flaky. 'I'll leave it for now. Can't hurt. In the meantime, I've got to focus on something to do. The police haven't got back to me about the toxicology report, so I can't arrange a funeral, and I'm at a loose end.'

Louisa started loading the dishwasher.

'Why don't you call Charlotte? You know she's wanted to see you since hearing the news and seeing her and the baby might cheer you up a bit. James is quite a little character, isn't he?' She closed the door of the dishwasher and smiled at Fiona as she headed to the door.

'He is, and I haven't seen them for weeks. Good idea, I'll ring her. See you later.'

As Fiona drove through the elaborate iron gates of Charlotte and Andy's Victorian villa, she couldn't help grinning. The impressive entrance and drive, leading to the stuccoed villa, shouted 'class', a description that also fitted Charlotte herself. A relative newcomer to the island after falling in love with Andy, a local architect, it was known that Charlotte originated from landed gentry in England, but she had no airs and graces and was fun to be with. And she had excellent taste in property, Fiona thought, parking at the side of the freshly painted house, oozing period charm. The gardens encircled the house, nestled among trees near Le Guet, with commanding views over Cobo Bay. Fiona stood for a moment admiring the vista of golden beaches and deep blue sea. A spring breeze carried the smell of the sea upwards, and she took a deep breath.

'There you are! I heard your car arrive, but then you disappeared.' Charlotte appeared around the corner from the front and threw her arms around her. Fiona gave herself up to the embrace, glad of any hugs offered.

Charlotte released her, saying, 'You're looking peaky, my dear. Not surprising under the circumstances, but let's see if we can put some colour in those cheeks. Lunch is ready, prepared by my own fair hands, and a bottle is chilling nicely. Shall we eat out or in?' Charlotte tilted her head, causing her hair to fall in thick waves around her face.

'Oh, inside will be fine, it's a little cool today,' she said, swept up by her friend's energy. Having a baby didn't seem to have slowed her down.

'We'll compromise and eat in the conservatory, shall we? James will be awake any minute, and he loves being in there. Such a good view of the garden and the sea.' Charlotte led the way into the hallway, leaving Fiona to admire again the restored mahogany staircase which, according to Charlotte, had been in a terrible state when they bought the house. And apparently, the rest had been in poor condition as well, having been owned and lived in by an elderly gentleman who no longer had the means to maintain it. Fiona loved this style of house, all corniced ceilings, marble fireplaces and solid panelled doors. The 1930s home she and Nigel had inherited from their parents was solid, well-built, but without the flourishes.

Charlotte turned into the huge drawing room which led to the newly added Victorian style conservatory. It was like walking into something from a glossy magazine such as *World of Interiors*. Fiona gasped at the brightly coloured Moroccan divans and chairs spread around the conservatory, as wide as the house and, she guessed, fifteen feet deep. All was colour and light, the view of lush gardens falling away to the coast the icing on the cake.

'How gorgeous! You'd barely started building when I was last here. And I love the Moroccan theme.' She grinned. 'What did Andy say about that?'

'Oh, he was a little unsure to begin with, he'd have gone for a neutral modern look, but he loves it now,' Charlotte said, laughing. 'I think he imagines himself as some sheikh, lounging on divans, surrounded by his harem, composed solely of the housekeeper and myself. Not much of a harem! But I think he's happy.' She smiled her warm, wide smile.

'How could he not be? He's got a gorgeous wife, beautiful home and handsome son – what more could a man want?' They both giggled.

'We're both happy, and James is such a good baby. I've been very lucky. Now, I'll ask Mrs B to serve lunch in the conservatory, meantime I'll fetch the wine.' Charlotte bustled off to the kitchen leaving Fiona to plop herself down on a squashy blue and yellow divan from where she could admire the view. Quite different from Louisa's the garden sloped away into a wooded area leading down to Cobo, with its expansive sandy beach now dotted with rocks at low tide, with a few walkers hugging the sea wall. The wind was keeping potential sunbathers away. For the first time since the death of her parents, Fiona considered the idea of selling the family home and moving near to the coast to catch the sea views. And since Nigel's death, the memories would be more poignant. Perhaps it was time to move on...

'Here we are. I thought Prosecco would go down well with the seafood salad I prepared. One of the joys of no longer breastfeeding is being able to imbibe without guilt!' Charlotte beamed as she poured two glasses, offering one to Fiona.

'Thanks.' Fiona took a sip. 'Lovely.'

'There's something decadent about a glass of anything bubbly in the middle of the day, don't you think?' Charlotte settled herself on a divan with a contented sigh. 'Not that I can drink much, as young Master James will want his lunch soon and I should be working on my book later.' She tasted the wine and leaned forward. 'And what are your plans for later?'

'Ah, that's the problem. I'm at a loose end until...until I can organise the funeral. And I can't just keep going out for walks or imposing on friends.' Fiona sighed.

'None of us would see it as an imposition. We're here to love and support you and I, for one, cherish your company. So, enough said!' Charlotte wagged an elegant finger at her, and she couldn't help but laugh.

'Thanks. I'll try not to become a nuisance. You mentioned your new novel, how's it coming along?'

'Let's just say, it's progressing slowly. I'm lucky in that my publisher isn't pushing me yet, allowing me extra time after having the baby. But I am enjoying it. Victorian Guernsey is a far cry from eighteenth-century England and the wars with the French of my first book, and Victor Hugo is ripe for a fictional story about his stay here.' She chuckled. 'Bit of a lady's man, wasn't he?'

'So I understand. But what a genius!' They became caught in an animated conversation about Hugo while Mrs B, Charlotte's daily housekeeper, began laying out food on the small dining table in the conservatory. Once she had finished, they took their seats and began piling their plates with crab, smoked salmon, prawns and a mixed salad accompanied with crusty French bread.

Between mouthfuls of food, they carried on a conversation about books and writing.

'I've had to let the V&A know that my book's delayed, and they've been very understanding. Have they broached it with you yet?' Fiona was commissioned by the museum to write a history of the V&A, and published by Charlotte's company, Townsend Publishers, based in Bloomsbury. One of those coincidences that happen rarely, but had brought the two women closer together. So much so, that Charlotte had invited Fiona to stay in her London house in Bloomsbury a couple of times when she was over undertaking research. The house was also handy for trips to her old uni, UCL.

'I'm not sure. Tony hasn't said anything yet, but I only get a weekly update from him. He's proving to be an excellent MD of the firm and I hardly ever need to get involved. Allows me to concentrate on James and my writing. Oh, and Andy of course!' She giggled an infectious deep, throaty laugh that made Fiona's mouth twitch. Her friend really was the tonic she needed.

A heartfelt wail transmitted by the baby alarm stopped Fiona from replying, and Charlotte, with a quick, 'Excuse me,' accompanied by a grin, left the room. Fiona chewed her food, gazing at the trees stirring in the wind, growing in strength and whipping up white caps on the waves. She could sit here all day watching...

Charlotte swept in carrying a wriggling James and followed by Mrs B holding a high chair which she set at the table.

'Here, let me hold him for a minute. It's been a while since my last cuddle.' Fiona reached out for the baby, who, after a moment's hesitation, beamed at her and lifted his arms.

'He's taken to you, Fiona, he doesn't let everyone hold him, the little monkey. Right, be good for Fiona while I go and fetch your lunch.' Charlotte dropped a kiss on James's head and rushed off.

Fiona sat him on her lap, and James studied her with his big brown eyes. He'd grown since she last saw him and, at eight months, was becoming quite a sturdy little boy.

'He's getting more like Andy by the day, don't you think?' asked Charlotte, returning with something gloopy in a bowl. She settled James in his chair and began spooning him what looked like green blancmange, but was probably blended vegetables.

'He's certainly got his eyes. Whoever he takes after, he's bound to be gorgeous with such good-looking parents.' Fiona smiled, enjoying the simple domesticity of a mother and child.

Charlotte blushed.

'That's sweet of you to say. Certainly, the grandparents are besotted by him.' She laughed, planting a kiss on her son's sticky face.

'How is your mother these days? Been over lately?'

'She's doing very well, thank you. Came over a couple of weeks ago for some treatment at La Folie and everyone seemed pleased with her continued progress. Apparently, the cancer's still in remission, which is all we can hope for.' She paused to wipe James's sticky hands after he'd tried to use them to scoop up the food. 'Silly boy, look at the mess you're in!' His answer was to gurgle in delight and wave his chubby hands in the air.

'That's great news. Did she spend much time here with you?' Fiona had only met Lady Townsend once, at James's christening, and found her a bit intimidating, so unlike Charlotte who had an easy manner with everyone.

Her friend laughed.

'She practically took root here! I'm convinced most of her trips are more to do with spending time with James than needing treatment at the centre. But I don't mind; I want him to see as much of her as possible because one never knows...' Her voice trailed off and Fiona caught the tremor in her voice. Charlotte gasped. 'Oh, that was crass of me! After all you've been through, I'm so sorry.' She patted Fiona's arm, her expression remorseful.

'Don't worry, you're right about not knowing what's around the corner, and I'm glad you and James are seeing more of your mother.' Fiona pushed down any maudlin thoughts trying to take over and asked after Andy.

Charlotte's eyes lit up.

'He's fine. Absolutely throws himself into the role of doting father when he's around and has had to take on more staff at work he's so busy.' She went on to describe Andy's latest project, and they continued chatting while James finished his lunch. Later, Charlotte suggested Fiona stay for the afternoon, and they could all go for a walk with James, and she was happy to agree. After all, there was nothing to rush back for.

◆◆◆

John was buried in the Priaulx Library; the island's go-to place for old island records as well as books. Fortunately, it was a pleasant place to be, ensconced in a quiet, book-lined room while scrolling through microfiched parish records. John was searching for a record of the marriage of Leo and Teresa, but nothing showed up. He wasn't surprised, it was more likely they had married in her home town, but it was disappointing. He then went on to check births, and here he struck lucky. Judith Bichard's birth was registered by her father as being 30th August 1939. His address was Le Vielle Maison, Route des Talbots, St Andrew. John rubbed his eyes, tired from staring at the small screen. Time for some fresh air before heading for the office and the computer.

He left the library to walk through Candie Gardens, and the invigorating sight and scent of the abundant spring flowers encouraged him to detour to the Victoria Café and sit outside with a coffee. The gardens lay spread out before him, sloping down steeply towards St Julian's

Avenue and the main Town, with the harbour and islands on the horizon. Sipping his coffee, John considered his next step. He had two main objectives. One, to trace Leo's descendants and rightful heir or heirs to the Renoir and other valuables and two, to find the person who killed Nigel Torode. Ideally, he'd like to nab the killer asap, but as yet there was little to suggest a likely suspect. Except for Ernest's mysterious son who may or may not prove of interest.

As yet he hadn't been back to see Mrs Domaille. He'd phoned the home and told she had another infection and couldn't have visitors. John didn't even have the son's name... He hit his forehead. 'Come on, Ferguson, use your brains! Check the register!' he said out loud, to the obvious consternation of the couple at the next table. Flashing them a smile, he finished his coffee and returned to the Priaulx.

Half an hour later, John had found what he was looking for and strode once more through the gardens, heading straight to St Julian's Avenue before cutting across the road to Hospital Lane and the police station. He wanted to ask Woods a favour.

'So you think this guy, Duncan Domaille, might be involved in Nigel Torode's death? Bit of a long-shot, isn't it?' Woods eyed him warily from across the desk in his office, looking none too pleased. He'd always made it clear he favoured a suicide verdict, thought it highly unlikely such a murder could happen in peaceful Guernsey.

'There's a chance, Ron. After all, he's the son of the old owner of the shop where the death took place, and I gather he was estranged from his parents. All I'm asking is for you to check him out for me, see if he has a record or anything. And to see if he shows up on the electoral roll.' John crossed his legs, trying to look as if it was no big deal whether or not Ron helped. But his gut instinct told him it *was* important.

'Huh. All right, I'll set someone onto it. Shouldn't take too long. Give you a ring later, shall I? Don't want you cluttering up my office longer than necessary.' Woods was overtaken by a fit of coughing and waved at John to go. Reluctant to do so, he had no choice but stand and leave. At least he could do some internet searching while he waited.

It took him five minutes to reach his office in Le Pollet, picking up a takeaway coffee on the way. While the computer booted up, John checked his notes. According to Judith's birth records, Teresa Spall was her mother's maiden name. Family from Suffolk. How many Spalls lived in Suffolk? Sounded like a local name, so perhaps not too many. John began tapping the keyboard as he downed his coffee.

By later that afternoon John's eyes were sore and itchy from screen watching, but he'd found what he wanted. And more. He was reaching for the phone to call Fiona when it rang.

'It's Ron. Got some interesting information about your Duncan Domaille.'

Chapter 18

Guernsey, June 1940

The war came to Guernsey on Friday, 28th June. Leo was one of a large crowd gathered in Smith Street to hear the latest announcement by Ambrose Sherwill, the recently elected President of the Controlling Committee, the island's emergency government. A lovely summer evening had encouraged islanders to come into Town and listen to Sherwill's speech before going down to White Rock for the departure of the mailboat. Leo had hoped to hear more about why the German plane had flown over the day before, but Sherwill had little to say.

Reluctant to return to his empty home, Leo joined the throng heading for White Rock. He liked watching the coming and going of ships and that evening the mailboat, *Isle de Sark*, was joined by the SS *Sheringham* and SS *Ringwood*, ready to take on board the latest crop of tomatoes destined for the UK. Leo smiled as the lines of lorries queuing to unload stretched back to the Weighbridge, glad to see it was business as normal. Passengers were embarking on the mailboat, bound for Southampton.

Suddenly he heard the throb of engines and Leo looked up, horrified to see three German Heinkels approaching from the south-east. Bursts of machine-gun fire erupted from the planes and puffs of smoke told him bombs had been dropped. Leo bent down and ran for cover towards the shelter under the pier as the lorries, Cambridge Sheds and the Information Bureau were hit, flames shooting upwards into the sky. Through a thick pall of smoke, he heard screams. Glimpses of people hit by debris, falling to the ground. Others fleeing, screaming in terror. He grabbed at a woman running past, crying and frightened, pulling her with him to safety in the shelter.

The muffled sound of answering gunfire from the mailboat reached them in the shelter, and he recalled reading it was armed recently. The noise seemed to last forever, when it could only have been a matter of minutes, replaced by the sound of anguished cries. Leo did his best to comfort those around him until the all-clear sounded at 8pm. Leo, leading the sobbing woman, came out to see the devastation, catching his breath at the sight. The whole of Town's front, as far as his eye could see, was damaged. Piles of rubble filled the piers and the street, and the dead and injured lay scattered like broken dolls.

Leo watched, stunned, as police and ambulance crews frantically pulled the injured from under lorries and the wrecked buildings. Adrenaline kicked in, and he rushed to lend a hand. Faces unrecognisable, coated in dust and blood. Bodies missing limbs. The moans of the badly injured. As he helped load the injured into ambulances and move the dead to the side, anger began to burn deep inside him. What cowards were the Germans to attack defenceless people! The anger drove him on until he was too tired to stand.

'Here, mate, have a breather and drink some of this. You've earned it.' A man with a smoke-blackened face handed him a flask, and Leo took a gulp, gasping as the brandy slipped down his throat.

'Thank you,' he spluttered, returning the flask.

'You're welcome, mate. We'll show those bastard Jerries what we're made of!' He shook his fist at the now empty sky. Leo could only nod his agreement. Their peaceful little island was dragged into the war at last.

In a state of shock and disbelief, Leo drove home as the light was fading, almost expecting German soldiers to appear out of the shadows. As he drove up the lane to his house he was concerned, but not surprised, to see the light on. Elsie was waiting in the kitchen, and she rushed at him as soon as he stepped in the door.

'Oh, my lord! What happened to you? Are you hurt?' Her hands clawed at him and, looking down, Leo saw dried patches of blood, mingled with soot, dirt, and God only knew what else.

He took her hands in his saying, 'I'm not hurt, Elsie. Calm down. I helped those injured by the bombs...' He sat her down and told her what had happened and her old face crumpled in horror. She had heard the bombs but didn't know where they'd hit, and she told him she heard more landing around the west coast. He finally managed to calm her enough to send her home after she'd insisted on serving his supper, kept warm in the oven.

After she left, Leo looked at the chicken pie and vegetables, not sure if he could swallow a morsel after what he'd witnessed. Deciding he needed something stronger to drink than the beer left out by Elsie, he took a bottle of Burgundy from his small wine collection and poured a large glass. After a sip, he felt able to try the food and, once he'd eaten a mouthful, found he was ravenous and wolfed it down, accompanied by the wine. He wanted to blot out the evening's horror as much as possible. The food and most of the wine finished, Leo took himself off to bed, missing his daily call to Teresa, knowing he couldn't tell her what had happened.

In Town the next day, Leo learnt the full aftermath of the bombings. He was horrified to hear that thirty-four people had died at the harbour, with many more injured and that the planes had then dropped more bombs and machine-gunned different points of the island, including Vazon and St Andrew, causing more damage but no casualties. Leaving Ernest to man the shop, Leo walked down in the direction of the harbour, but at the last minute, realised he wasn't yet ready to face the devastation. Instead, he turned up High Street and then into Smith Street, arriving at the offices of *The Guernsey Evening Press*.

'Good morning, Mr Bichard. I heard you was quite the hero last night, helping the injured, according to PC Piesing down at White Rock,' the man at the desk greeted him.

Leo waved his hand dismissively.

'Oh, I wouldn't say that, Joe. Everyone was doing their bit.' He coughed. 'I heard people were blaming the British government for leaving us without any defence. I understood the Germans knew about this, so they did not need to attack us like that. Do you know different?'

Joe leaned forward, lowering his voice even though there was no-one in earshot.

'Apparently, Mr Sherwill raised this with the Home Office last night, and it seems Jerry wasn't told we had no defence. Pah! Blooming Brits let us down badly, all right. Anyhow, apparently it was on the BBC news last night, so the Germans know now. Bit late, though, ain't it? Especially for those who died, poor souls.' Joe shook his head.

'It is. I got home too late for the news last night, but I expect it's going in the *Press*?'

'Yes, with the latest news that shipping's suspended to the islands. So I'd say that's ominous, wouldn't you, Mr Bichard?'

Leo nodded, said goodbye and left. His feelings of anger were now equally directed at the British government and the Germans, something he'd never expected to happen. As he walked down Smith Street the air raid siren sounded and, his heart pounding, he joined others rushing towards the nearest shelter. This time he heard no bombs or machine-gun fire, and thirty minutes later the all-clear sounded. A constable told him a plane had been spotted circling the island, probably checking the damage caused the previous evening. Leo hurried back to the shop, telling Ernest they were closing for the day, but to come back on Monday when he would reassess the situation.

Back at home, Leo telephoned Teresa, no longer able to hide the truth from her.

'I think invasion's imminent, my darling, and I'm not sure how long we'll be able to talk like this. Now we've lost contact by sea I fear there could soon be total silence.'

He heard Teresa catch her breath, but her voice remained steady when she answered.

'Then we can only pray this war ends soon.'

'After the Allies retreat from Dunkirk and the French armistice with Germany, I'm not optimistic. We must both be brave, my darling, and look forward to when we are reunited. And how's Judith? Still troubled by her teething?' They spent a few minutes chatting about their daughter who, he was relieved to hear, was now happy and sleeping again. Promising to call the next day, Sunday, Leo said goodbye.

The sense of foreboding he had felt of late was becoming stronger as each day passed. How could Guernsey – and the other islands – survive if cut off by sea from Britain? Where would their food come from? There was only so much a small island could grow, and they imported most of their meat.

Leo stepped outside into the summer sunshine where barely a leaf stirred. Bees buzzed unconcerned as they drew the precious nectar from his wife's colourful flowers. There was something to be said, he thought, for the simple life of a bee, thrusting his hands into his pockets as he breathed in the idyllic scene. The strident ringing of the telephone broke his reverie, and he rushed into the house. Teresa! Had something happened?

Chapter 19

Guernsey 2011

Fiona tapped the steering wheel in frustration. Why had everyone chosen this fine Friday morning to come into Town and park on the Crown Pier? She had circled the parking area twice and was about to give up and head to the Albert Pier when a car pulled out of a space in front of her, and she slipped in, breathing a sigh of relief. Quickly setting the parking clock, she locked the car and jogged down to the pedestrian crossing.

She hated being late for appointments and had arranged to meet John in his office at ten, and it was now five past. He'd sounded excited when he phoned the previous evening, and Fiona was anxious to hear his news. The lights changed, and she shot across the road and up the Crown steps at a more sedate pace in honour of their steepness. Sidestepping shoppers, she managed to arrive within another two minutes, hot and out of breath.

'Sorry, John. Car park chaos.' She gasped as he held the door open for her.

'No problem. I'm not going anywhere. Glass of water?'

She nodded, and he filled a glass at the tiny sink.

Fiona took a long gulp and saw him grinning at her.

'Okay, out with it. What's too important to tell me on the phone?'

'A couple of things. First off, I've tracked down Teresa's family home to an address near Sudbury and believe it or not, there's a Mrs T Bichard still registered on the electoral roll.' His eyes gleamed with excitement.

'You're joking! Leo's widow is still alive? Wow! But she must be ancient, surely?' She grinned. 'What incredible news.'

'She's about ninety-four. Remember she was much younger than Leo and, according to the records, married him when she was twenty-one in 1938. But I presume she's quite frail, and the electoral record shows a Mrs Judith Collins at the same address. And Leo's daughter was called Judith, so it's possible it's her. Mind you, she'd be in her seventies. And if it is her, then she married, but there's no Mr Collins registered. Worth waiting to hear?' John leaned back in his chair, a satisfied smile spread across his face.

'You bet! But you said there were two things to tell me.' Fiona's head buzzed with excitement. Fancy finding two generations of the family in one go.

'The other news concerns the mysterious son of the Domailles called Duncan. My pal Ron Woods did a bit of digging for me and found out that young Duncan was a bit of a bad lad as a teenager, getting into trouble with the law on occasion, resulting in a couple of short stays in prison. Nothing major, but he left the island abruptly in the early 80s and disappeared off the radar. But then,' John added, his smile even broader, 'he popped up again a few weeks ago, and is still on the island.'

'Oh! So, he could be Nigel's killer. Do you have a description of him?' Fiona's stomach clenched at the thought of this man being free to wander around. And possibly try again to steal the painting.

'Better than that, Ron emailed me a photo. It's an old one, but it's something to go on.' He pushed a sheet of paper over to her.

She stared at the mugshot, presumably taken when Duncan was arrested as a young man. Tall, heavy set, with long hair framing a scowling face. A thug. Fiona shuddered. What had Nigel said? A big man? Well, this man was big back then so...

'Not someone you've seen, I suppose?'

'No, not to my knowledge. Would Inspector Woods be able to get an up-to-date photo?'

'I can ask, but I'm planning to revisit Mrs Domaille and will ask her for a description of him. And I'd like to know where he's been and what he's been up to for the past thirty years.' He rubbed his hands together. 'Then I want to talk to Mrs Bichard or her daughter. Might have to go over.' John hesitated. 'It may be an idea for you to come with me. After all, you found the painting and know the story. Would you feel up to it?'

Fiona pursed her lips. It was tempting. To be the one to talk to the original owner of the Renoir, and to hear what had happened during and after the war at first hand. But there was Nigel and the funeral.

'It depends. I haven't been given the all clear for the funeral yet, so if it's going to be a while, I could go. Your pal didn't say anything about that, did he?'

John shook his head.

'No, and from experience, I'd say it'll be at least another week before toxicology comes back. And then you'd have to give it another week or so to make the arrangements.' He cleared his throat. 'Let me try and make contact with the family, and we'll take it from there, shall we?'

Fiona straightened her shoulders. Nigel would want her to meet the Bichards. She could imagine him telling her not to worry about his funeral. It could wait. The funeral was for the comfort of the living, not the dead.

That night Fiona curled up in her bed, clutching Nigel's photo, the room lit by moonlight streaming through the unclosed blinds. It had been a few days since he had last appeared and she was keen to share with him what John had discovered. She allowed herself to relax, focusing on Nigel's face. Moments later, she sensed him in the room and opened her eyes to see his hazy figure just out of reach. She spoke quietly but quickly, telling him about John and what he'd found. 'He's committed to finding the man who killed you, just as I am, and we're making such progress, darling. You said he was a big man. Is there anything else you can tell me?' She held her breath.

Nigel's form seemed to grow more solid, and she ached to touch him, to hold him.

'Odd accent. Guernsey...something else...could be...Oz. Cropped hair. Lined face. Only a...glimpse. Big...hands.' Nigel's voice grew fainter. 'Love you, Sis,' he said before his body dissolved into the semi-darkness of the room.

Fiona murmured, 'Love you, too,' to the emptiness in front of her. A lump formed in her throat as, once more, she was alone.

◆◆◆

John didn't usually go into the office on a Saturday, but he wanted an excuse to get out of the house. His wife was holding one of her regular coffee mornings, and the noise level wasn't conducive to serious phone conversations. He had managed to track down a phone number for the Sudbury household and now waited impatiently as the line rang out on loudspeaker in the quiet of the room.

'Hello.' The voice, female, sounded impatient.

'Good morning. I'm looking for Mrs Bichard. Mrs Teresa Bichard. Do I have the right number?'

'You do, that's my mother. But who are you and what do you want? If you're trying to sell something –' The woman's voice rose in anger.

'No, not at all, in fact quite the opposite. Am I talking to Judith, Leo's daughter?'

'Yes. How do you know about my father?' her voice faltered.

'My name's John Ferguson, and I'm a detective in Guernsey, employed to trace the owner of some property which is thought to have belonged to Mr Bichard,' John said, keeping his voice calm while feeling a mounting excitement.

'Oh!' the woman gasped. John heard a voice in the background, and there ensued a muffled conversation for a few moments. 'Sorry about that, my mother wants to speak to you. Just a minute.' Silence while the phone was transferred and then an older, less confident voice came on the line.

'Mr Ferguson? Teresa Bichard. I believe you said something about some property belonging to my late husband. Would that be a painting by Renoir, among other things?'

He heard a tremor of excitement in her voice and smiled.

'Yes, a possibly valuable painting's been found, and we're checking the provenance. And there are more, less valuable pictures, too. It's a rather sensitive and complicated issue and I, and the lady who found them, would like to visit you if that's convenient. We can go into more detail at that point.'

'Would you bring the paintings with you?'

'No, we can bring a list of the less valuable pictures, and the suspected Renoir's in safe-keeping in London. It's being tested for authenticity, but we have a photocopy of it. Do you have a photograph of your missing picture for comparison?'

'Yes, my husband was very thorough and kept records of all the family valuables.' There was a pause, and another whispered conversation. 'I'd be happy for you to come here as I'm not able to travel these days. Age, you know.' A sigh. 'I would like my grandson to be here as well, but he's in London. Can we ring you back to arrange a suitable date?'

'Of course.' He left his mobile number and rang off. Then he jumped out of the chair, pacing around as he phoned Fiona with the news. She was equally happy at the news, saying she would advise Sam about the breakthrough. John left the office and headed straight to the Ship & Crown for a celebratory pint. He'd earned it.

Chapter twenty

Guernsey 2011

Fiona was sharing a coffee with Louisa in the garden when John rang with his news. She immediately told her friend.

'That's amazing! I bet you can't wait to meet this Teresa,' Louisa said, smiling.

'No, I need some good to come out of Nigel's death. And this poor woman lost so much thanks to the Germans and whoever betrayed Leo. I'm glad she's around to see their painting again, it might bring her some comfort.' Fiona drained her mug, staring out to sea and the distant shape of Jersey on the horizon, a mix of emotions swirling around inside. 'It's the waiting that gets to me. I have to wait to hear from the police, wait for the coroner, wait to arrange a funeral, wait to hear when we can go to England...' She stood up, her hands thrust into her pockets as she continued staring into the distance.

Fiona swung round to face Louisa.

'I hate not being in control of what's happening to me. As a teenager, whenever I felt at the mercy of my teachers or my parents, I'd slink over to Herm for the day and pretend I was the boss-lady, in my head, anyway. Walking around, hardly meeting a soul, it was easy to believe it was my domain and no-one could tell me what to do.'

Louisa nodded.

'I can relate to that. Not being able to make your own decisions. And Herm does have a special kind of magic, doesn't it? Why not go over now? Reclaim yourself, if that's what you need.'

The answering flutter in her stomach convinced Fiona.

'Think I will. I just need to do something for *me* at the moment. You won't be offended if I stay there for a night or two? Assuming I can get a room at short notice.'

'Don't be silly. Ring the hotel now. The phone book's in the kitchen.' Louisa punched her arm playfully, and Fiona grinned as she headed inside.

She was in luck. The White House had had a late cancellation and could offer her a room for the Saturday and Sunday nights. Perfect. After telling Louisa, she threw clothes and toiletries into a bag, and her friend offered to run her down to the ferry, the next one due to leave in thirty minutes. Louisa dropped her off at the Weighbridge with time to spare, and she joined the queue for tickets at the Trident kiosk. A bubble of anticipation surfaced, and Fiona knew she'd made the right decision as soon as she stepped aboard the ferry. The cheerful chatter from the day trippers was uplifting after the pain of the past two weeks, and for the next couple of days, she was determined not to dwell on what had happened.

A light sea breeze accompanied them as the boat steered the well-worn route to Herm, basking quietly ahead under the late May sun. The following weekend would be the May bank holiday and half-term, and Fiona knew from experience how busy the island would become. Standing on deck as the boat neared the harbour, she gripped the rail as her eyes swept over the familiar scene. Motorboats and small yachts bobbed at their moorings offshore and small groups of people could be seen making their way along the coastal path. Fiona released a contented sigh. It all looked so *normal*.

She grabbed her bag and jumped onto the jetty, keen to check in and grab some lunch. Every time she visited Herm her appetite redoubled, probably thanks to permanent sea air on such a small place and all the walking needed to get around.

The White House was a sprawling country house style hotel, determined to encourage guests to relive the joys of being off-grid, without televisions, clocks or telephones and this suited Fiona's current frame of mind. She'd packed a couple of paperbacks and although she'd brought her mobile, only planned to check for any text messages from John. She was delighted to be offered an upstairs sea-view room in the main hotel, and it wasn't long before she'd unpacked, admired the view towards Guernsey and returned downstairs to walk to the adjoining Ship Inn for an al fresco lunch. As she sipped her wine, Fiona realised, with some surprise, she hadn't been over to Herm since moving back to Guernsey to join Nigel. Well, she would make up for it now. Reclaim her old love for the tiny slice of paradise that had soothed her so often in the past.

Later, having changed, Fiona set off past the island shop and pub, taking the path towards the common and then round to the beaches on the far side. Along the way she returned the smiles of those she met, their sun-kissed faces testament to a morning's sunbathing. She arrived at the top of the stairs leading down to Belvoir Bay and gave herself a moment to take in her favourite beach. As a child, no trip to Herm was complete without spending a few hours here. Smaller and more sheltered than the adjoining Shell Beach, it bore an air of seclusion in spite of the popular café.

Fiona smiled as she noticed only a handful of people stretched out on the sand and trotted eagerly down the steps. She found a spot backed into the cliff and spread out her towel before stripping down to her bikini and walking the few yards to the sea. An icy shiver ran through her as she dipped her feet in the water and she took a deep breath before plunging in full-length for a swim. After a few minutes of sustained swimming, Fiona acclimatised and carried on until her leg muscles ached.

Stretched out on the towel, it was easy to let the sun soothe her into a doze, accompanied by the gentle lapping of the waves on the shore. With her eyes closed, she could imagine herself the only one on the island. Her domain. She found herself smiling as she drifted away.

Two children, a boy and a girl, played at the water's edge, splashing each other and screaming with delight. Then they moved up the beach to start building rival sandcastles with battered buckets and spades. They had their backs to her, and she couldn't see their faces, but there was something familiar about them. The boy stood up, saying his was the best and he'd ask their parents to judge. He turned around and walked towards her and Fiona saw it was Nigel, and when the girl looked up, she recognised herself. About ten years old. Her heart skittered in her chest as Nigel drew closer.

'Mummy, come and tell us which is the best castle. I'm sure you'll agree it's mine, but Fiona says it's hers. Please, before the sea washes them away.'

Fiona didn't move, too lethargic in the heat. She opened her mouth to speak, but nothing came out.

'Come on! You need to move, now!' The voice was no longer Nigel's.

She opened her eyes, groggy. A shadow blotted out the sun, and she recognised the tussle-haired young lad she'd passed earlier. Something wet touched her feet and realisation kicked in. The tide! Fully alert, she stumbled to her feet, and he helped her collect her things.

'Thanks, I must have drifted off and lost track of time.' She felt the heat in her cheeks, whether from embarrassment or the sun she wasn't sure, but he just grinned, saying, 'It's easily done. You'll be okay over there,' he pointed a few feet away, before moving off.

Fiona decided a cup of tea would be welcome and walked the few yards to the café. She sat on a bench under a bright umbrella to sip her tea and make some sense of what had happened. Could the sandcastle incident have been a real memory? It was possible. They'd spent so much time here and had loved their buckets and spades and making castles. And they'd been quite competitive. But it was odd how it had morphed into the stranger, warning her of the encroaching tide. She dragged a hand through her hair as she considered whether or not Nigel had 'followed' her to Herm and had been trying to warn her, or whether it was her mind playing tricks. Neither answer provided much comfort.

Later that afternoon, Fiona made her way back to the hotel via the Manor Village, nestled in the middle of the island. Not a proper village, but a collection of self-catering stone cottages huddled around an old chapel and the Manor House, the traditional home of the Tenant of the island. As a family, they had enjoyed holidays spent in one or other of the cottages, and Fiona found herself dawdling, noting any changes over the years. The gardens were full of colour, bursting with spring flowers and she exchanged greetings with holidaymakers sat outside enjoying the view down to the sea. Her favourite cottage from her childhood, Lower Bailiff's, was on the corner, opposite St Tugual's Chapel and she smiled as she drew level to it. Fiona was about to walk on when she recalled the chapel had recently been reopened after months of restoration and the discovery of skeletons hundreds of years old. Intrigued, she entered the tiny eleventh-century church.

The chill hit her immediately. The old granite walls shut out the heat of the day, and Fiona picked up the faint musty smell she remembered from previous visits, even though the doors were wide open. Light streamed through the stained glass windows, illuminating dust motes floating through the air. She didn't see any significant changes, but as ever sensed an air of peace enfold her. The only visitor, Fiona took a seat near the small, plain altar table and closed her eyes, planning to say a quick prayer for her parents and brother. She became aware of an even greater drop in temperature and shivered. In her head, she saw Nigel's face and heard his voice.

'Darling Sis, I know you feel alone, but you're not. I'll always be by your side and in your heart, as you are in mine. Love you always...' His face and voice faded away, and when she opened her eyes, her face was damp. She breathed deeply, experiencing a release, a letting go. The heavy lump of sorrow which had settled in her stomach for the past two weeks, lightened. Whispering, 'Thank you,' she stood and left the church to return to the hotel.

Fiona slept so deeply that night she nearly missed breakfast Sunday morning. Arriving at five minutes to ten in the Conservatory restaurant, she apologised to the young waitress hovering near the door.

'No problem, no-one's early on a Sunday,' she said with a grin, going to fetch a pot of coffee.

After settling at a table in the window, Fiona gazed out over the front lawn edged with bushes and flowering shrubs over to the sea, sparkling under another blue sky. Part of her mind dwelt on the experience in the chapel and on the beach, which she now recognised as connected. Nigel wanted her to know he was there for her, to warn her of danger – or wet feet! – if necessary. By the time her coffee arrived, she was smiling, ready for a chilled-out day by the pool or on a beach.

Chapter 21

Guernsey 2011

John was sauntering up High Street when his mobile rang. It was Judith Collins, advising him her son, Michael, would be free to meet them in Sudbury on Wednesday if that suited. After saying he would confirm with Fiona, he rang her with the news.

'Okay with me. I'll book us on the early Gatwick flight and will stay overnight to see Sam, but you can return the same day. Could you check the trains, please? I'm in Herm, but will be back this afternoon.'

'Sure. I'm also going to ring the nursing home, see if Mrs Domaille's up for visitors.'

'Good luck with that! We'll catch up later.'

Back in the office, John confirmed Wednesday with Judith, checked the times of the trains and then rang the nursing home. He was relieved to hear she was better, although 'not quite with it', according to the nurse, who agreed he could visit that afternoon. He rubbed his hands. Action, that's what he enjoyed most. Not sitting in front of a computer screen. That wasn't real detective work. Going out and about and interviewing people was what counted.

Sorry as he was that a man had died, and violently too, John relished the task of tracking down his killer. Since transferring from the Met to Guernsey Police he had mainly dealt with white collar crime and the occasional serious assault or theft, and it stirred his detective's soul to be involved in such a case. The last time had been when he worked for Louisa and her father, Malcolm. He'd been looking for a killer then, and they nailed two. Good stuff. Standing up, he decided to go home for lunch before visiting Mrs Domaille. And he could tell his wife about the trip to England.

'Ah, Mr Ferguson, isn't it? You'll be wanting to see Mrs Domaille, I suppose?'

The sister he'd met last time stood, her arms folded, in the hall. As if to bar his way. He hoped not.

'Yes, Sister, I did phone earlier...' He offered a smile and mentally crossed his fingers.

'So I understand. Well, you can visit her if you wish, but I have to warn you she's regressed somewhat since your last visit. Dementia, you know.' She spread her hands and shrugged. 'I'll take you down, but please, at the slightest sign of agitation, call for a nurse.'

'Of course.'

He followed her down the corridor and into the old lady's room. As before, she sat huddled in a chair by the window, covered in blankets. He made to walk closer when the nurse bustled forward.

'Mrs Domaille. I have a visitor for you. It's Mr Ferguson who came to see you recently. He won't stay long if you don't mind answering some questions.'

The watery eyes turned slowly towards him, and the look was blank. John's stomach sank.

'Who are you? What do you want?' Her voice wobbled.

The nurse opened her mouth to say something, but he cut in, 'It's all right, Sister, I'm willing to try and refresh her memory. I'll call you if there's a problem, shall I?'

'Well, if you promise not to distress her,' she said, giving him a stern look. Turning to Mrs Domaille, she said, 'I'll leave you for a few minutes, dear. The...nice gentleman only wants a chat.' With another warning look at John, she turned on her heel and left. Letting out a sigh of relief, he pulled a chair near the old lady who still looked puzzled, but not frightened.

John explained about his last visit and repeated what he'd told her about Nigel and the ownership of the shop.

A slight glimmer appeared behind her eyes.

'I sold the business to that poor young man. They don't want their money back, do they?' She began twisting a blanket, her gaze flitting around the room as if looking for a way out.

'Don't worry, Mrs Domaille, they don't. I'm here to ask you about your son, Duncan. He came to see you a few weeks ago, didn't he?' John kept his voice gentle, but firm.

She frowned and pulled harder on the blanket. 'My son? I have a son?'

'Yes, his name's Duncan, don't you remember? He left the island a long time ago, but he's back now.' He pulled out the photo Inspector Woods had unearthed. 'Here, this is how he looked before he went away, about thirty years ago. He's in his fifties now'. He passed her the photo, and a trembling hand reached for it. She stared at it, her forehead creased in concentration. John imagined the cogs slowly whirling in her diminished brain and felt sorry for her. Fancy not remembering you had a son.

'I'm not sure. Don't remember a son. But he does look a bit familiar. Duncan, you say?'

'Yes. Take your time. No rush.' John summoned all the patience he'd learnt over the years when questioning witnesses.

'I don't know. Is this the man who died?' She looked up at him, a puzzled look on her face.

'No, it isn't, Mrs Domaille. It's an old photo of your son, Duncan. Before he went away.'

He watched the old lady continued to gaze blankly at the photo, wondering if he was wasting his time.

Then, it was if a switch was flicked and she became animated.

'Duncan. Yes, sweet little boy, he was. Till he got older. Always in trouble.'

She looked at John, and her eyes were moist.

'What kind of trouble? With the police?'

'Yes, but he also stole from Ernest. From the till. He couldn't get a job, so Ernest took him on. When he found out about the missing money, his father told him to leave.'

'I see, that must have been upsetting for you.'

She nodded. 'For all his bad ways, I loved him, Mr – who did you say you are again?'

'Ferguson, John Ferguson. I came to see you before. Don't you remember?'

She stared at him and shook her head.

'I don't know you, do I? What do you want?' She gripped her blanket tight, her eyes searching the room.

'We've met before, Mr Domaille. I want to talk about Duncan, your son. In the photo. Did he leave Guernsey after he fell out with Ernest?'

'Eh?' She studied the photo. 'Yes, he did leave. Never said where he was going. I was that upset, I was.' She pulled out a handkerchief and blew her nose.

'I'm sorry to hear that. Would have been hard for you as a mother. So when he turned up recently, you must have been so pleased to see him again.' John leaned forward and patted her arm.

'What? He turned up here?' She looked surprised.

John's stomach sank again. It was worse than pulling teeth.

'Yes, the sister said he came to see you a few weeks ago. He'll have changed from that photo, and I was hoping you'd be able to tell me what he looks like now.'

She gazed, unseeing, at a spot above his head.

'Perhaps he brought you flowers or chocolates?' John prompted.

'Duncan bring me flowers? No. He was never one for presents, even as a boy.' She looked at the photo again. 'Now you mention it; I do remember him coming here. He wasn't happy. He was angry, that's it, he was angry with me.' She nodded, the memory stirring.

'But why was he angry? You hadn't seen him in years!'

'To do with the business. Can't remember. What was it, now?' Her face screwed up in thought. 'I'd sold it, that was what made him angry. Duncan said it was his inheritance; I shouldn't have sold it without telling him. But I didn't know where he was, did I?' She looked at John as if for reassurance.

'No, you didn't, Mrs Domaille. Did the advocate say you could sell it?'

'Yes, he did, or I wouldn't have, would I?' She nodded her head. 'Duncan said Ernest had told him it would be his one day, before they fell out, that is.' Mrs Domaille became agitated, and John filled a glass of water from the jug on the table and passed it to her.

'So what did Duncan say then?'

'Kept going on about what was rightfully his. He marched around the room, his face getting redder. I offered him the money I got for it, but he was still angry. What had I done wrong?' She looked at John, her eyes glistening with tears.

'You didn't do anything wrong, Mrs Domaille, don't upset yourself.' He paused, wondering if he could risk asking more questions. He had to take the chance. 'Can you tell me where Duncan's living? He might be able to help with my search for the original owner.'

'He didn't say. Stormed off. Need his address for the advocate to send him the money. He'll be back sometime, will want the money.' Her voice was bitter, and John felt even sorrier for her.

'If he does get in touch, I'd be grateful if you'd let me know. You can ask the sister to contact me.' He stood up, saying, 'One last thing, can you tell me what he looks like now? In case I bump into him.'

'He's a big man, even bigger than he was. Big muscles. Short hair, going grey. And his skin was tanned.'

'Did he say where he'd been living all those years?'

'Somewhere far away. Met a woman, he said, married her. I didn't get the chance to ask if they have children. My grandchildren.' Her face crumpled.

'Thank you; you've been extremely helpful, Mrs Domaille. I'm sorry to have intruded on you like this.' He shook her hand, and she nodded.

'Goodbye, hope you find who you're looking for.'

He left the room, glad the poor woman didn't know who he really wanted to find. Her son.

Chapter 22

Guernsey 2011

Fiona arrived back from Herm late Monday afternoon, convinced the island had worked its magic on her. The image of Nigel as a boy on the beach stayed with her, a reminder of the many happy times they'd shared together. No-one could take those memories away, and it helped to erase the awful image of his poor, dead face.

She walked to the taxi rank and was soon on her way back to Icart. At the top of the Val de Terres, where it met Fort Road, she glanced briefly towards Colborne Road and her home and sighed. She was even less inclined to want to return there permanently after days spent looking at the sea. And heart and mind told her she needed to start afresh. The problem was the business. Could she consider going back? At the moment, no. But she needed an income. The V&A had paid her an advance for the book, but it wouldn't last for much longer.

As she arrived at Louisa and Paul's house, John phoned her with the update on his meeting with Mrs Domaille. Fiona listened carefully as he gave her Duncan's description. It sounded like the man Nigel had described, and she experienced a flutter in her stomach. Should she tell John? Deciding to leave it until they met again on Wednesday, she went inside to receive a warm welcome from her friends, keen to know how the weekend had gone.

The seven o'clock plane from Guernsey to Gatwick wasn't called the red-eye without reason. As Fiona looked around at their fellow passengers, she spotted a mix of bleary and red-eyed people stifling yawns. She was no brighter and nursed a cup of coffee as she sat next to John while they waited to board.

'It feels strange, knowing we'll be meeting all of Leo's family except him. After all, it's his story, isn't it? Why all that's happened has led us to this point,' Fiona said, glancing at John.

'He's the central character, yes, but there's another one. I suspect the person who stood to gain the most from Leo's arrest was Ernest. And I'd bet good money he betrayed him and somehow took over the business. Also, I suspect his son knew about the hidden paintings, and that's why he was so angry about the sale of the business.' John turned towards her. 'Adds up, doesn't it?'

Fiona nodded.

'I think you're right. I'm hoping Mrs Bichard will be able to tell us more about what happened when she returned to Guernsey after the war. About Ernest, in particular. I–' She was interrupted by the tannoy announcing the boarding of their flight, and she swallowed the rest of her coffee before they joined the queue. Fifteen minutes later they were airborne, tacitly agreeing to leave any further discussions about the case until they had more privacy.

Two hours later they were in a First Class carriage on a train from Liverpool Street to Sudbury, enjoying the comfort and peace of a virtually empty carriage.

'John, I have something to say which you might find a bit off the wall, and you don't have to believe me if you don't want to.' Fiona cleared her throat. 'Do you believe in ghosts?'

His eyebrows rose.

'Well, that's quite a question! Is this to do with Nigel?'

'Yes. So, do you?'

'I'm not big on the afterlife stuff, and I've no experience with ghosts, but I know people who have, so,' he shrugged. 'Tell me more.'

She told him about her conversations with Nigel, including his description of his attacker. At this point, John's eyebrows shot up higher, and he let out a short whistle.

'That is interesting. Seems to point the finger at Duncan, doesn't it? Of course, it's not evidence we could use, but it makes it even more urgent we track this man down.' He studied her for a minute. 'Did you believe in ghosts before your brother died?'

Fiona shook her head.

'Not entirely, although a friend of mine saw ghosts in a house she bought last year, verified by a vicar too, but I was a bit sceptical. I believe her now.'

'Once I'm back in Guernsey I'll focus on tracking down Duncan Domaille. And I always get my man,' John said, with conviction.

They arrived at Sudbury station late morning, having arranged that Michael Collins would collect them. The tiny station, on the edge of town, was unmanned and there was no car park. As they strode out towards the road, there was no sign of a waiting car.

Pacing up and down, John said, 'If he doesn't arrive soon, you could return to the platform and take a seat. I'll look out for him.'

'I'm okay, been sitting down for hours. Did you exchange mobile numbers?'

'Not with Michael, no. But his mother has my number if there's a problem.' John frowned.

Fiona's hackles rose as the minutes ticked by. She and John had gone to the trouble, let alone the expense, to come there to give what she assumed to be a wealthy family, the opportunity to claim a picture worth millions. No doubt Michael, when he eventually turned up, would be driving some flash Rolls or similar. She tried not to think about what had happened to Nigel because of the damn painting.

Twenty-five minutes later a battered Land Rover skidded to a halt in front of them. By then Fiona was hot and thirsty and only gave the jeep a cursory glance. Surely that wasn't their transport? A man climbed out, leaving the engine running. Her heart sank. It looked like he was coming for them.

'Hello, are you Fiona and John? I'm desperately sorry to have kept you waiting, but the old girl had a hissy fit in one of the lanes and cut out. I've managed to get her going again, but can't risk switching her off.' While he said this, at top speed, he quickly shook their hands before picking up Fiona's overnight bag and depositing it in the back of the jeep.

Wondering if, judging by the vehicle, they had sent the gardener, she allowed herself to be helped into the front passenger seat while John hopped into the back. She murmured a polite 'Thank you,' and he smiled and returned to the driver's side.

'I'm Michael, by the way. Did you have a good trip?' he asked, putting the jeep into gear and setting off at a brisk rate.

'Yes, thanks, after an early start.' Her voice cool. So he wasn't the gardener, but Teresa's grandson. He did have a posh voice, she acknowledged. Like her friend Charlotte.

'Oh, right. Well, my mother's arranged a decent early lunch as she guessed you'd be hungry after all the travelling. It's about twenty minutes from here to Oak Tree Farm if you can last out?' He grinned at her.

'Of course.' Still cool.

John butted in to ask if his grandmother would be able to meet with them and Michael said she would. While the two men talked, Fiona observed Michael unnoticed. Tall with brown eyes and dark hair slightly too long, touching his collar. Dressed in well-worn jeans and an open-necked cotton shirt, he gave the impression of someone not bound to an office job. Hence her thinking he might be the gardener.

Finishing his chat with John, he turned his head towards her, catching her scrutiny, and she averted her eyes quickly. Michael didn't comment, and Fiona fixed her gaze on the lush countryside as they sped by.

'We must be near Constable country, aren't we? Dedham can't be far from here.'

He smiled. 'You're right. There's a story in our family that Constable spent time as a guest in our house and included it in one of his paintings. Unfortunately, we've not been able to trace it. But it makes a nice story to hand down the generations.'

'Yes. It seems as if both sides of your family have a connection with famous artists or their paintings.' She glanced at him, but he kept his eyes on the road.

'Indeed. I'm looking forward to what you tell us about the Renoir. My grandmother is what you'd call uber excited.' He chuckled. 'I've not seen her so animated for years. I'm only concerned with her heart. It's not the strongest.' His face clouded.

'I'm sorry to hear that, but at least it's good news we're bringing.'

'A bit like winning the lottery, eh?' He flashed a smile, and she nodded. They lapsed into silence once more, and Fiona concentrated on the pretty cottages and houses flashing past, nestled under thatched roofs and surrounded by leafy trees and hedgerows bursting with colour. Open fields lay spread out on both sides of the road; some centred around an ancient oak spreading its branches, like a king laying claim to his land. She turned to see what John's impression might be and saw he'd nodded off, his mouth wide open. She smiled. Michael caught her glance.

'Won't be long now. Food will wake him up. Are you travelling back today?'

'I'm not, but John is. I'm staying with a friend in London for the night. I understand you live in London, do you travel much for work?'

'I'm my own boss, so only travel when I want to or absolutely have to. My studio's in my backyard, so hardly a commute.'

'You're an artist? How interesting, I studied art history and used to work at the V&A.' Fiona perked up, allowing herself to thaw towards him.

'Mainly I sculpt. Though I like to draw and paint for fun. Ah,' he said, turning sharp right into a tree-lined drive, 'we're here. Welcome to Oak Tree Farm.'

Fiona heard John stir in the back as the jeep lurched onto the drive, edged by three-bar fencing which had seen better days. She caught a glimpse of a house in the distance as they swayed on the uneven surface. Horses grazed unconcerned in a field.

'Sorry about the bumpy ride, the drive's overdue for repair, like other parts of the property. A modern car wouldn't cope as well as Sheila does.' Michael gripped the steering wheel as he negotiated the potholes.

'Sheila?' John asked.

'The jeep. Someone else's name for her and it stuck.' Michael grinned.

Fiona was struck speechless by the emerging house, now fully visible at the end of the drive.

'What a beautiful house!' Her eyes swept over cream-washed walls of a rambling L-shaped farmhouse, topped with a weathered red pantile roof, resplendent with numerous tall chimneys. Small-paned windows, like beady eyes, gazed back at her as Michael drew to a halt.

'It is, isn't it? We're all rather fond of the old place, even though it's showing its age a bit. Some bits go back to the fifteenth century, but luckily, most rooms have tall ceilings, or I'd have a stooped back by now,' he chuckled, stepping out of the jeep.

Fiona followed suit, mesmerised by the house basking peacefully in the sun. John jumped down to join her.

'Nice place your grandmother has, Michael. Been in the family long?'

'Centuries. Hard to believe nowadays, but it's true. The Spalls have farmed here forever, though the land's been sold off now. Down to five acres.' His jaw tightened, and Fiona saw a flash of anger cross his face. What had happened to bring the family so low? John had said Andre Bichard mentioned Teresa came from a posh family, and she'd assumed that meant wealthy. Must have been a fairly recent change of fortunes.

Michael flung his arms wide, ushering them towards to the huge oak door.

'Come on in, and meet my family. And have lunch,' he added with a lazy smile.

They entered a wide, dual aspect dining hall with beamed ceiling and walls and featuring a walk-in inglenook fireplace. Dishes and plates of food covered an old oak dining table. Fiona was aware of the hollowness in her stomach. It had been a meagre, early breakfast. As they walked across the herringbone patterned brick floor, Michael called out, 'Ma, we're here!' A door leading into what looked like an inner hall opened, and a woman came through, pushing a wheelchair holding an old lady. Leo's widow.

Michael moved forward, dropping a kiss on the old lady's head. 'Let me introduce you all. My mother,' he motioned to the woman behind the wheelchair, 'Mrs Judith Collins, and my grandmother, Mrs Teresa Bichard,' squeezing the old lady's shoulder, 'please meet Fiona Torode and John Ferguson. And it's my fault we're so late, Sheila had a tantrum, and I'd left my phone behind and couldn't let you know. Sorry, everyone.'

His grandmother reached out a hand to first Fiona and then John.

'So glad you could come, and I do appreciate you making the journey. As you can see, I'm not able to travel far these days, but I've been most anxious to meet you and hear the story in detail. But first, you must have some refreshment. Please, be seated.' She motioned towards the dining table as Fiona murmured, 'Pleased to meet you.' Judith looked about to say something, then clamped her mouth shut and steered the wheelchair to the head of the table. Judith sat on her left, Michael on her right and Fiona was ushered into a chair next to Michael while John sat by Judith.

The initial polite conversation about their journey drifted into silence as they helped themselves to the food; a cold collation of new potatoes, a homemade quiche, various salads, cooked chicken pieces and a big plate of crusty bread. Yummy. Fiona studied the women as she ate. Mrs Bichard, although painfully thin and frail, had a brightness about her face that could almost make you imagine her as the young woman with whom Leo fell in love. Her eyes held a sparkle, and her smile was wide and warm in the barely lined face, and she held herself erect in the wheelchair, as if in defiance of her ageing body.

Mrs Collins, on the other hand, although bearing a strong resemblance to her mother, with her fair colouring and high cheekbones, had deep lines on her forehead and around her thin mouth. Fiona guessed at deep unhappiness and wondered where her husband was. Michael hadn't mentioned him, and it seemed impolite to ask. Fiona overheard Judith asking John about the Renoir, but was tartly reminded by her mother they'd agreed not discuss it until after lunch. Judith's mouth tightened into a thin line. Not much love lost between those two, Fiona thought.

Michael became embroiled in a debate with Teresa about whether or not the Land Rover would survive much longer. 'Cost of a replacement' was mentioned. Looking around more closely, she noticed the furniture and furnishings were past their best, and a general air of neglect hung over what once must have been a glorious room. Curtains with ragged edges, rugs with worn patches and chipped tableware. Again, she wondered about the decline in their fortunes and now understood Teresa's excitement about the return of the Renoir.

Lost in these thoughts, she didn't hear Michael ask her a question until he tapped her arm.

'Sorry? Did you say something?' She felt the heat rise in her face as he grinned at her.

'I asked if you wanted more to eat as I see your plate's empty. Can I pass you anything? Or get you more coffee?'

'No, thanks, I'm fine. It was delicious, thank you, Mrs Bichard.' She smiled at the old lady.

'Oh, don't thank me, Judith prepared all the food. She has a talent for preparing tasty meals from the poorest of ingredients, don't you, darling?'

Judith flushed, and Fiona sensed the underlying tension behind the words and experienced a twinge of sympathy for the woman.

'I also enjoyed the meal, thank you, Mrs Collins,' John said, smiling at his neighbour.

Michael stood. 'If everyone has finished, I'll help you clear the table, Ma, and then we can get down to business.'

With nods of agreement all round, Fiona half stood to offer to assist, but Michael pushed her down, saying as a guest she wasn't allowed to help. He and Judith piled plates and dishes onto trays and left, leaving the three of them at the table.

'I think we'll retire to the drawing room where the chairs are more comfortable. And I do find this room rather dreary; the drawing room is much brighter.' Teresa smiled.

At this point, Michael and his mother returned, and Teresa informed them of the move. Michael took hold of the wheelchair, and the others followed him through to the inner hall. They passed several closed doors and a carved heavy oak staircase before arriving at an open door leading into the drawing room. Fiona had to agree with Teresa, this room was not only enormous, with sofas and chairs facing another large inglenook fireplace, but it enjoyed a triple aspect over the gardens, allowing a mass of light to reflect off pale painted walls. Light oak beams rather than dark added to the overall impression of lightness.

'What a wonderful room.' Fiona's eyes widened as she gazed around, albeit noting how shabby the furniture was. But at least the chairs looked comfortable.

'Thank you, my dear. It's always been my favourite room, even as a child. It seemed even bigger to me when I was small, and my parents told me it was where I learnt to walk. Plenty of floor space.' Teresa chuckled as Michael set the wheelchair next to a large, high back chair before giving her his arm to help her stand and move a couple of steps to the chair.

'That's better, thank you. I can pretend I'm not as infirm when I'm in this chair.' She gave him a big smile and waved to the others to make themselves comfortable.

Fiona settled on a sofa next to John, and Michael and his mother sat together on another, all facing Teresa.

'Shall I explain, or will you?' she asked John, suddenly shy of being the focus of attention.

'I will if you wish.' Clearing his throat, he told the story of the discovery of paintings in the basement of the shop by Fiona and Nigel, and the suspicion that one was a genuine Renoir. He went on to say how Fiona had gone to London to have it verified by Professor Wright and his conclusion that it was undoubtedly a Renoir. At this point, Teresa asked Michael to fetch a folder from a side console. She lifted out a photograph and handed it to Fiona.

'This is a photograph my husband took of his painting before the war. Naturally, it's not in colour, but does it correspond to the one you found?'

Fiona studied the photo, then compared it with the photocopy John pulled out of his briefcase. Even allowing for the lack of colour it was clearly the same picture.

Nodding her head, she handed them both to Teresa. Michael and Judith leaned forward expectantly.

Teresa let out a sigh.

'Yes, it's the same. Oh, I can't begin to thank you and your brother for finding this and for tracking us down.' Tears glistened in the old lady's eyes, and Judith went and stood by her, patting her shoulder.

Michael gave Fiona a questioning look.

'Where is your brother? As Grandmama says, we owe him our thanks too.'

'I'm afraid Fiona's brother was killed in a burglary at the shop recently. We think the killer was looking for that painting.' John squeezed her hand as she fought to keep control of her emotions.

Teresa's hand flew to her mouth, her eyes widening in horror, a response reflected in the faces of both Judith and Michael.

'Dear God! I'd no idea, I'm so sorry, Fiona. Please accept my condolences. I'd never have asked you to make the journey here if I'd known about your loss.' Teresa, visibly shaken, seemed to shrink in her chair.

Michael leaned forward, his face puckered in a frown.

'I'm equally sorry, particularly if you think finding our painting led to your brother's death. Can you tell us what happened?' His voice was gentle, and Fiona felt her eyes prick. John must have sensed her distress and intervened.

'If I may answer for Fiona, I'll explain what happened and how I came to be involved.' He proceeded to relay the whole story, occasionally looking at her for confirmation, as she sat mutely by his side. When she and John had discussed how much to tell the family, they had concluded it was better to wait and see when they met. She knew it would have to come out about the burglary and Nigel's death eventually, but had hoped to put it off until they found the killer. She watched as the faces of the family registered various degrees of shock, sorrow and curiosity as John relayed all they knew to date. When he finished, the room was silent for moments afterwards.

Teresa, Judith and Michael exchanged glances, as if deciding who should talk and what they should say.

Eventually, Teresa spoke, her voice cracked.

'My dear, we are all saddened and humbled by what John has told us, and I, for one, consider you both brave and unselfish in undertaking the task you've set yourself. This painting,' she waved the old photo in her hand, 'may be returning to us, the rightful owners, but it comes stained with your poor brother's blood, and possibly that of my husband.' Teresa paused, taking what sounded like a painful breath and Fiona reached to grip her hand. This woman had suffered great loss, too. Their eyes met in acknowledgement.

'You believe your husband was betrayed for what he possessed, not for being a Jew?'

'I wasn't sure at the time what to think. Remember I only found out what happened to Leo after the war ended and I was able to travel to Guernsey. His Red Cross messages had stopped years before, and I had no idea why. I went to our house and found it in a terrible state. Soldiers had used it.' She shuddered. 'Then I called in on our old housekeeper, Elsie, and she told me of his arrest and deportation.' She looked up, her eyes bright. 'I was shocked he'd been accused of being a Jew, which was untrue. And knew he was unlikely to return after the...camps were found. A friend, Clem Le Page, confirmed the details to me later. He was, I think, ashamed that the then government hadn't been able to save him.'

'How awful, I'm sorry. Did you visit the shop at all?'

'Yes, and found Ernest now owned it.'

John and Fiona exchanged a brief look. She cleared her throat.

'Did you knew Ernest? We assumed he'd bought the business from your husband, but didn't know if they had any previous connection.'

'Oh yes, he worked for Leo and before him, his father, Henry. I met him before the war. He seemed a good worker and Leo trusted him, but I...I didn't take to him. Something in his eyes.' Teresa looked down at her hands, twisted together.

Fiona's mind raced at the implication of Teresa's words and opened her mouth to ask a question, but John beat her to it.

'From what you say, it seems possible, in fact, highly likely, that Ernest knew about the paintings and other valuables in the basement. What exactly did he tell you when you met?' Fiona caught his sense of excitement. The pieces of the jigsaw were sliding into place.

Teresa frowned.

'Let me think. Ah, yes, I remember. He showed me a piece of paper confirming the sale of the business from Leo to himself, at a particularly low price and dated before Leo's arrest. Ernest said the value was negligible as the shop was closed from the day of the Occupation. I did find it strange Leo had entered such an agreement but could hardly challenge it. There appeared little in the way of stock when I saw it.'

'Did you know about the basement?'

'I...I don't think so. If Leo had ever told me about it, I'd forgotten.' She looked from John to Fiona and sighed. 'The business was the least of my concerns after learning of my husband's fate.' The old lady removed a handkerchief from her sleeve and dabbed her eyes. 'I could no longer see myself living in our home after its violation. Or anywhere in Guernsey.' She sniffed. 'We'd been so happy during the few years we had together, and I saw my only choice was to return to England and my parents.'

Fiona's heart contracted at the thought of what Teresa had endured. It was bad enough to lose a loved brother, but a husband and the father of your child.

'It's looking more likely that Ernest hatched a scheme to keep the hidden valuables for himself. Which leads to the conclusion he was the informer. But did Leo have Jewish blood? We've found a descendant of Leo's uncle who knew nothing of it.'

Teresa lifted her head, looking at her daughter and grandson.

'His French grandmother was a Jew by blood, but she married a Gentile and converted to Christianity. Their daughter, Leo's mother, was brought up a Christian and married Henry Bichard, also a Christian. In normal times, Leo would not have been accounted a Jew and he certainly never thought of himself as such. But in the eyes of the Nazis, it appears it was enough to condemn him.' Tears now fell unchecked, and Judith moved to her side, holding her bony shoulders as Michael knelt beside her, taking her hands in his.

Again, John and Fiona exchanged glances, and she inclined her head in answer to his unspoken question.

Teresa's tears slowed, and she removed her hands from Michael's, giving him an affectionate pat. Addressing Fiona and John, she said, 'You must think me a silly old woman to cry about something which happened so long ago, but the finding of Leo's precious painting has brought back so many memories.'

'Of course, we understand. May I ask you something?' She nodded, and John continued, 'Is it possible that Ernest knew about your husband's family history? About the French grandmother being a Jew?'

'I've no idea. Leo made it clear to me it wasn't something the family spoke about. Not quite a skeleton in the cupboard, but a guarded secret. And with Guernsey being a small island...' she spread her hands.

'Quite.' John coughed. 'Another important question concerns the provenance of the Renoir. Do you know how it came to be in Leo's possession?'

By now Fiona was virtually on the edge of the sofa. So much had been learnt already and this, for her, was the burning question.

'Yes, of course.'

Chapter 23

Guernsey June 1940

His heart beating fast, Leo picked up the receiver.

'Bichard.'

'Leo, hope I'm not disturbing you?' He let out a deep breath as he heard his old friend Clem Le Page's voice.

'Not at all. What can I do for you?'

'You might regret asking that!' His friend chuckled. 'I've been roped into working for the Controlling Committee, in the department for Essential Commodities. With things hotting up everyone's working all hours, and we're going to need some steady hands at the helm. That's why I thought of you, my friend.'

'You mean you want me to come and work for the Committee?' Leo sat down, surprised. Work for the government? 'But I'm a businessman, Clem, not a civil servant.'

'Exactly my point. We need someone like you with good business experience and who can be trusted. There are many out there who will be looking to profit from this war, and I know you as an honest man.' Clem cleared his throat before adding, 'Let's be clear *when* we're invaded there won't be any call for a business like yours, Leo. You'll end up having to close the shop and will have time on your hands. Why not join me working for and being paid by the government? The pay's low, but it's better than nothing.'

Leo thought about it. Clem was right; he'd have no business to run while the Germans were there. He owned the building so he wouldn't be paying out rent, a plus. It would mean letting Ernest go, but what choice would he have?

'I'd like to know more about what's involved first, but in principle I'm interested.'

'Good man! Could you meet me tomorrow at the Committee's offices at nine? You can ask as many questions as you like, and if you're happy, we'd be glad to have you start immediately. Sorry to interfere with your Sunday, but every hour counts.'

Leo agreed, and Clem ended the call, saying he had work to do. Pouring himself a beer, Leo returned to the garden while he mulled what his friend had said. Clem, in his sixties, was a retired businessman and a friend of Teresa's father and would make a good work colleague. And becoming a civil servant might give Leo some protection from the Germans if needed.

The meeting went well, and Leo agreed to join the team. His decision was reinforced when Clem informed him three German planes had landed at the airport the previous evening, the pilots staying a short while before taking off again. Reconnaissance, Clem had said. It could only be a matter of time before they landed and stayed. Leo worked through the day, drawing up endless lists for the committee, before heading home tired, but with a sense of achievement.

It was nearly eight when he arrived home, and as he parked the car, the air raid warning sounded. He stood, searching the sky and within minutes he spotted five dots approaching from the south-east, and as they drew closer, he realised they were heading in the direction of the airport at Villiaze, losing sight of them as they descended.

Leo rushed inside to ring Teresa, but he couldn't get a long-distance line. With a groan, he guessed everyone had the same idea. He walked into the kitchen and discovered a note from Elsie, saying there was a stew in the oven. Aware he hadn't eaten since breakfast, he shrugged off his jacket and tie and filled a plate before fetching a jug of beer from the larder. Once he'd finished his meal, he retired to the sitting room with the beer and picked up the phone. The line was still busy, and throughout the evening he kept trying to get through. By ten o'clock he gave up. It was too late to disturb the family and Leo went to bed planning to try again early on Monday morning.

He rose soon after six and ran down the stairs to make the call. Again there was no long-distance line available. As he turned to walk back upstairs the telephone rang and he rushed to pick up the receiver.

'Teresa? Is that you?' His heart thumped loud in his chest.

'Sorry, old boy, it's Clem. There won't be any calls between us and Britain for the foreseeable future. I was calling to warn you we've been occupied. The bloody Jerries arrived last night and are here to stay.'

Chapter 24

Suffolk 2011

Fiona held her breath as Teresa settled back in her chair, briefly closing her eyes. She felt a pang of guilt for putting the old lady through the ordeal but didn't see they had any choice.

Teresa opened her eyes and smiled tiredly.

'It's a sweet story, which Leo shared with me when he first showed me around his home. I remarked on the painting, and he confirmed it was by Renoir. His grandparents had seen an exhibition of his work in Paris shortly after he returned from Guernsey and loved the scenes of Moulin Huet with the group of children. They were passionate art collectors and fond parents and asked if Renoir could replicate the picture, but with their three children as the subjects.'

Fiona let out an involuntary gasp. A private commission! No wonder the painting wasn't listed anywhere.

The old lady nodded.

'Renoir knew the family and was happy to oblige. He'd returned with a number of semi-finished pictures from Guernsey and simply completed one with the children as the principal subjects. It became a family favourite, having special significance as, sadly, the two younger children died a few years later. Adele, my husband's mother, inherited a considerable estate as well as the painting. She's the eldest of the group,' she pointed to a tall girl in the photocopy.

'Wow! That's some story, Mrs Bichard,' John said, his eyes alight with excitement. 'Everything finally makes sense, doesn't it, Fiona?'

She nodded, too overcome with the various revelations to speak. This family's story was like something out of a novel, particularly with the surprise news that Leo's mother was in the painting.

Teresa seemed to think of something.

'You mentioned other paintings? Were they by any chance local scenes by Naftel and Toplis among others? My husband had a large art collection, of which he was extremely proud.'

'Yes, they were. I'm afraid it looked as if an unknown number of items stored in the basement had gone, presumably sold. But there were about a dozen paintings left, and I have a list here.' Fiona handed her a typed sheet of paper.

Teresa gave them a cursory glance.

'To be honest, I can't remember the details, but is it fair to assume these were Leo's and not general stock?

'It is, they had been wrapped in the same oilcloth as the Renoir and had been there years. I'm happy for you to have them when I can arrange it.'

'Thank you,' Teresa whispered, looking pale.

She watched as Michael whispered something to her, before turning around and saying, 'My grandmother's very tired and needs to rest. I'm happy to answer any other questions you may have before you leave. Okay?'

They agreed, and Judith stood ready with the wheelchair as Michael again assisted his grandmother into it. Teresa reached out a hand to first Fiona and then John.

'It's been a pleasure to meet you both and no doubt we shall be in touch again soon.' To Fiona, she added, 'And again, please accept my condolences for your loss. I do hope you find the man who killed your brother soon.'

'Thank you, and I enjoyed seeing you as well, Mrs Bichard.' Fiona watched as Judith wheeled her mother out of the room, leaving her son pacing up and down, running a hand through his hair.

'Were you surprised at what your grandmother told us?' Fiona said.

He swung round and grinned ruefully.

'Not really, I'd heard most of the story before. But it still has an effect when told again in such detail.' He slumped in a chair.

'And your parents knew?' John asked.

'My mother yes, but I doubt my father was aware of it, particularly about the Renoir. He wasn't someone you could entrust with such information.' Michael's voice sounded bitter.

'I'm assuming your parents are not together?' Fiona ventured, hesitant to intrude.

'My father died last year, but they'd been apart for years.' He crossed his legs and gazed out of the window.

She muttered, 'I'm sorry,' but he didn't respond. A sore subject, then. An uneasy silence ensued, broken by Judith's return, twisting her hands.

'Mother's resting and asked me to offer you some tea and cake before you leave. I made a carrot cake this morning, and we also have shortbread.' She stood next to Michael, briefly touching his arm. He jumped up, saying, 'I'll sort it, Ma, you sit down and relax.' He turned to Fiona and John. 'Earl Grey okay with you two?'

They nodded their agreement.

'You have a beautiful home here, Mrs Collins. I presume it's where you grew up?' Fiona asked. Judith looked up from gazing at her lap, the sunlight emphasising the lines and dark circles on her face, making her look older than her years.

'Yes, with my mother and grandparents. It was a working farm in those days, idyllic for a single child. So many places to explore,' she said, a smile hovering on her lips.

'I noticed the horses in the field as we arrived. Do you ride?'

'Only occasionally now, but Michael rides when he's here. It's such wonderful riding country, and makes a refreshing change for him from London.' Judith smiled properly for the first time. 'Do you ride, Miss Torode?'

'Please, call me Fiona. Yes, I do, but not for a while. We're limited in Guernsey as there are few wide-open spaces like you have here. My favourite was always galloping on the beach at low tide.' For a moment the image of her and Nigel racing each other along L'Ancresse beach, laughing from pure joy, reignited the agonising ache of loss and she took a deep breath to calm herself. She was saved from saying more as Michael arrived with a tray of tea and cake and cups and plates were passed around.

'Did I miss anything interesting?' he said, his head on one side.

'Fiona and I were chatting about the house and of how wonderful it was to grow up here.' Judith's voice faltered as Michael's face clouded.

Fiona, sensing tension, changed the subject.

'We haven't discussed with Mrs Bichard what happens next regarding the Renoir. Should we do that now?'

'Absolutely. My grandmother's happy for me to be her representative from now on, with me being based in London,' Michael said, handing her a slice of carrot cake.

'I'm meeting Professor Wright tomorrow morning to update him on the provenance and ownership of the painting. As a leading authority on Renoir, his accreditation will be critical if Mrs Bichard wants to sell. For my part, I'm happy for the painting to be returned to the family.' She paused, struck by a thought. 'You're welcome to come along with me if you're free.'

Michael glanced at his mother.

'I'd planned to spend another day here, what do you think, Ma? Can you manage if I leave today?'

'I think you should be at the meeting, but the doctor's coming at five if you can wait.'

'Would this work for you two? We could travel back together by train.' Michael looked at them.

John shook his head.

'Sorry, I must leave within the hour if I'm to catch my plane. I can get a taxi.'

'No worries, I'll get Steve, our handyman, to run you to the station. Fiona?' He turned to her, his smile warm.

'I can wait. It'll give me time to explore your garden if I may.' In spite of herself, she felt a twinge of excitement at the thought of spending time alone with him. She hadn't dated in the past couple of years, partly because of spending more time with Nigel and partly because she hadn't met a man she found attractive. And Michael was attractive.

'Great!' Michael's eyes seemed to light up a little, and Fiona assumed he was thinking about the family reunion with their valuable heirloom. Which reminded her, no-one had asked how much a Renoir would be worth.

'Do you plan to keep or sell the painting?'

'Oh, sell.' He waved his arms around the room. 'As you can see, the house needs money spending on it, and my mother and grandmother have few savings,' he glanced at Judith, who flushed, 'so what's the point of having a pretty picture on the wall when we can fix the house?'

She nodded. It was what she'd expected. Only the wealthiest people kept such valuable art on their walls these days.

'I'm sure there'd be a lot of interest from collectors and museums. It's rare an unknown Renoir comes to the market.'

'What sort of figure are we talking? Hundreds of thousands? I don't follow auction prices these days unless it's sculpture.' He took a sip of his tea.

Fiona cleared her throat.

'You're a bit out.' Her gaze took in Michael and Judith. 'It's difficult to predict at this stage, and an auction house would advise more accurately, but I'd say three or four million pounds is possible.'

'You're kidding!'

Fiona grinned as Michael slapped his leg in surprise. His mother's jaw dropped.

'We weren't expecting that, were we, Ma?' He hugged her.

Judith seemed lost for words and had to take a deep breath.

'No, Mother had hoped for a few hundred thousand, but certainly not millions! It's...hard to take in.' She took a swallow of tea, her hands shaking.

'Sorry to interrupt,' John said, standing, 'but I do need to leave soon.'

Michael jumped up. 'Of course. Follow me, and I'll round up Steve. I've just thought, Ma; we'll be able to buy a new jeep after all!' He rubbed his hands.

John exchanged goodbyes with Judith and Fiona, telling the latter he'd see her on Friday. The men left, leaving the women with the remains of the tea on the table in front of them.

'Do you have to manage the whole house on your own, Mrs Collins? Looks a lot for one person.'

Judith didn't appear to have heard, her eyes unfocused.

'Mrs Collins?'

'Oh, sorry, my dear, I'm still trying to take it all in. You asked if I manage on my own. Yes, for the most part, but I do have a cleaning lady a couple of times a week. And Mother has a carer who calls once a day.' She gazed at Fiona and smiled. 'We'll be able to afford more help once the painting's sold. Will that take long, do you think?' For a moment she looked anxious like someone offered a present and then seeing it snatched away.

'I'm no expert, but I'd say months at least. The auctioneers will want to attract as many potential buyers as possible. So, I'm afraid you'll have to carry on as you are for a while.'

'I've managed for the past twenty years so I can wait a few more months.'

At that point, Michael appeared in the doorway.

'What's this about waiting a few more months?'

Judith explained about her conversation with Fiona while he sat down and helped himself to more cake. Michael and Judith, in light-hearted mood, started drawing up a mental list of all the things they could spend the money on, leaving Fiona to enjoy their fun. A few minutes later, Michael turned to her, saying, 'Please forgive our rudeness, this must be boring for you. Would you like to walk around the gardens now? Ma and I need to wait for the doctor.'

'Yes, please.'

He took her through the French windows facing the garden. Fiona realised they were at the back of the house and saw what appeared to be an unfinished attempt at a formal country garden. Untidy hedges, overgrown herbaceous borders and strips of ragged pathways.

'Not in great shape, is it? My grandmother wanted to establish a proper garden once her parents died and the family no longer farmed.' He followed her gaze as she surveyed the dereliction. 'Unfortunately, for various reasons, money became a problem, and there was no-one to help keep it in shape. Ma did her best, but it's got too much for her lately.' His expression was solemn.

'Well, I guess employing a gardener's on the list once the painting's sold,' she said with a grin.

He laughed.

'Too right! I expect Ma will have written a Wish List as long as my arm by the end of the day. Anyway,' he added, pointing to the left, 'you'll find the remnants of a kitchen garden down there, and if you follow the path around the house, you'll end up by the fields with the horses if you want to say hello.'

'Thanks, I'll do that.'

'Here are some mints, you'll be friends for life with these,' he said, grinning.

She watched him return inside then picked her way along the paths towards a copse, from where she wanted to look back at the old house. Along the way, she spotted brave roses and irises raising their heads above tangles of weeds and long-dead stalks of indeterminate flowers. Fiona was saddened by the state of the garden, emphasising as it did, the downfall of what was once a proud and successful farming family. She liked old Mrs Bichard, she had spirit and hadn't lost her pride. Whereas her daughter seemed cowed and somewhat diminished by their misfortune. Whatever it was.

As Fiona reached the edge of the wood, she turned to view the house stretched out behind. Now she could see where additions had been made over the centuries, offering different coloured brickwork and varied window sizes, from small single pane to the large French windows serving the drawing room. Although a hotchpotch, the overall effect was beautiful. No-one had painted the bricks like the front elevation, now gleaming red in the sun. Fiona hoped whatever plans the family had for this house; they'd keep its character. Not that it made any difference to her, of course, as she might never return. But still...she sighed as she made her way back towards the kitchen garden, and beyond. Something about this place called to her.

Fiona was fussing over the horses eagerly sniffing her pockets for treats when a car drove up to the house. A man with a medical bag emerged and was promptly ushered inside. Glancing at her watch, she saw it was ten minutes past five. Pretty much on time, then. Good. She wanted to arrive in London early enough to share a meal with her old uni friend. It was less than three weeks since she'd seen her, but so much had happened. Her life turned upside down – clearing her throat, she bent to kiss the soft muzzle of a horse before reaching for the mints. Frantic whinnying ensued, and she couldn't help laughing as both horses vied for attention, the mints soon gone. They were happy to stay by the fence and be stroked, and Fiona found it soothing. She must get back into riding, she thought, envious of the openness of the surrounding countryside.

The closing of a car door alerted her to the doctor's departure, and she took a fond farewell of her new friends, who trotted alongside in the field as she walked back to the house. Michael must have spotted her as he was waiting by the open door, his hands shoved into his pockets and a smile on his face. She had to acknowledge he was gorgeous even in his scruffy jeans and felt a small frisson of desire in the pit of her stomach. Perhaps it wasn't a good idea to travel back with him...

'Hi, did you enjoy your walk? Looks like my horses fell for your charms,' he said, chuckling.

'It was the mints, as well you know. Cupboard love.' She smiled and glanced back at the horses straining at the fence to join her.

'They may have had something to do with the attraction, but it looked to me as if you have an affinity with horses. If you're ever this way again, perhaps you'd like to join me for a ride?' His eyes locked onto hers and she took a deep breath to stop the heat rising to her cheeks.

'I'd like that, thanks. Although–' she shrugged, as if to say, it's not likely to happen.

'Good. In the meantime, if you're ready, we can leave for the station. Steve will drive us as he needs to run some errands for my mother.'

She raised her eyebrows.

'Your mother doesn't drive?'

He shook his head.

'No, at least not nowadays. Do you want to come in and freshen up before we go?'

Fiona followed him into the hall, and he directed her to a cloakroom near the kitchen. When she returned, Judith was standing in the hall to wish them goodbye.

'I hope the doctor's visit wasn't urgent?' Fiona said as they shook hands.

'No, just routine. He likes to keep an eye on her, been a friend of the family for years.'

'Right, let's go. I'll give you a ring later, Ma.' Michael lifted Fiona's overnight bag and led the way outside where Steve was waiting with the jeep, the engine running. She hopped in the back, and Michael took the passenger seat. Her new four-legged friends galloped to the fence and followed them down the drive. Fiona waved, receiving an answering whinny from the bay and a toss of the head from the grey. As they neared the end of the drive, she settled back in the seat, the men deep in conversation about cricket.

Once at the station they only had to wait ten minutes for the London train to arrive and soon found a vacant table with facing seats. Fiona, confronted with the intimacy of an hour's journey alone with Michael, shifted uneasily in her seat. Would it be rude to read her paperback? Of course, it would. They would have to make conversation, which should be easy as they had stuff in common.'

'I don't know about you, but I could murder a glass of something alcoholic. Care to join me?' He raised his eyebrows in enquiry.

'Love to, thanks. Dry white would be good.' Phew! What a relief. She'd feel much more relaxed with a glass of wine in her hand. Michael disappeared to the refreshments carriage, allowing her to reflect on the events of the day.

The family had been so different to what she'd expected and Michael, well he was something else. Not that she wanted a relationship with anyone, her heart was too fragile after losing her beloved brother, but a mild flirtation might cheer her up. She didn't even know if he was married or in a relationship. Idiot. Why wouldn't he be taken? Nice guys were hard to come by these days. More frogs than princes. A flicker of disappointment caught her by surprise at the thought. Stupid woman. Anyway, they might not meet after tomorrow. She and John had done their bit. Now Leo's family would take over the rest of the story while she...what? Well, they had to find Nigel's killer and bring him to justice. There would be a funeral to organise soon and then she had the rest of her life to plan. By the time Michael returned with their drinks, Fiona had talked herself into a low mood, barely raising a smile when she saw he'd bought two small bottles of white for her and a couple of red for himself.

'Thought we could celebrate my family's good fortune, or is that insensitive of me?'

He must have seen the sorrow in her face as his smile disappeared.

'No, it's fine. You have a right to celebrate, and I'm truly pleased for you and the family. I'll be hitting the vino later with my friend, so what the hell?' She managed a smile, appreciating his concern. Sod it; she may as well drown her sorrows while helping him celebrate.

After giving her a long look, he opened a bottle each and poured the wine into the unprepossessing plastic glasses.

Raising their glasses, they touched them briefly, with a muted 'Cheers!' Before taking a sip. Fiona grimaced, catching the same reaction on Michael's face and within seconds they were both laughing. In her case, verging on the hysterical.

He wiped the tears from his eyes, saying, 'Sorry about the wine. Bloody typical rail fare, but they'd run out of Dom Perignon so...' He grinned at her.

Grabbing a tissue, she blew her nose and patted her eyes before she could reply.

'You're forgiven. But next time you invite me to share a celebratory drink, I'll expect something with a little more class.' She took another swallow, urging her taste buds to get used to it. At least the alcohol would relax her.

'I'll bear that in mind. So, you're meeting a friend tonight? Someone close?' He took a swallow of wine and sat back.

'Yes, a friend from uni. She and I were in the same year and shared a flat together. Since I've been in Guernsey, we've not seen as much of each other.'

He nodded.

'I made some great friends at college, but seem to have lost track of most of them. That's the trouble when you get involved with a girl when you're young, your mates drift away cos you're never available.' He stared at his glass, a fleeting look of sadness crossing his face.

'Did you get married young then?' He wasn't wearing a ring, but she knew from experience that not many men did.

'No, didn't get that far. Got engaged, but,' he said, looking up, 'it was a long time ago. We've met up a few times since and she's happily married with three kids. There were no hard feelings. What about you? Is there a doting husband or boyfriend waiting for you back home?'

'No. It might sound sad, but I live, I mean lived, with my brother. He developed MS a couple of years ago, and he needed my support. I don't regret it, but I guess it impacted on my love life as I spent so much time with him.' She swallowed more wine, determined not to cry.

Michael's eyes widened.

'I'm sorry, must have been awful for you both. What will you do now?' He topped up her glass, and for a split second their fingers touched, and Fiona felt a tingle pass through them. She pulled back, not daring to look at him.

'No idea. I'm not making any plans until we've caught the bastard who killed Nigel. It's the main reason I hired

John, and already we think we know who did it. We just have to prove it.'

'Right. I'd assumed that was a job for the police.' He looked puzzled.

'Long story. And it involves your painting and how Nigel died.' She went on to tell him about the police viewing Nigel's death as a suicide and how, as yet, they hadn't been told about the Renoir. Michael leaned forward, giving her his full concentration as she talked. When she finished, he gripped her hand, saying, 'I want to help in any way I can. And I think I should come over to Guernsey.'

Chapter 25

2011

Fiona wasn't expecting that. Why would he want to help, even taking time to travel to Guernsey? And what was with the holding of her hand? Her face must have registered her surprise as Michael, looking serious, went on to tell her his reasons.

'Firstly, my family owes you a huge debt of gratitude for what you've done and suffered, and it's only right you're not left alone to finish the search for the killer.' She mentioned John, but he brushed that aside. 'He's a professional and knows what he's doing. Going after a killer is very different to tracing an owner of a painting.' He kept his fingers curled around hers, and she was reluctant to pull away.

'I know, but–'

'I *need* to do something, Fiona. What happened to my grandfather and your brother has to be atoned for, and I want to be involved. Family honour, if you like.' He took a deep breath. 'And secondly, after hearing my grandmother's story again, I want to see the island where Leo and my mother were born. I must be about a quarter Guernsey myself. Do you understand?' His eyes searched hers, and she nodded. He had every right to visit Guernsey. Her problem was whether or not she could deal with him being in her 'space' if he helped in their search.

'Right, that's agreed. As soon as we've set the ball rolling with an auction house, I'll fly over. The project I'm working on can wait.' He grinned, releasing her hand.

'What is it?'

'A giant metal sunflower for my client's garden. Fortunately, he's on his yacht in the Med for a few weeks, so no pressure.' He opened the remaining bottles of wine. 'I've got accustomed to the taste, how about you?'

'I guess. So, tell me more about your work, sounds fascinating.'

By the time they arrived at Liverpool Street, Fiona had relaxed enough, thanks to the wine, to enjoy Michael's company, hearing about his work and discussing art generally. They separated at the station, Michael going south to Battersea and Fiona north to Camden. After the merest hesitation, he kissed her on the cheek before rushing for his train. Once on the Tube, she mulled over the events of the day as she gradually succumbed to the effects of the early start and the alcohol. Yawning, she hoped her friend wasn't geared up for a late night as was their norm. Not only did she need an early night, but she was meeting Sam at nine in the morning at UCL and would have to brave the rush hour. Oh, joy!

A bright-eyed Michael was waiting for her outside the main university entrance the next morning when she arrived at five to nine. He greeted her with a peck on the cheek and a warm smile.

'This is it. I finally get to see the painting which meant so much to my family. I only wish Grandmama was able to be here.'

'If you have a computer at the farm, we could set up a Skype link with my netbook; I always have it with me when I travel.' She patted her bag.

His eyes lit up.

'Brilliant! Ma has a laptop, and I could ring her when we're ready.'

Pleased to have solved the problem, Fiona led the way to Sam's office in the art department.

'Fiona, my dear girl. It's good to see you.' She was wrapped in a bear hug that was both comforting and poignant, reminding her of their last meeting. Sam was a big man in all ways, tall and broad with a mass of grey curls and a tidy beard.

She pulled back and smiled, saying, 'Good to see you, too. And this is Michael Collins, the grandson of the last owner of the painting.'

The two men shook hands before they all sat down round Sam's untidy desk, overflowing with paperwork. Fiona had written down Teresa's story of how the painting came to be in Leo's possession and passed it to Sam. As he read, she saw the glint of excitement in his eyes and knew all would be well. She winked at Michael, who relaxed back in his chair.

'Wonderful!' Sam sighed. 'You know, it's a first for me, being involved in the discovery of a piece of work by such an artist as Renoir. Congratulations, young man. I'm happy to validate the painting. I assume you'd like to see it?' His eyes twinkled as he looked at Michael.

'Sure thing. Is it here?' Michael glanced around the cluttered room, filled with filing cabinets, shelves and a lone artist's easel.

'It's in our vault. I'll go and fetch it, won't take long.' He stood to leave, and Fiona asked if they could set up a Skype link with Michael's family, and Sam agreed. Michael rang his mother to warn her and then paced around the limited floor space until Sam returned. He removed the protective blanket and placed it on the easel. Fiona, lost in thought, gazed across at the object which had cost her so dearly. It was almost too painful to look at. Nigel would have been so excited to have been proven right about its authenticity. And delighted to find the true owner.

'There you are. What do you think?' Sam beamed at Michael who stood silently in front of the painting, hidden away for so long.

'To be honest, I'm not a great fan of the Impressionists, but seeing it in the flesh is quite, well, moving.' He pointed to the older girl playing on the sand with a younger boy and girl. 'And to think that's my great-grandmother. Quite something. Thank you, Fiona'. He turned to face her, and she summoned up a smile.

'You're welcome. Shall we set up the Skype call now? I know Sam's a bit short of time.'

The connection was soon set up, and Michael showed his mother and grandmother the painting, while Fiona remained in the background with her thoughts. She heard the oohs and aahs coming over the ether and was happy for them. Sam came and stood by her.

'How are really, my dear? This must be difficult for you.' He gripped her shoulder.

'It is, but at least something positive's come out of it.' She dropped her voice to a whisper. 'The family's pretty broke so the money will come in handy. It's so sad, they have a beautiful house but can't afford to look after it.'

'I see. Have they decided who to sell it with?'

'I was going to ask your opinion, but how about Christie's? I know they also offer private sales as well as the big auctions. Might suit the family better if they want to avoid publicity.'

'Excellent choice.' He coughed. 'I've pushed my luck a bit, keeping it here, and now we know its provenance, the sooner it's moved to somewhere more secure, the better. Insurance, you know.'

'Yes, I'd wondered about that.' She chewed her lip. 'If I can arrange an appointment with Christie's today, we could take it off your hands, but I'll need to check it's okay with Michael. Fortunately, I do have a contact there from my time at the V&A.'

Sam glanced at his watch.

'I need to give a lecture in thirty minutes, assuming any students can be bothered to get out of bed at what they consider to be an ungodly hour,' he grinned. She laughed, she was one of the few who always made it to Sam's lectures, and he knew that.

Michael switched off her computer, and she told him about her thoughts for an auction house.

'Sounds good to me. Can we call them now?'

She checked her phone for their number and dialled, keeping her fingers crossed her contact, Charles, was free. He was, and she was put through, explaining quickly about the Renoir. Charles sounded suitably excited, which she expected and said he'd set up a meeting with the senior valuation expert for after lunch, but they were welcome to bring the painting now. Fiona relayed this to Michael, and his grin said it all.

'I'd better order a cab, don't think we should risk the Tube, do you?'

She hugged Sam goodbye, thanking him for his help and promising to stay in touch. He and Michael shook hands, Michael also offering his thanks.

The Renoir wrapped once more in its anonymous grey blanket; they returned to the entrance to wait for the taxi.

'Thanks for giving up more of your time, Fiona. If you need to catch a flight home, I could carry on alone once we've dropped off the painting.' He held it tight under his arm.

'It's okay; I haven't booked my flight yet, thought I'd see how things went this morning.' She felt her face flush. 'I'd quite like to be there for the valuation if you don't mind.'

'Of course not, in fact, I'd be glad. And the very least I can do is offer you lunch. With a decent bottle of wine,' he added, straight-faced.

'You're on. Looks like our taxi. Good, I feel vulnerable standing here with you holding onto millions of pounds worth of art.' She flashed him a smile before getting into the taxi.

'Christie's, King Street, driver, please.' Michael sat beside her, the painting on his lap. 'My grandmother was over the moon to see this on Skype, as you probably gathered. I think it made it seem more real for her, no longer a daydream. She got a bit emotional.'

'It must be reviving memories of Leo and all she lost,' Fiona murmured.

They remained lost in their thoughts as the taxi weaved its way to St James's and the splendid Georgian building belonging to Christie's. Michael jumped out, offering a hand to Fiona, while still holding the painting under his other arm. Once inside, she asked for Charles, and two minutes later he arrived to guide them to a small office down a corridor. After the initial introductions, Michael unwrapped the painting for his inspection. Charles grinned.

'I say, Fiona, you were right. What a find! And thanks for bringing it to us. I've managed to fix an appointment for two o'clock with Roger Baines, who's our expert in Impressionist paintings. Bit of luck he was in today as he's due to fly to New York tomorrow.' Charles signed a receipt for the painting before seeing them out with a cheery wave.

'Right, now what? It's a bit early for lunch, so how about coffee and a stroll in Green Park before we find somewhere to eat?'

Fiona was happy to agree; the sunshine was too good to miss. They picked up takeaway coffees near the entrance and wandered off to find a quiet spot. Being too early for the lunchtime brigade, they found a place near one of the many trees and flopped down on the grass, facing towards the back of the Ritz Hotel.

'You'd find a good bottle of wine there,' Fiona said with a grin, pointing to the hotel. 'I hear they provide a pretty good lunch as well.'

Michael looked where she was pointing and laughed.

'And I hear men have to wear a tie in the restaurant, so no can do, sorry.' He indicated his T-shirt. 'But there are other great places around here, including one in Jermyn Street I quite like and isn't as stuffy.'

'I was only joking. I'm not keen on places like the Ritz myself. When I lived here, I used to take pleasure finding good value eateries off the beaten track.' She sipped her coffee, enjoying the feel of the sun on her face. It was good to be away from her problems in Guernsey for a while, even though she'd be back later that day. To face – what? With a sigh, she looked up to find Michael gazing at her, an odd expression on his face.

'What's the matter?'

'Nothing. This is a bit awkward,' he said, swirling coffee in the paper cup. 'My grandmother phoned last night as she'd been thinking about you and what you've done for us. If this guy at Christie's confirms what you've said, we stand to make millions, and we should be paying you a reward–'

Fiona, her face flushing, cut him off. 'I didn't do this for a reward! I did it for love of my brother and...and justice. I actually expected you to be a wealthy family and not in need of money.' She almost choked on her drink and Michael had to pat her back. It took her a moment to recover and breathe normally.

'Okay now?' He looked shocked. 'Why did you think we were wealthy?'

'Because I was told by someone that Teresa was from a posh family. Which is true, isn't it?'

'Yes, you're right.' He pushed a hand through his hair. 'I've lived so long with us having lost almost everything that I forget how grand the family once was. Grandmama hasn't forgotten, though. As I'm sure you could tell.' He grinned ruefully.

She laughed.

'Sure did. But I respect her for it, family pride and all that.'

'Hmm. In any case, we're all agreed on offering you something to say thank you. You've obviously spent money on employing a detective and flights, so,' he said, leaning forward, 'we think ten per cent of what we sell for would be fair. And no arguments.'

Stunned into silence, Fiona didn't know what to say. She hadn't given a thought to ask for a reward, only concerned with restoring the painting to the rightful owner. Although she and Nigel had joked about a reward when they first found it, after his death it had been the last thing on her mind. And she was far from broke, owning the house and business. But she didn't have a long-term income...oh, what to do, what to say.

'Just say yes and accept gracefully. I'd hate for us to fall out over it, Fiona. And what's a few hundred thousand pounds to a multi-millionaire, eh?'

'Could we settle for five per cent? Even that would be more than generous.'

He shook his head.

'Nope. Grandmama was insistent, and no-one argues with her. Please, shake hands on it?' He held out his hand.

'Oh, all right, but it's under protest.' She shook his hand, again feeling a tingle as their fingers touched. His brown eyes smiled back at her, and she felt the heat rise to her face. This was stupid. She was reacting like a teenager not a woman of thirty-four. And they were not potential lovers, more like business acquaintances.

'Great, I can report back to my grandmother that mission is accomplished. Now, ready for a walk before lunch?' He helped her up, and after discarding the empty cups in a bin, they walked down one of the tree-lined avenues. People lounged on either side in the park's green and white striped deckchairs.

'Michael, would you mind telling me what happened to your family? Why you're not as well off?' She hoped he didn't think her rude, but she thought it might help her understand them better.

He frowned.

'My father happened.' His voice was bitter. 'It's no big secret, but it's not something we talk about.' He took a deep breath and continued. 'Ma didn't meet my father until she was thirty, and fell in love with him, head over heels. A real charmer, apparently, though I never saw that in him. Bruce Collins; had a good job in banking, not bad looking and everyone was happy. I came along a few years later, and I understand the marriage was reasonably smooth. My parents bought a house in Surrey, and my father commuted to the City. At eight I was packed off to boarding school, which I hated.' He picked up an errant drink can from the path and tossed it in a bin.

'I'm sorry about the school. Did you miss your parents?' Fiona had this image of a small boy crying himself to sleep at night in an unfriendly dormitory and reached out to touch his arm.

'Not so much, hardly ever saw my father and Ma, well, Ma had all her clubs and societies to attend, the usual for a woman of her class. No, it was my friends I missed the most, from my local primary. I remember begging my parents not to send me away, but my father was adamant. I was to go to his old school. As it happens, I wasn't there too long as everything changed three years later.' Michael stopped to watch the antics of a grey squirrel, running in circles around a tree, as if searching for something.

'So, what changed?' she asked softly.

He turned, his face stricken. 'I'd been aware my father was a heavy drinker, but it turned out he was also a gambler, losing hundreds, sometimes thousands, on the horses. He got so desperate that he began stealing from his firm, setting up bogus accounts to cover his losses. I was eleven when he got caught. We lost our home, everything. The only good thing was I had to leave that dreadful school.'

Fiona's heart ached for him.

'How awful! Did he get sent to prison?'

'No, that's why the family's broke. My grandmother paid back all the money my father stole to save his skin. I think she should have let him be arrested, the bastard. But it was to save my mother from total disgrace. So it was all hushed up, and Ma and I had to move in with my grandmother, which was great for me, but Ma found it hard. She totally lost her confidence and self-respect and been living in her mother's shadow ever since.'

Fiona, in spite of, or perhaps because of, her past tragedy, felt a swelling of sympathy for him. 'What happened to your father?'

'He and Ma divorced, that was non-negotiable as far as my grandmother was concerned. Although I didn't learn about any of this until years later. Apparently, my father was forbidden to have any contact with me, but I just thought he'd stopped loving me and wasn't interested in seeing me. We'd never been close, but still...' He shoved his hands in his pockets, turning his head away.

She moved closer, linking her arm through his and he didn't comment.

'And you didn't see him again?'

'No, he simply disappeared. I think Ma did try to find him, in spite of what he'd done, she still loved him, never loved anyone else. And then five years ago, we heard he'd died in Spain, running a sleazy bar. Cirrhosis of the liver.' His jaw tightened. 'Karmic justice, I suppose.'

'Your poor mother. No wonder she seems unhappy. But at least the family fortunes are about to be repaired.'

'Thanks to you.' He smiled faintly. 'Come on, time for that lunch I promised.'

Within ten minutes they were sitting at a table in Franco's, which Michael assured her was one of the best Italian restaurants in the area. Happy to take his word for it, she perused the menu as he ordered the wine. Moments later the waiter arrived with a bottle of Laurent Perrier and two champagne flutes. Fiona laughed. 'You really didn't have to...'

'But I do. After that crap we drank last night, I must make amends. And don't worry, I'm getting well paid for the sculpture I should be working on.' Michael grinned, and her stomach flipped. He had the most devastating smile.

They raised their glasses in a toast as Michael said, 'To the painting, and may it sell for millions.'

Fiona sipped her wine, allowing the bubbles to fizz through her. Not having eaten since seven, the alcohol went straight to her head. She reached for the basket filled with fresh ciabatta and began nibbling.

'Sorry,' she mumbled, 'but I'm starving. I'm ready to order if you are.'

Their order taken she relaxed. She loved Italian food, and her stomach juices were flowing at the sight and smell of the food on nearby tables. The familiar Italian herbs of oregano, thyme and sage with an overlay of garlic. Delish. Michael had good taste in restaurants.

'If I can settle the necessary with the bloke at Christie's today, I should be able to come out to Guernsey at the weekend. Can you suggest somewhere I could stay?'

Fiona gulped. So soon! She hadn't had a chance to discuss it with John yet, although he was unlikely to object, as long as she still needed him. Which she did. If Michael was coming over, then there was one obvious place for him to stay.

'How about my house? I'm staying with friends, so it's empty. John upgraded the security after we realised the killer might burgle the house and it might be good to have you there.'

He slapped the table, causing bemused glances from their neighbours.

'Great idea! We could work out some kind of lure for the guy, catch him in the act. We need him to try again, and this way you'll be safe.'

'Sounds good. I'll run it past John tomorrow. Welcome to our team,' she raised her glass and Michael reciprocated.

'Thanks. We'll make a good team. Ah, our food,' he added as the waiter arrived bearing their starters. Parma ham and fried parmesan for him and linguine with crab for her. 'Looks wonderful, doesn't it? All I need now is the right valuation from Christie's to make this day perfect.'

Chapter 26

London 2011

As they walked to Christie's, Michael's heart and brain were full of anticipation, matching his full stomach. One object of anticipation was walking quietly beside him, and he sneaked a glance while she gazed at a window display. Her profile showed him one of her blue eyes, the neat, small nose, full lips and light brown curly hair. Together with her slim figure, he thought she was perfect, and he wanted to get to know her better. The air of sadness she projected added to her attraction for him, but also told him she was, for the near future at least, off limits. He was happy to wait. Although he'd had no ulterior motive when he said he wanted to visit Guernsey, Michael was pleased with the outcome. Staying in her house would allow him to find out more about Fiona, and if he could help bring her brother's killer to justice, that would be even better. Might even earn him a few brownie points, he smiled to himself.

The other object of anticipation, the valuation, came closer as they approached Christie's entrance and Michael turned to her, saying, 'Fingers crossed.' She grinned, holding up her crossed fingers as they entered the building. The receptionist announced their arrival and moments later a thin, middle-aged man wearing heavy black-rimmed glasses came through to greet them.

'Roger Baines. And you must be Miss Torode and Mr Collins. Please, come along to my office. Charles has gone to collect your painting, which I haven't seen yet, but I gather he's rather excited about.' He led the way to a beautiful panelled room with a large antique desk and leather chairs. They had just taken their seats when Charles arrived with the painting wrapped in its grey blanket. With a quick grin of acknowledgement, he pulled back the material with a flourish, presenting the picture to Roger.

'Hmm, I see. Let me have a closer look.' He took out a magnifying glass and studied the picture inch by inch while Michael held his breath. Roger's face remained inscrutable as he asked about provenance. Fiona handed over Teresa's statement and explained about Sam's validation. His eyebrows raised a fraction before he read Teresa's story. Michael noticed Charles shifting from foot to foot in barely concealed anticipation. Fiona, on the other hand, looked composed, leaning back in the chair, legs crossed.

Finally, Roger looked at Michael, a faint smile hovering around his mouth.

'Well, I have to agree with our esteemed Professor Wright's conclusion. This is a genuine Renoir, no question. And we would be more than happy to act on your behalf in a sale.'

Michael sagged with relief.

'Thanks. And your valuation?'

'At auction, it might fetch around four and a half million, if we catch enough interest. Which, be assured, we would. At the very least it wouldn't go below three million.' The smile grew a little.

'That's even better than I'd hoped, thank you.' He glanced at Fiona, whose smile stretched from ear to ear, probably matching his own, he thought. 'And if we decided to sell privately? I understand you offer this option?'

'Yes, and it might be worth considering if you want a quicker sale. Our next Impressionist Auction is not until November and will be well attended. Auctions tend to achieve a better price, outdoing our highest valuations sometimes,' he added, stroking his chin, 'but I think we could safely ask for three and a half million privately. I know keen collectors who would be interested in acquiring a new Renoir privately.'

'I'll need to discuss the options with my grandmother, the legal owner. What about the commission and costs involved?'

Roger quoted him their terms. Their services didn't come cheap, but Michael knew that. They'd still come out considerably better off than they were now, he reminded himself. They agreed Michael would confirm which path they would follow by the next day and shook hands. Roger finally allowed himself a warm smile.

'It will be a pleasure to represent you, Mr Collins. We'll talk soon. Goodbye, Miss Torode.'

Charles escorted them to the entrance, a smug expression on his face.

'Old Baines doesn't give much away, does he? You wouldn't know from his expression he's over the moon about your painting. It's a real feather in his cap to take on the sale of an undiscovered Renoir, you know.' He kissed Fiona on the cheek. 'Thanks again for thinking of us. Some of the fairy dust will be sprinkled on me when my bonus is calculated.'

Fiona laughed. 'I'm glad, Charles. Take care.'

The men shook hands and Michael took Fiona's arm to lead her out of the building, trying to keep a straight face.

'Fairy dust!' he cried when they were clear. 'Does he need more fairy dust?'

'Now, behave yourself, Michael. He's very sweet, and every girl needs a gay friend in her life, and he got us into the big man's office pretty darn quick, didn't he?' She smiled at him, and for an insane moment, he wanted to pick her up, whirl her around and plant a lingering kiss on her lips. It took a huge effort of will to hold back.

'You're right, I apologise. I have some gay friends myself from college days.' They stood on the pavement, his hand on her arm. 'Where to now?'

'Victoria for me. I need to get the Gatwick Express.'

'How about I get you a cab?'

'No need, it's the next stop from Green Park, as I'm sure you know. But thanks for the offer. What about you?'

'Might as well go home and get organised for my trip. So, Victoria will suit me too.' Michael grinned, glad to spend a bit longer in her company. He picked up her bag and they headed back to Green Park station. Once on the Tube, they found themselves squashed together in the crush, their bodies bumping into each other. Fiona kept her eyes down, as if uncomfortable with their closeness. Neither spoke during the short journey, and it was with some relief Michael jumped out, Fiona close behind.

'Aren't you travelling on?' she asked, looking surprised.

'Soon. I thought, as a gentleman, I should escort you to your platform.' Placing a hand under her elbow, he steered her through the crowd heading for the elevators. Later, they stood on the platform where the Gatwick Express was waiting to leave. It was time to say goodbye.

'Thanks so much for coming over, Fiona, and I look forward to catching up at the weekend. I'll give you a ring when I've booked my flight, okay?'

'Sure. See you soon.' She smiled at him.

Moving closer, he kissed her on both cheeks. 'Bye. Have a good flight.'

He waited while she boarded the train and found a seat and waved as the train left. She waved back. Thrusting his hands into his pockets, Michael headed back towards the Underground, his head nearly bursting with a myriad of thoughts.

◆◆◆

Fiona arrived back at Louisa and Paul's house somewhat drained. The time in England had been more of an emotional rollercoaster than she'd expected. A mixture of grief, sadness, pleasure and celebration. Her friends welcomed her with their usual consideration, not pressing her for details as they shared a supper. She told them all had gone well and that the grandson, Michael, was coming over at the weekend to help. Paul's eyebrows rose at this, but he didn't comment. Fiona said she'd explain more the next day, but needed an early night. Once in her room, she unpacked on auto-pilot, barely able to concentrate and feeling close to tears. She'd arranged to meet John the next morning at ten and crawled into bed seeking a dreamless sleep.

Friday morning she was a different woman. Refreshed and energised, ready to focus on the aim of catching Nigel's killer. Michael sent her a text earlier to say he'd booked a flight for Saturday morning and she replied saying she'd collect him. At breakfast, she gave her friends a potted version of events during her time in England, not mentioning the times she'd spent alone with Michael. They were particularly impressed with the painting's valuation.

'I'd no idea it would be that much. I know you'd said it could be in the millions, but thought you were a bit optimistic. Not that I know anything about art, Charlotte's more au fait with that world.' Louisa beamed at her.

'It's never entirely predictable, but whatever it finally goes for, the family have insisted I receive ten per cent as a reward. I tried to refuse, but they stood firm.'

'Quite right too,' chipped in Paul. 'Without you, they might never have got the painting back.' He stood, collecting his phone and keys. 'I'm off, see you at work,' he said to his wife, 'and catch up this evening, Fiona. Have a good day.'

Louisa eyed her warily.

'So what's with this Michael coming over? And what's he like?'

'He wants to help us catch the killer and also see the place where his grandfather and mother were born. Nothing unusual. He'll stay at my house.' She stirred her muesli as she thought of how to describe him. 'He's a sculptor and lives in London, visiting the family home occasionally. In his late thirties and seems nice.' Her voice neutral.

'I see. Is he married?' Louisa asked, head on one side.

'Don't think so; he didn't say.' Fiona realised that he hadn't said anything about a wife or girlfriend, only that he'd come close to marrying when young. Surely, if he were involved with someone, he wouldn't have suggested coming here to help?

'Well, I look forward to meeting this "nice" sculptor when he's over,' Louisa said dryly, standing to clear the dishes. 'We must have him over for dinner one night. How long's he staying?'

'No idea. I assume a matter of days. It's a long weekend isn't it, with bank holiday on Monday? Are you two working?'

'I've got the three days off, but Paul will be working tomorrow.' She stacked the pots in the dishwasher and turned around. 'We must do something, meet up with the others, perhaps. If you feel up to it?'

'Sure, why not, would be fun.'

Fiona had just parked on the Crown Pier when her mobile rang.

'Miss Torode? Inspector Woods. How are you?' He sounded cheerful.

'I'm fine thanks. Do you have some news for me?'

'Yes, the toxicology results are in, and they're negative, and I've arranged with the coroner to hold the inquest next Friday. In the meantime, the death certificate can be issued and the body collected by the funeral directors. I'm sorry it's taken so long.'

'Thank you; I'll organise it.' She swallowed, the horror of Nigel's death rushing back into her mind. 'Do you still intend to recommend suicide to the coroner? I believe John's spoken to you about our investigation.'

She heard a fit of coughing on the line before he replied.

'Sorry about that, know I should give up the fags. Yes, John did explain things to me, but unless you have concrete evidence, my hands are tied. However, if you can provide genuine doubt, we might get an open verdict, as I said to John. Have you made any progress?'

'Yes, and as it happens, I'm on my way to John's office now. We need to discuss a few things, and perhaps he could phone you back?'

'No problem. Goodbye for now.'

Fiona's mind swirled as she made her way up Pier Steps and into High Street. The thought of organising the funeral was scary. Knowing you had to do it one day was different to being told you could go ahead. When her parents died, Nigel was there to help and did most of the organising. She gritted her teeth to stop a cry bursting out. She couldn't let her beloved brother down, but it was hard.

By the time she was a couple of doors away from John's office she would gladly have downed a stiff vodka, but settled for a large cappuccino, buying one for John at the same time. Once in his office, she thrust his cup at him and collapsed in a chair without speaking. He waited until she'd taken a scalding gulp, before asking, 'What's happened?'

Through tears, she told him of the phone call.

'Ah, I see. Here,' he passed her a box of tissues.

She blurted out how alone she felt, with no-one to help her with the funeral arrangements. He took her cup, putting it down on the desk and hugged her.

'I'm sure any of your friends will help, and I'd be honoured to offer my services. You're not alone, Fiona, far from it. Come on, drink your coffee and we can talk.' John returned to his chair behind the desk, taking a sip of his drink. 'Thanks for my coffee, by the way.'

Fiona slowly calmed down, taking sips of coffee as her tears dried. She knew John was right, she did have people who would be only too happy to help her, and his offer touched her. He'd become more than a hired detective, he was a friend, as reliable as Louisa had promised.

'Before I forget, Michael's flying over this weekend, arriving tomorrow.' She explained why and where he'd be staying. John's face creased into a smile.

'That's good news, I liked the man, and having him stay in your house is inspired.' He tapped his fingers on the desk, and Fiona could almost hear the cogs whirring in his brain. John would have a plan, she was sure.

She told him about the valuation and authentication, including the family's offer of a reward.

'I'm pleased for the family, only wish I could have been there at Christie's to see Michael's face. Well done.' John drained his cup and leaned forward. 'We now have to decide what we tell Woods. With the painting verified and owner found, the situation's changed, hasn't it?'

'Yes, and Michael could confirm to Woods about the Renoir's history and the connection to the Domaille family.' Fiona pushed the thought of the impending funeral to one side, galvanised by the idea of proving Nigel's death was no suicide.

John nodded.

'Exactly! We're building up the links, but it's still circumstantial, and we haven't a clue about Duncan's whereabouts. We need to draw him out.' More drumming of fingers on the desk ensued, and Fiona waited patiently.

'With Michael's permission, we could get an article in the *Evening Press* about the find of a valuable work of art and the owner coming over from the UK to claim it. It can mention a Guernsey connection and that more will be revealed later. We can't say anything about you and the shop, or about Michael staying in your house, but that doesn't matter. Duncan will make the connection and hopefully try and steal it. What do you think?' His excitement was palpable, and she was caught up in it.

'Brilliant! But we can't leave Michael like a sitting duck. Duncan, if it is him, is dangerous.' The thought of anything happening to Michael made her grow cold.

'That's okay; we'd have the police on our side, remember. Once I tell Ron what we know, I'm sure he'll cooperate. We could have men watching the place, and I'll be one of them,' he said, grimly. 'Somehow, we need to make it look like you're back at your house. He's not going to try anything in daylight, so if Michael has your car and it's in the drive, he'll think you're in. So far the cameras I installed haven't picked up anyone arriving other than the postman. I guess our friend's been lying low. From his viewpoint, there was no urgent need to try again soon.'

'Yes, but wouldn't he prefer to break in when I'm not there? Safer, surely.'

John shifted in his chair.

'Not if he wanted to know where the painting was, and you're the only one who could tell him. He couldn't assume he'd simply find it, unhidden, in the house.'

The penny dropped.

'Oh! You mean he'd force me to tell him like he tried with Nigel?' She remembered her brother saying the man had hurt him and shivered.

'Exactly. And it's another reason why I think he's stayed away from Colborne Road. You've not been there. He must be wondering where you are, so if we tell the media the finder of the valuable work of art has been away, trying to trace the owner, then he'd have an answer. Right?'

Fiona let it sink in, looking for a catch. She nodded.

John rubbed his hands together.

'I'll go and see Ron, explain what we've discussed and see if he can find out more about Duncan and where he's been for the past thirty years. It might give us a clue as to where he's holed up here. When's Michael arriving? Do you think he'll agree to be bait?'

'Tomorrow morning and I'm picking him up so will run it past him. I'm sure he'll be happy to be bait, as you put it.'

Fiona sat on a seat watching the waves break on the shore at Bordeaux Harbour, one of her favourite little spots on the island. She was drinking another much-needed coffee after spending time at the funeral directors' at The Bridge, a few minutes away.

The same firm had provided a wonderful funeral for her parents, some of the staff remembered her and Nigel, and it had added to the emotion. When people are kind and solicitous, as these were, it tended to make her more tearful. They took her gently through the options, and she managed to choose a coffin and decide on Le Foulon in St Peter Port for both the funeral service and burial. Their parents were also buried there, although their funeral had been at the Town Church because of a large number of mourners. Fiona wanted Nigel's funeral to be more private, solely family and friends, which she thought would have been his choice. Never one to be the big centre of attention and not keen on crowds, he'd struggled to cope with their parents' grand funeral.

She stood, needing to stretch her legs, and taking her shoes off, walked onto the sand, her head still full of unwanted images and thoughts of past funerals and the plans for Nigel's. A date was yet to be confirmed but was likely to be about ten days. Once a date was set, a notice was to be placed in the *Evening Press*. There was much still to do; the vicar, hymns, prayers. Fiona wished she could press a 'forward' button, such as those on machines, and it all be over. And then her life could begin again.

Chapter 27

Guernsey 2011

'Hi!' Michael said, kissing her on both cheeks.

Fiona grinned. It was good to see him again, that lazy smile of his...

'Morning, have a good flight?'

He hoisted a large rucksack on his back, saying, 'Fine thanks. Probably one of the shortest flights I've been on in a while. It took longer queuing through security,' he said, walking alongside her to the exit. 'My mother and grandmother send their regards, and I have to file a detailed report of everything I see and do when I return. Strict orders from Grandmama,' he laughed.

'Does she talk about her time here at all?'

'Not much, but from what I gather, she loved the few years she lived here. The way she left poisoned the memories a bit, I think.'

She nodded, opening the car boot for his rucksack before sliding into the driver's seat.

Michael slipped in beside her.

'What's the plan?'

'There's no food in the house, so I suggest we stock up at Forest Road Stores, round the corner from here. Then it's off to Town and my home. There's a lot to tell you, but it can wait till we get there. And John will be joining us.' She cast a quick glance at him before starting the car.

'Sounds good to me. Let's go,' he answered with a smile.

After filling several bags of groceries at the store, Fiona drove on towards St Martins, giving Michael a running commentary about the areas they drove through and told him of the parking clock system on the island for when he ventured out alone.

'You mean you have free parking here? On the whole island? I love this place already!'

'Hopefully, you'll find other things to love, too. Fabulous scenery, beaches, loads of bars and restaurants.' She laughed.

'Oh, I'm sure there will be, don't worry.' He gave her an odd look before turning to face the road.

Fifteen minutes later she pulled into the drive in Colborne Road and switched off the engine. She opened the front door as Michael collected his luggage.

'Say, what a lovely house. 1930s, right?'

'Yes, it was my parents', and where we grew up. Come in, and after we've unloaded the food, I'll make coffee. I'll show you around after John's been.' Fiona led the way into the kitchen, and together they unpacked the groceries. She filled the espresso machine and set out two cups.

'Actually, there's something we need to discuss before John arrives.' She told him about his plan to use him to lure Duncan out of hiding and try to steal the Renoir, her eyes fixed on his face, watching his reaction.

'Great idea! Looks like I'll be of more use than I'd expected.' His eyes lit up with excitement.

'John's hopefully enlisted the support of the police so that you won't be in any danger. But I've heard Duncan's a big, strong man. So don't be too heroic, will you?' she said, offering him a cup of coffee. She couldn't quite quell a hint of fear – and doubt. Something niggled her about the plan.

Michael drew himself up taller. 'I'll have you know I'm a karate black belt. I'd be no pushover.' He banged his chest, Tarzan-style.

'Good,' she said, picking up her cup, 'shall we sit in the garden while we wait for John?' She led the way to the back garden, composed of a large, now overgrown, lawn area and various borders looking equally neglected. Her mother would turn over in her grave, she thought, guiltily. When she and Nigel had lived in London, they employed a gardener to keep it tidy between their visits but had taken it over themselves since being back. At least the patio area was tidy, set with low maintenance rattan-effect table and chairs.

Michael remained standing, surveying the scene.

'I could cut the grass for you, tidy it up a bit. I'm not so good at weeding, I'm afraid.'

'That's kind of you, but please don't feel you have to.' Fiona was touched by his offer.

He grinned. 'It's no big deal. The exercise will do me good.' He sipped his coffee, striding around the patio, his eyes darting around. 'You're not overlooked, which is good. And they provide security,' he added, pointing to the high brick walls on all three sides. He swivelled around to face the back of the house. Fiona followed his gaze to the fences either side, one holding a gate, providing access from the front.

'The gate's always locked and John's installed cameras and alarms around the front and back, so it's as secure as we can make it.'

'Don't worry, I'll be fine. And if we have the help of the local plod that'll be a bonus.'

Fiona wished she shared his confidence but smiled at him. It was odd, having him here in her home, even though she wasn't staying. It created an intimacy, a connection, knowing he'd be free to flick through her books and music collection, look at family photos scattered around the house and take note of the ornaments and pictures accumulated over the years. Her family's history was on show and she felt exposed. Daft, she knew, but, after all, until a few days ago they'd never met, and now he was ensconced here. Don't be silly, she told herself, he's no nosy parker, he's a nice man who wants to help.

'I think a car's just arrived, will it be John?'

Fiona roused herself from her reverie.

'Yes, I'll let him in. Stay here, and we'll come out.' She nipped through the French window into the sitting room and through to the hall.

'Hello, John, please come in.'

'Morning. Michael got here okay?' John followed her inside.

'Yes, and he's agreed to be the bait. Would you like a coffee?' She hovered by the kitchen door.

'No thanks, I'm good.'

She led him outside to join Michael, and the men shook hands before taking seats at the table with Fiona.

'How did it go with Inspector Woods?'

John beamed.

'Very well. I think he was impressed with our mutual detective work, tracing Michael and his family and Ernest Domaille's connection to it. He agreed it was too much of a coincidence to be ignored. He's initiated an international search on Duncan's background; where he's been since the 80s, and if he's got a criminal record anywhere. Prioritising Australia because of the possible accent,' he said, tapping the table.

'And is he up for trying to trap Duncan?' Fiona asked.

'Yes, he thought it a good idea, but he made an observation which I should have thought of.' He cleared his throat, giving her a look of apology. 'Ron pointed out that if you weren't in the house, he wouldn't be able to ask where the painting was, and if he did break in, the only charge would be burglary.'

'That's it! That's what's been bugging me! I knew something didn't fit, but couldn't work out what,' Fiona cried, looking at the men. 'So I need to be here, don't I?'

Michael shook his head.

'I don't like that idea, at all. There must be some other way, surely? We can't put Fiona's life at risk.'

'I'm not keen either, but as you told me, Michael, you're a karate black belt, and you'll be here and won't the police be around?' The thought of having to face the monster who'd killed Nigel made her feel sick. She wouldn't consider it on her own, far too dangerous.

'Ron and I discussed it and, assuming Fiona was to agree, he'd arrange to have a policeman hidden in the grounds and Michael would be in the house, of course.' He paused, looking from Michael to Fiona. 'It's possible Duncan will have the brass neck just to turn up and ring the bell. After all, there's been nothing said publicly about the possibility of this being a murder inquiry and attempted theft. He wouldn't come during the day in case he was seen; I'm sure of that. But he might not wait until the middle of the night, either.'

'Basically, you're saying I'd have to move back in with Michael, and he'd need to keep out of sight?' They'd be living under the same roof. She hadn't expected that and for a moment wondered about changing her mind. It would have been fine if she didn't find him attractive. But it was more important to catch Duncan, so she'd have to cope. And Michael, who looked thunderous, had offered to take the risk.

John shifted in his chair.

'It's not ideal, I'll grant you, and neither of you has to agree. We could try and think of something else and you, Michael, don't need to be here if the police are in the house.'

'No, I came over to help catch the guy who killed Nigel while hoping to steal my family's painting, and I'm not going to back out as soon as I've arrived. It's Fiona I'm worried about. We have to ensure her safety.' His concern touched her.

'Absolutely. Ron assured me his men wouldn't give Duncan a chance to hurt her and if you're there as well, that's even better. So, does this mean you both agree to be here at night?' They nodded. 'Right, the next point I've agreed with Ron is the "leak" to the *Evening Press*, and we should see that in Monday's edition. Assuming it does go in, you'll both have to be here Monday night onwards.

We're saying that the owner of the artwork's due over on Thursday, limiting Duncan's chance to steal it to three nights. Okay with that?'

Michael nodded, his expression clearing. Fiona took a deep breath. In a few days, it could all be over, and she could focus on laying her brother to rest.

'Yes, fine by me. Just a thought, what if Duncan doesn't read the paper?'

'Good question and I'd thought of that. We're making sure the story gets picked up by local radio and television. After all, it's big news – valuable artwork found on the island, mystery finder, etc.' John, his eyes shining, leaned forward. 'Now, the really exciting news is that I know where Duncan's staying!'

'You do? How...how did you find out?' Fiona's eyes widened.

'I had a brainwave, which does happen occasionally,' he chuckled. 'I thought it likely he'd have seen his father's advocate about the will and would have given his contact details. So I rang the nursing home and had a quick chat with Mrs Domaille, who, fortunately, was reasonably with it, and asked her for the advocate's name. She wasn't sharp enough to query why I wanted to know and gave it to me.' He smiled at them both and Fiona could see how much he was enjoying it.

'But surely an advocate wouldn't divulge their client's details, would they?' Michael said.

'You're right, except Duncan wasn't the client, Ernest was. As it happens, the advocate's a pal of mine, and we had a chat this morning, off the record, and he told me Duncan's renting a place in St Sampson. I have the address here,' he patted his pocket.

'Awesome, John! Well done.' Fiona smiled at him, happy to acknowledge his brainwave.

'Are we going to stake him out?' Michael asked, looking keen.

'Not us, I'm sorry,' John grinned at him. 'I rang Ron, and he'll organise a watch on him from Monday. It'll mean we should get a warning if he's on the way here, a real bonus. So,' he leaned back, 'any questions?'

Fiona looked at Michael, who raised an eyebrow. She shook her head.

'I don't think so. I assume we carry on as normal over the weekend and Monday, being a holiday, and then I'll move back that evening. Now we have a plan set up from Monday, wouldn't it be better if my car's not here until then? Just in case Duncan swings by.'

'Good point. You okay with that, Michael?'

'Sure, it's only a couple of days.'

'Right, I'd better get off. Promised the wife I'd take her out for a late lunch,' he glanced at his watch, 'a very late lunch.'

Fiona saw him out and rejoined Michael in the garden.

'It's turning out a bit different to what we'd planned. You still okay with me staying here? I could move to a hotel for a couple of nights.'

'It's fine. Silly for you to not stay here when the house is empty.' She collected the coffee cups. 'Shall we make some lunch and then I'll show you round? Oh, and you've been invited to join us for supper tonight if that's okay?'

'Sounds good. You'd better tell me more about your friends while we prepare lunch.'

They headed into the kitchen and, deciding on a salad, between them they chopped and prepared the ingredients, Fiona filling him in about Louisa and Paul. Finished, they returned outside to enjoy the sun, Michael opening a can of lager while Fiona settled for juice. As they ate, she explained how he could walk into Town, with a choice of two routes, and where to hit the shops, cafés and bars, all near the harbour.

'I saw the harbour from the plane, looks pretty amazing. And you've got a great coast here, haven't you? Would you take me along to Moulin Huet sometime? So I can see the famous bay for myself.' He looked relaxed as he ate, a lazy smile hovering around his mouth. Fiona had to stop herself thinking about the nights they'd be spending together here. With a bit of luck, it might only be one night if Duncan turned up on Monday. Then she could escape back to the safety of her friends' house.

Lunch over, she showed him around, starting with the kitchen and explaining the various gadgets and appliances. Then the sitting room, full of their family mementoes. She tried not to look at them, focusing instead on the television and its remote control. He made the occasional comment about the décor and paintings as they moved around. Fiona pointed out her study next door but didn't go in, the door remaining closed. Then it was the dining room and cloakroom before she showed him upstairs.

This was the hardest part, more personal, more intimate and with Nigel's bedroom, more painful. Again, she pointed out the rooms, but left the doors closed, as she did her bedroom. Michael seemed to understand her discomfort and squeezed her arm. Then it was the guest bedroom at the end of the landing, thankfully en suite as were the other bedrooms. No embarrassing meetings in a shared bathroom for them.

'This is great,' he said, dumping his bag on the bed. 'And being at the back, I won't be showing any lights in my room if anyone's snooping. Can you explain the alarm system to me before you go?'

'Sure. Let me fetch you clean towels first. There are basic toiletries in the bathroom, but is there anything else you need?' She raided the airing cupboard on the landing, returning with a set of towels.

'No, I'm good, thanks.'

Fiona repeated the tour, this time pointing out the almost invisible cameras and security devices on the doors and windows before giving him the security code for the alarm housed in the hall.

Michael grinned.

'A mini Fort Knox! John's done a good job; I shall feel totally safe.'

'Yes. I'll get off now, then, and pick you up about seven. Will text you first so if you could wait outside on the pavement, just to be safe.' She swung her handbag over her shoulder and stood uncertainly by the front door.

'Thank you, again, Fiona. I look forward to this evening.' He held her arms as he kissed her on both cheeks.

'Bye, see you later.' She virtually ran out of the house and into the car. As she started the engine, Michael remained framed in the doorway, waving. She gave a quick wave and drove off towards Fort Road, feeling as if her life was even more out of control than it had been. And was likely to get worse, with an attractive man under her roof.

Chapter 28

Guernsey June 1940

Leo drove his car into Town for the last time on that fateful Monday. At the offices of the Controlling Committee, he learnt the Germans had been busy issuing numerous orders in the early hours since their arrival, including the banning of private vehicles. Heavy-hearted, he made his way to the shop to meet with Ernest, waiting pale-faced in the office.

'Good morning, Mr Bichard. I see the Germans are here. What's going to happen to us?' he asked, hopping from foot to foot.

'I've no idea, Ernest, but it looks as if we're facing enormous changes.' He went on to tell Ernest of his new work and his reluctant decision to close the shop. A red flush appeared on Ernest's face.

'But what about me, Mr Bichard? You promised to keep the shop going, you did. How will I survive without a job?' His truculent tone annoyed Leo.

'I have no choice but to close. The Germans are already placing restrictions on businesses, and there will be little need for antiques. I'm sorry, Ernest, I'd hoped to stay open, but now see I can't. But I'd be happy to put in a word for you with the Committee when they're hiring staff.' Leo tried not to sound too irritated, having some sympathy with Ernest. The ones to be angry with were the Germans, not each other.

The young man sniffed.

'I'd appreciate that, sir. What are you going to do about the stock? An open invitation to thieves, leaving it here.'

'A friend has offered me secure storage in his warehouse, so if you could get hold of the delivery men, we'll need to do it today. From tomorrow lorries are only to be used for moving essential supplies, and it would take forever with a horse and cart.' He glanced around the shop, full of personally curated items representing his deserved reputation as the best antiques dealer on the island. He sighed, would he ever be able to start again? Or would he want to?

'Mr Bichard? You okay? I said I'd be off to get the lads.' Ernest's words broke into his thoughts.

'Yes, of course. Oh, and Ernest, I'll pay you a month's wages to tide you over.'

'Thank you, sir.' Ernest nodded and left.

Leo, his feet leaden, went up the steep stairs to the attic for boxes and packing material. He wasn't looking forward to dismantling the family's business. His father would turn in his grave.

Six hours later, he surveyed the now empty shop. Marks on the walls showed where the paintings and mirrors had hung, and the old wooden floor bore the imprints of the feet of the furniture. Even the office was empty. Anything small enough was stored in the safe place with his personal valuables, only the larger items were now in the warehouse. After making sure everything was stored correctly, Leo had returned to the shop with Ernest to whitewash the windows. A subdued light filtered through the painted glass and Leo shivered in spite of the day's heat.

Counting out the notes, he handed Ernest his promised wages.

'Thank you for your hard work today, and in the past, Ernest. I'll be in touch if there's a job available. Good luck.' He held out his hand.

Ernest shook it after pocketing the money.

'Thank you, sir, and good luck yourself.' Ernest limped out of the door and Leo, with a last look around, followed, locking the door behind him. As he walked towards the Committee offices where he was due to put in a few hours work, groups of German soldiers marched past, the soles of their leather boots striking the cobbled streets with a sound like gunshots. There were few islanders to be seen in the normally bustling Town centre, acknowledging each other with a tip of the head rather than the usual friendly smile. As he passed The Royal Court, Leo kept his eyes averted from the hated Nazi flags flying overhead. The Guernsey flag was nowhere to be seen.

Over the next few months, Leo was kept busy working for the Essential Commodities department. The role became more complex as the island's pre-Occupation supplies dwindled and the Germans constantly demanded updated lists of everything, from flour and potatoes to coal and fertiliser. In one way Leo was glad his work was so demanding, though dull, as it kept him from thinking too much about Teresa and Judith and their old life together.

There was no contact between the island and the mainland, although there was talk of asking the Red Cross to facilitate messages via France to the UK. It was if the rest of the world didn't exist, except through the BBC news bulletins on the radio. And the news wasn't good: the Germans continued to make huge advances in Europe and Leo, for the first time, and to his shame, began to doubt if the Allies could ever win.

German propaganda was constantly broadcast through the local newspapers and the cinemas, and the old Guernsey ways were replaced by German efficiency and bureaucracy. Although Leo considered himself well-organised, he preferred and missed the slow, personal approach of the Guerns.

In late October, Leo was enjoying a drink with Clem Le Page after work when Clem brought up the subject of the innumerable lists the Germans required.

'Do you know, they even want a list of Jews and Jewish businesses in the island?' he said, sipping a beer.

Leo's hand shook. 'But whatever for? What's different about Jews, for heaven's sake?'

'Nothing, as far as I'm concerned, but there have been rumours the Germans are running some vendetta against them in Germany and France. I have Hungarian Jewish friends who fled to England when Hitler came to power, saying he'd vowed to wipe them out. I'm sure it was an exaggeration, but it's odd they're asking for this list, although I doubt there's many left on the island. Most foreign Jews evacuated back in June.'

Leo grunted, burying his face in his glass as a frisson of fear shot through him. He tried to reassure himself it was simply the Germans being over-zealous about the background of islanders.

'They'll be wanting a list of Catholics next,' he said, with a forced smile.

Clem laughed and went off to order more beer while Leo tried to push away the increased feeling of foreboding. He must be safe, surely?

Chapter 29

Guernsey 2011

Fiona had barely said hello to Louisa when her phone rang. It was the funeral directors, saying they had the vicar booked for the funeral service at Le Foulon Chapel, followed by the internment, at twelve-thirty on Monday 6th June. She and the vicar now had to meet to confirm the Order of Service and could she do that at the earliest opportunity? Fiona noted the vicar's number and said she would. The excitement induced by the plan to trap Duncan drained away as Fiona once again faced the reality of the funeral. With a sigh, she followed Louisa into the kitchen.

'Sorry about that. The funeral's set for a week on Monday and I'm dreading it.' She slumped into a chair, with her head in her hands, tears leaking from her eyes.

'Oh, you poor thing, I understand how you feel.' Louisa threw her arms around her and squeezed. 'When Mum died, I left everything to my aunt to sort, and I've regretted not being more involved ever since. It was me being in denial that Mum was actually dead. Could that be true for you?' Louisa stroked Fiona's hair, soothing as you would a child in distress.

She reached for a tissue. After blowing her nose, she considered what Louisa had said, seeing the truth in it. One part of her did know Nigel was dead, the logical, grown-up part, after all, she'd found his body. But another more fanciful, wishful part of her wanted to deny it to the heavens.

'Could be. The funeral's always considered the definitive moment after a death, isn't it? Not for the benefit of the deceased, but for those left to mourn. It's supposed to help us finally let go and move on. But we don't want to, do we?' She looked at Louisa, whose face was etched with concern.

'Do you need help with the planning, choosing hymns and things? I'd be happy to help.'

'Would you? It's something I was dreading. I have to see the vicar soon and need to decide on what I want first.'

'Right, why don't we make a start before Paul gets home? We can get inspiration from the internet if necessary. Okay?' Louisa squeezed her hand.

'Okay. Let's do it.'

Two hours and several cups of coffee later, they had produced a rough draft of the service, incorporating what Fiona remembered as Nigel's favourite hymns from their childhood and quotes from poems she loved. One which made them both cry were the lines from Kahlil Gibran's *The Prophet*, describing death –

'Only when you drink from the river of silence shall you indeed sing.
And when you have reached the mountain top, then you shall begin to climb.
And when the earth shall claim your limbs, then shall you truly dance.'

The hardest part was deciding about the eulogy. Fiona knew it had to come from her, no question. But would she able to stand up in the chapel and read it to the congregation? Louisa suggested someone else who knew Nigel could read it if necessary, and Fiona said she'd think about it.

Louisa stood and stretched. 'I think we deserve a glass of wine, don't you? To help us relax before this evening.' She grabbed a bottle from the fridge and brought it over with two glasses. 'Want some?'

Fiona nodded. 'A small one, please, I'm fetching Michael later. Thanks,' she added, as Louisa handed her half a glass.

'Let's go outside, soak up some vitamin D.'

They sat looking out to sea, watching a group of white-sailed boats making slow progress across the bay. 'Too little wind,' Louisa observed, 'that race is going to take forever.'

They watched in silence, sipping their wine and Fiona began to unwind. It had been quite a day, and there was still dinner to get through. With Michael. Hmm.

'Paul suggested we had a barbecue tomorrow, so I phoned around this morning, and we've got three couples coming; Jeanne and Nick, Charlotte and Andy, and Natalie and Stuart. Should be fun. If a little noisy with the children running around,' Louisa chuckled and took a sip of wine. She gave Fiona an oblique look. 'Should we invite Michael to join us? Would he mix with the others?'

'Don't see why not. He's bright, good conversationalist, creative. Why don't you wait and see for yourself this evening? I doubt if he has much else to do, you know how little happens here on Sundays.' Fiona kept her eyes down in case her face gave anything away. Too much had happened since Wednesday. From thinking she'd never meet the man again, she was being forced to spend hours with him and then spending nights together under her roof. At this point, she remembered what they'd planned that morning, pushed to the back of her mind by the funeral, and wondered whether to tell her friend. Might be better to wait and ask Michael's opinion, she thought. Although she'd have to come up with a darn good reason for moving home on Monday.

'Will do. I've stocked up with so much food; we could invite the street,' Louisa said, smiling.

◆◆◆

Michael chose to walk down George Road and Hauteville to reach the centre. The mainly Georgian houses reminded him of parts of London, but with the bonus of the wonderful sea views he caught sight of in the gaps of houses. Even while admiring the architecture, his mind strayed to the morning's meeting with John and Fiona. He was happy to put himself at risk to catch Nigel's killer, but he wasn't comfortable with Fiona being involved, in spite of appearing to agree. Being brought up in a female-dominated household after the divorce, he'd learnt to respect women and admire their toughness, but still felt it was his duty to protect them. He adored his grandmother, although he knew she gave his mother a hard time for marrying his waste of space father. It wasn't fair, in his book, to be judged for who you loved. His mother didn't have the strength of character to cope with disaster, and Michael dreaded to think what would have become of them without Teresa's intervention.

His thoughts were interrupted when he spotted Hauteville House, the onetime home of Victor Hugo, and was surprised to see a French flag flying. Drawing closer, he saw the noticeboard indicated France owned the building. Explained the flag. Deciding he must make time to visit the house while on the island, he carried on down the street, his thoughts once more on the reason for his visit. If all went according to plan, the suspect would be caught by Thursday, and he would no longer have a reason to stay. Except for Fiona. And that was a bit one-sided. He sensed she liked him, seemed to find him attractive, but he couldn't ask for more, yet. Michael grinned to himself. He could wait.

At ten minutes to seven, Fiona sent Michael a text to say she was on her way and he checked around the house before setting the alarm and leaving. He looked forward to meeting her friends and had made an effort to look suitably smart casual, which for him was clean black jeans teamed with an open-neck crisp cotton shirt. A light splash of aftershave and he was ready. The evening was warm, and he breathed in the scent of freshly cut grass, having mowed the lawn. More brownie points, he hoped.

He was standing in the street a few yards from the house when she arrived and quickly jumped in. He leaned over to kiss her briefly on the cheek, inhaling her light perfume.

'Hi, did you have a good day?' she asked, giving him a brief smile.

'Yes, thanks, had a wander around the town and harbour before coming back to mow the lawn. Think I've earned my supper,' he said, grinning.

'You have, I'm grateful.'

Michael sneaked a look at her profile. Something had changed since this morning when she had shown real interest in the plan they had proposed. Now, there was a detachment about her, a quietness. Was it him? Only one way to find out.

'Is everything okay? You don't seem too happy.'

She was gripping the steering wheel as if to help her hold something in.

'I'm sorry, it's...it's the funeral and...the inquest and I feel a bit overwhelmed. Ignore me; I'll be fine later.'

'I don't know what to say; I guess I thought they had already happened. Must be tough for you. When are they?' He was out of his depth, not having had to deal with grief and the awfulness of funerals and genuinely couldn't imagine what Fiona was going through.

She cleared her throat.

'The inquest's on Friday and the funeral the following Monday. With all the other stuff going on, the timing's not great.' She bit her lip, staring straight ahead.

'Ah, a bummer. Anything I can do to help, please ask.'

'Won't you be returning home, assuming we've caught Duncan?' Fiona turned to face him, her eyes pools of utter sadness.

'Haven't thought that far ahead. I don't have to rush back, but if you want me out...' Irrationally, he couldn't bear to think of leaving so soon. Their lives had become entangled and he didn't want an abrupt parting of the ways.

'That's not an issue; I can stay with my friends. And we've arrived,' she added, pulling to a stop at a gated entrance to a white property set in what Michael could see was a large, well-kept garden. He'd been partly conscious of their surroundings as she drove, going along a main road before turning into a narrow road signposted 'Icart', and then along winding lanes towards the coast, the sea shimmering in the distance. Some view, he thought, as Fiona pressed a button to open the gates and drove in, parking in front of a detached garage away from the house.

'This is quite a place,' he said, climbing out of the car. 'Are your friends millionaires?'

She shook her head, a glimmer of a smile appearing.

'No, they're a hard-working couple, but Louisa's father's wealthy and I think he helped them buy it. Come and say hello.' Instead of entering the front door she headed to the side of the house and followed a path around to the back and a patio area, enjoying one of the most beautiful views he'd ever seen.

'Wow! This is amazing!' Michael cried, taking in the deep blue sea, dappled with pale evening sun, and rugged cliffs spread out to either side. Gulls swooped overhead, looking for their supper.

'It is, isn't it? We're very lucky,' came a voice behind him.

He turned to see a fair-haired woman, with a smiling, freckled face, walking towards him. 'Michael, I presume? I'm Louisa; I'm so glad you could come for supper.' She reached out, and they shook hands.

'The pleasure's mine.' He handed her a bottle of wine and a small bouquet of roses.

'That's kind of you, thanks. Let me put these in water while Fiona shows you the garden. We thought drinks on the terrace before supper inside,' Louisa smiled and went through what appeared to be a sun lounge.

'Your friend seems nice,' he said, as they walked towards the edge of the garden, close to the cliff path.

'She is and so is Paul. They make a great couple. You'll meet him shortly, he only arrived home from work a few minutes ago and needed to shower and change. They've been brilliant since...Nigel died.'

Michael squeezed her arm, not knowing what to say. Fiona seemed to make an effort to cast off her sadness and pointed out Jersey in the distance and Moulin Huet Bay to their left. He stood lost in thought, staring at the view so beloved by Renoir, inspiring, among others, the painting responsible for his presence here.

'Shall we walk further? There's a fruit and vegetable area over there,' she pointed to their right, 'and a large terrace they use for parties further round. They have a gardener to help them as they're both so busy at La Folie.'

He asked what it was, and she explained it was the natural health centre Louisa's father owned and Paul managed. Michael was intrigued; this small island was full of surprises. As they walked and talked Fiona appeared to relax, and by the time Louisa caught up with them, she was smiling.

'You have the most wonderful place here, Louisa, I'm quite jealous.' He smiled, spreading his arms.

'Thanks, we love it. Come and meet my husband and have a drink.'

A tall, slim man with fair hair and deep blue eyes stood watching them, looking relaxed in chinos and a polo neck shirt to match his eyes.

'Hi, Michael, good to meet you. At last I'm not outnumbered by women!' he laughed as they shook hands. 'What can I get you? Beer, cider, wine, gin or vodka? We have local versions of all but the wine and vodka.'

'Impressive. I'll try a local beer, please.' Michael sat at the table set with small dishes of nuts and crisps. Paul hugged Fiona before taking her order for a glass of white wine, dittoed by Louisa, who sat next to Michael.

'I understand you live in London, Michael. It was my home until I met Paul, so tell me where you're based.'

They began a discussion about London, their favourite places and pet hates, occasionally joined by Fiona. Paul returned with a tray of drinks and also added his opinions, having spent some years working in London himself. Michael relaxed, enjoying the unexpected bonus of a common connection. At some point Louisa disappeared to the kitchen, returning fifteen minutes later to ask Paul to give her a hand. Alone with Fiona, Michael asked her how she was feeling.

'Better, thanks. But there's one thing bugging me. I haven't told them of our plans for next week and wondered what you thought?'

'Having met them, I'm sure they're not the sort to blab, so I think we need to tell them. They'll know something's up anyway when you move back home with me in situ. We don't want them to get the wrong idea, do we?' he said, mischievously.

Fiona blushed.

'Oh! No, we don't. Will you tell them? Think it might come better from you.'

'Sure, but I'll wait until after the meal.'

Paul called them in, and Michael followed Fiona inside to find a round table groaning with food set to one side of the full-width sun lounge.

'This looks marvellous, Louisa, as does your house,' he said, looking around admiringly.

'Thanks. Now tuck in everyone and enjoy,' Louisa beamed, taking a seat between Paul and Michael. Wine was handed round as they helped themselves to colourful dishes of vegetables, salads and a whole poached salmon. Michael picked up the scent of herbs scattered on the food and his mouth filled with saliva. Lunch seemed a long time ago.

'What do you think of Guernsey so far?' asked Paul, after they'd filled their plates.

'I love what I've seen today, your town and coast are amazing.' He went on to describe in more detail what he'd seen, and the conversation rolled around to various topics, including history and the arts and finally to the work Paul and Louise did at La Folie. While they talked, Michael's attention kept drifting to Fiona. He watched her mouth as she talked, even occasionally laughed. Listened to the sound of her voice, light and warm. It was clear she was well liked by her friends and continuously kept pushing the attention away from herself. He liked that about her; not one who wanted to be the centre of attention. Being here with her friends helped him to see a different side of her. And it increased his attraction towards her.

Once the dessert of strawberries and cream was eaten, they drifted back to the sofas in the sun lounge, facing the blackness of the evening sky. Michael spotted a web of light around the garden, formed, he guessed, by small LED lights. The effect was magical. Certainly beat the view from his ground floor flat, overlooking a yard full of scrub grass and strategically placed pots hiding uncleared rubbish. He must do something about that, he thought, taking a proffered glass of whisky from Paul. When everyone was settled, Michael raised his eyebrow at Fiona, and she nodded.

'As you know, Fiona's keen to catch whoever tried to steal my family's painting and ended up killing Nigel. Well, there's been a breakthrough, and we're setting a trap to catch him...' he went on to explain the plan, causing Paul and Louisa to look at each other, and then Fiona, with worried frowns.

Before they could comment, Fiona said, 'I know what you're thinking, and believe me, I wasn't too keen at first, but the police are involved and can track Duncan, so I feel a lot safer.' She drew a deep breath, watching their faces. 'I'm doing this for Nigel, and I'm sure he'll be by my side, watching out for me.'

Paul, sitting next to her, squeezed her hand.

'You're very brave and, you're right, you'll have a good backup, including Michael, who looks more than capable of protecting you,' he said, smiling at him.

Louisa, not looking as convinced, said nothing.

'I won't let him touch her. As I told Fiona, I'm a black belt in karate, so...' he shrugged, returning Paul's smile.

Her face brightening, Louisa said, 'Okay, you're on your honour to keep her safe. Now, on a brighter note, would you like to join us tomorrow afternoon for a barbecue? We've a few friends coming, and it should be fun.'

'Love to, thanks. Can I bring anything?'

'No, just yourself, we've heaps of food and drink. Say about three?'

Michael nodded, glad he wasn't in disgrace for appearing to put Fiona at risk. Suddenly aware it was growing late, he asked for the number of a taxi firm, and Paul offered to ring for him. While waiting for it to arrive, Paul made coffee for everyone, and the conversation turned to the forthcoming Wimbledon Tournament, and what Andy Murray's chances were of getting to the finals for the first time. The fact of his winning the Australian Open the year before, 2010, didn't seem to cut any ice with the pessimists. The somewhat heated debate ended when the taxi arrived and Michael, who didn't rate Murray's chances, was glad to escape.

Goodnights were exchanged; the men shaking hands and Michael kissing the women on the cheek, received with smiles. Fiona offered to pick him up the next day, waving him off at the door. He sank into the back of the cab, his mind full of the day's events. Guernsey was proving to be pretty full on, both socially as well as dramatically. As the taxi approached Colborne Road, he asked to be set down at the top. He walked the rest of the way, keeping an eye open for anyone lurking in the shadows, but he met no-one. The drive was empty, and no lights were visible, and when he entered the house, the alarm was still on. With a sigh of relief, he switched it off and headed upstairs. So far, so good.

Michael woke with a start. Where the hell was he? And what was that noise? It took him a minute to realise it was a phone, not his mobile as he'd switched it off, but a landline. Bleary-eyed and half asleep, he stumbled onto the landing, realising the sound was coming from Fiona's bedroom and echoed downstairs. He pushed open the door and picked up the phone by the bedside, trying to avert his eyes from the bed, displaying crisp white linen and a multicoloured throw.

'Hello?'

'Thank goodness! It's Fiona, just checking you were all right and when your phone didn't pick up I...' He heard the fear in her voice.

'Sorry, my fault. I always switch my phone off at night. Force of habit.' He moved onto the landing, feeling uncomfortable talking to her while in her bedroom. 'But I'm fine, thanks, no sign of an attempted break-in.'

'Good. I shall feel better when the police get onboard tomorrow. It's a bit nerve-wracking.' He heard a deep sigh.

'Yeh, well stay strong, with luck it'll be over soon. And I promise not to switch my phone off again.' He walked into his bedroom and, picking up his phone, clicked it on. 'It's on now.'

'Right. Any plans for this morning?'

'There's this Seafront Sunday on in Town, so I'm going to mooch around for a bit. Then maybe take a bus trip around the island, I'd like to see more of it.'

'Good idea, the bus takes you right around the coast so you'll get a real feel for Guernsey. See you later, okay?'

'Bye.'

Minutes later Michael was standing under a hot shower, the last vestiges of sleep draining away. One more night alone here, then Fiona would be back. And then the fun would begin.

◆◆◆

Fiona clicked off her phone, glad all was well but annoyed with herself for being so uptight about everything. She had spent the night tossing from side to side, and the odd times she slept the dreams had been unsettling, full of mysterious figures appearing out of the darkness and disappearing before she could see who – or what – they were. It was like being under siege. When she finally woke to bright sunlight pouring through the slats of the blinds, she was a wreck, and immediately phoned Michael, needing reassurance. When he failed to answer, she was convinced something awful had happened to him, completely overreacting. He'd sounded so laid-back, adding to her sense of foolishness. By the time she'd showered and dressed she was calmer, and the prospect of a fun afternoon with friends made her feel better.

'Morning, lazy bones. We've had breakfast so you'll have to help yourself,' Louisa greeted her as she entered the kitchen. Fiona spotted Paul outside giving the barbecue a thorough clean while Louisa was busy preparing kebabs.

'Didn't sleep well, I'll give you a hand after I've had something to eat.' Fiona slotted bread into the toaster and switched on the coffee machine before giving her friend a quick hug.

'No problem, I can manage.' Louisa brushed her hair back and grinned, adding, 'By the way, I thought Michael was more than "nice". Not only attractive but intelligent. And he obviously likes you.'

Fiona, spreading butter on her toast, paused the knife in the air.

'Well, I like him, too. Doesn't mean anything, so don't get carried away. Once this...business is sorted, he'll hot foot it back to London, and that will be that. And I'm not in the right space for a relationship, as you know,' she said, sharply, focusing on the toast, not meeting her friend's eyes. Why did happily loved-up couples try to play matchmaker with their single friends?

'Sorry, didn't mean to upset you. I won't say anything again, promise.' Louisa's voice was contrite, and Fiona was ashamed of her sharpness. She managed a faint smile, and Louisa smiled back. Swallowing her coffee, Fiona told herself to chill if she didn't want to upset her friends. At that moment her mobile rang. John.

'Hi, John, anything up?'

'No, but I've been thinking about Duncan and what he might get up to, so have decided to stake him out tonight, in case he surprises us and makes a move on your house. Thought I'd let you know and you can tell Michael.'

'Right, but are you sure? I hate to think of you losing a night's sleep.'

He chuckled.

'I'm used to it and anyway we've got my daughter and her baby staying over, so no-one's getting much sleep at the moment. I'll keep you posted. Enjoy your day.'

Fiona was relieved, at least she wouldn't have to worry about Michael that night. She could put her fears to the back of her mind until Monday night at least. And then she would need every ounce of courage to face her brother's killer.

Chapter 30

Guernsey 2011

Sunday had been fun. Fiona knew all the couples, and they had welcomed Michael like a long-lost friend. Reluctant to spoil the happy mood, she hadn't shared the news about the funeral, Louisa and Paul promising to keep it to themselves. It enabled her to push it to the back of her mind for a while and let her hair down. Jeanne's children, little Harry and Freya, kept everyone on their toes as they ran around playing games and generally being the stars of the show. By the time everyone left at nine, Fiona was ready for bed, praying for a good night's sleep. She was lucky, waking on Monday refreshed, feeling more like her old self.

As ever, she was the last to arrive in the kitchen to find her hosts munching on muesli.

'Morning, you look well. Help yourself to coffee.' Paul pointed to the cafetiére in the middle of the table.

She sat down with a mug of coffee and a bowl of muesli, smiling a greeting at her friends.

'Any plans?' Louisa asked.

'Yes, I'm taking Michael out in the car today as he wants to see his grandparents' house and the shop, and a bit more of the island. We'll probably take in Moulin Huet and spend some time there. What about you two?' She took a sip of coffee.

They shared a half smile.

'We plan to chill out and do nothing, so are staying in and eating yesterday's leftovers. No cooking, bliss!' Louisa laughed.

'Sounds good, you two deserve a day off. I'll take my stuff with me, ready to move back home later.' She grinned. 'You'll have your house to yourselves now.'

Paul, looking serious, said, 'We've been happy to help and please keep us posted. We both want this man caught soon, for your sake.'

'Amen to that,' Fiona replied, pushing down a feeling of foreboding.

When Fiona pulled into her drive, she found John's car parked to one side. He was talking to Michael in the kitchen, a copy of that day's *Evening Press* on the worktop. Her stomach lurched.

'Morning. Is it in?'

John nodded, and handed her the paper, tapping a headline on the front page.

'There, they've done us proud, considering there's no photos or quoted source.'

She read the headline, '*Valuable work of art worth millions discovered in Guernsey!!*' The article went on to mention the finder had been to the UK to trace the owner and they were due to arrive on Thursday. The work of art was also described as having an 'exciting local connection' and that the full story would be published once the owner had staked their claim.

'Great, isn't it? That should lure the bugger out,' Michael said, smiling broadly.

'It is, thanks, John.' She smiled from one to the other, part of her as pleased as the men, but another part feeling slightly sick. Roll on Thursday.

John made to leave, but stopped, tapping his forehead.

'Nearly forgot, Ron got back to me about the trace he put on Duncan. Turns out our friend married an Australian girl and moved there years ago. It appears he didn't mend his ways and ended up in jail for armed robbery, only released a few months ago, not knowing his father had died. Another piece of the jigsaw, right?' He grinned.

'Sure. Thanks for coming round, we're going out for the day, but our mobiles will be on if anything happens.'

She escorted him to the front door, having a quick word with him, before returning to find Michael pacing around.

'This guy sounds even more dangerous than I'd expected. Thought he was just a thug – but armed robbery! That's big time.' His face was creased with worry.

'Yes, I know. I asked John what difference it makes to the police operation, and he said the inspector is going to have armed officers on alert if it looks as if he's heading here. But, he might not have access to a gun now, and he's only expecting to find me here.' She was trying to convince herself as well as Michael. And somewhere in the back of her mind, Australia rang a bell. If only she could remember...

'Hmm, let's hope the police know what they're doing.' Michael drummed his fingers on the counter, looking thoughtful. Drawing in a breath, he said, 'Shall we get going? I've a strong need to get out and get some fresh air.'

'Yes. We'll go to your grandfather's house first. Nigel and I went there to discuss buying the business from old Mrs Domaille. I've no idea who owns it now; she sold it when she moved into the nursing home.' Picking up the car keys, she led the way to the front door, setting the alarm, before locking it.

'I'd forgotten old Ernest bought it from my grandmother after the war, at a knockdown price, too.' He got in the car, adding, 'Now we know he must have used the money he'd made from selling the stuff he'd stolen from the house.' Michael shook his head, 'What a bloody family! No wonder Duncan turned out as he did.'

Fiona, fixing her seat belt, nodded in agreement. It was about time the sins of the father were brought to light, though nothing could compensate for his betrayal of Leo. She drove off down Colborne Road, cutting across at the bottom to head uphill and the road towards St Andrew as Michael studied the *Perry's Guide* to follow her route.

'Grandmama said the house was beautiful, what was it like when you visited?'

'You could see it had been lovely once, but the Germans had badly damaged it and I don't think the Domailles had spent much on repairs.' She sucked her teeth, remembering how sad she thought the house looked. 'We got the impression Ernest had been a bit of a skinflint, liked to look posh, but didn't want to splash the cash.' She recalled the poor state of the roof, with slipped tiles and vegetation growing in the gaps and gutters, and the peeled paintwork of the doors and windows. Fiona couldn't help but compare the similarities of the two family homes: Teresa's rundown, but still achingly beautiful home in Suffolk, and what had been her marital home here. Which thought reminded her...

'I forgot to ask, did your grandmother decide which route to take in selling the painting?'

'Yep, the private sale. We're giving it six months, and if there's no great interest, we'll go to auction next year. But Roger seems confident he'll find a buyer soon. I hope so as, quite frankly, we need the money if my grandmother's to get the care she needs. Ma can't cope on her own much longer.' He frowned, tapping his fingers on the dashboard.

'Oh, with all the attention on the Renoir, I forgot to mention that the other paintings are worth a bit of money, too. Two or three thousand each, I'd say, so unless you wanted to keep them you could raise about twenty odd thousand quite easily.'

'Well, that's a nice surprise! I'll tell Grandmama and see what she thinks. I'm pretty sure she'll say sell, but how?'

'As they're both local artists and views, selling here is the obvious solution. We've got collectors asking to let them know when any come up for sale if you decide that's what you want.'

'Brilliant! As long as you don't charge the same commission as Christie's,' he said, laughing.

'Don't worry; I'd only put on a small markup to cover our time. It would be a pleasure to help.' She meant it, the paintings would be easy to sell and it would add to the reputation of the shop to handle their sale.

They lapsed into silence, both caught up in their thoughts and Fiona concentrated on her driving. The bank holiday traffic was less than on a work day, but narrow winding roads and lanes made it difficult to see oncoming vehicles until the last minute, forcing drivers to steer close to hedges and granite walls. By now they were in an area known as Talbot Valley, a lush, wooded area watered by tinkling streams.

'This is wonderful, what a great place for walking. Is it far now?' Michael gazed around in obvious delight.

'A couple of minutes, up that lane to the left. You'll see the house has the most amazing view down on the valley.' She was forced to drive even more slowly along what was little more than a track, up past a derelict barn and then, rounding the last bend, they arrived at the house. Leaving the car tucked into the side of the lane, they stood facing it and Fiona noticed the house had had a makeover, new windows and doors and a repaired roof. The soft grey granite of the walls gleamed in the sun. She guessed it was Victorian, a gentleman's residence with double-fronted bay windows and gardens stretching out either side. The driveway was short, leading to a parking area to the side, now empty of vehicles. Michael took photos with his phone.

'I'll email these to Ma, and she can show my grandmother, she'll be delighted I've seen it. The link to my grandfather and part of our family history.' He turned his back to the house to catch the view. Fiona copied him

Spread before them lay fields and the thick line of trees they had driven through, then glimpses of the fields on the other side of the valley. Birdsong competed with the sound of water gurgling over stones in the streams.

'Magical, isn't it? You could pretend there was no-one else living for miles around. No wonder my grandmother loved it.' Michael spread his arms, taking a deep breath.

'Yes, and now it probably looks more like it did when she lived here. I'm glad someone's given it some TLC, I hate seeing houses neglected, don't you?' She gasped, covering her mouth. 'Oh, I'm sorry.'

He grinned. 'Don't worry, I feel the same, but soon we'll be able to spend money on the farmhouse. Make it as beautiful as it was when I was a boy.' He turned once more to take a look at the house. 'Time to leave, I think. Where to now?'

'Thought we'd take a bit of a drive and end up at Moulin Huet in time for lunch at the tea room. Okay with you?'

'Sounds good, let's go.' He brushed his hair out of his eyes, giving her a wide smile. The answering leap in her belly unsettled her. They were behaving more like a couple on a date than two people intent on catching a killer. With an inward groan, she started the engine, turned the car around and drove down the lane and headed right at the junction. She planned to take a meander towards St Martin and then through the myriad of lanes leading to Moulin Huet. At least there'd be lots of people about on the beach and in the tea room and she'd be able to relax.

◆◆◆

Thirty minutes later they pulled into the car park at Moulin Huet, taking the last free space.

Michael looked around the wooded valley which he presumed led to the beach.

'I never expected to find so many trees on the island, doesn't look that many from the plane. Is it far to the beach?'

'A bit of a hike, but the tea room is nearer, about three hundred metres. There's a super view over the bay from there, and I'm hoping these people,' she waved her arms at the mass of cars, 'aren't all trying to eat at the tea room,' she said, with a rueful smile.

He'd noticed how quiet Fiona was in the car and wondered if she was feeling apprehensive about the possible confrontation with Duncan. For himself, he was alarmed at the possibility the man would carry a gun, as even karate would not be protection against a bullet. And she was even more defenceless. If it came to the crunch, he'd shield her body, even if it meant taking a bullet himself.

They collected their beach gear from the back seat and set off down the leafy lane, accompanied by the soothing sound of a brook heading towards the open sea. Michael noticed a party of walkers leaving the coastal path to make for the beach, rucksacks bulging with towels and mats. Everyone looked happy, smiling as they called out hellos. He and Fiona returned the greetings before she led him towards a long low-level building on the right, painted white with pale green windows and doors wide open to the sun. A large grassed area sloped away below, scattered with wooden benches and tables, covered by brightly coloured parasols and filled with chattering diners. Michael stood for a moment, absorbing the view. Renoir's view.

'Beautiful, isn't it?' Fiona said, shading her eyes from the sun.

'Sure is, no wonder this place is popular.'

'Here's a table.' She led the way to a small table set with two chairs at the end of the terrace immediately outside the café.

'That was lucky.' He grinned, glad of the relative quiet up above the grassed area set below. 'What a fab spot. I don't suppose old Renoir had a welcoming café when he set up his easel.'

Fiona laughed.

'He probably had to make do with a bottle of warm beer and a meat pie. We're lucky, this place is renowned for its great food, although no alcohol, I'm afraid.' She offered him the menu. 'I can recommend the crab sandwiches, which will be my choice.'

He scanned it.

'I'll go for that too.' He stood. 'What about a drink? I'll go and order.'

'Cappuccino, please.'

Michael joined the queue inside, and after placing the order carried their drinks outside.

'The food will be out in a minute. Excuse me while I take some photos for my mother.'

He clicked away, moving around the edge of the garden to catch different perspectives. At the very bottom, he was able to look down on the beach, recognising some of the rocks portrayed by Renoir. As he stood still, the idea began to form for a sculpture, figures leaning on a rock, similar to the image portrayed in their painting. Excited, he rushed back to tell Fiona.

'What a wonderful idea! Your homage to both your family and the painting. What medium would you use? And how big would it be?' Her eyes reflected his excitement, and he had to fight down an impulse to kiss her. Fortunately, their food arrived, and the sight of the thickly filled crab sandwiches nestled among salad and crisps made his mouth water.

He picked up a sandwich and took a bite. Delicious. 'Good choice, thanks. Not sure about the medium, there's quite a choice...' They had an animated discussion about the options and Michael drew a rough sketch on a paper napkin.

Fiona looked thoughtful, chewing on her sandwich. Finishing a mouthful, she said, 'It reminds me of one of Rodin's works. The woman emerging from stone looks like he didn't finish it...' she wrinkled her brow.

'You mean *Psyche*?'

'Yes! Do you see what I mean? The look of not being quite separate from the rock.'

'I do, and it could work with a group of three figures, like those in the painting.' He leaned back, pleased. It would be a challenge, and expensive to produce, but it could be something for the family, a tribute to his great-grandmother and her unfortunate brother and sister. He told Fiona, and she agreed.

'Your family need a replacement for the Renoir – so why not a sculpture by that up and coming sculptor, Michael Collins?' she said, grinning.

In a relaxed mood, they finished their lunch and walked down to the beach to find the exact spot Renoir had painted. Laughing, they took photos of each other in roughly the right place before finding a space to stretch out their towels and chill. Closing his eyes, Michael imagined what it would be like if he and Fiona were an actual couple, out for a day's fun on the beach. The more time he spent with her, the more he enjoyed her company. But, and it was a big but, he would be leaving soon and when would they meet again? He couldn't see how a relationship could work, even assuming Fiona would consider one while she was grieving for her brother. He'd have to be patient; not his greatest virtue.

The sun was losing its heat by four, and they decided to call it a day. They'd enjoyed a, decidedly bracing, swim before drying off on the towels. Now changed into shorts and T-shirts Michael bid a reluctant goodbye to the beach.

'London's great, but I do envy you the easy access to such fantastic beaches. And that air!' He took an exaggerated deep breath, making Fiona giggle.

'I know we're never more than ten minutes from the sea here.' She picked up her bag, 'Let's try and beat the queue out of the car park. Then I thought we'd take a look at the shop before heading home.'

He nodded, looking forward to seeing the business his grandfather had owned, but conscious it was where Nigel met his death. He clenched his fists. He'd love to get Duncan in a Katawa Guruma hold, not called the cripple wheel for nothing. He'd be on the floor with his balls crushed.

On the way back to Town, Michael phoned his grandmother to tell her about the value of the remaining paintings. As he expected, she agreed Fiona could sell them and he was happy to pass on the news to her.

She parked the car in a tiny lane in what she referred to as The Old Quarter. He could see why; some of the buildings, either shops or restaurants, looked to be hundreds of years old and the main street was cobbled. She walked a few yards and pointed out the smartest shop in the area, 'N & F Antiques', a large double-fronted building on the corner.

'This looks great, Fiona. Has it changed much since Leo owned it, do you know?'

'Not that much. I've seen old photos, and apart from the paintwork and our signage, the frontage is as it was. Come on; we need to go round the back to get in.' She led the way and unlocked the solid back door before switching off the alarm. They were standing in a small office, cluttered with a too-large desk and filing cabinets. But it was extremely tidy, Michael noticed.

'I've a guy running the place for me until I decide what to do long-term. And as you can see, he's meticulous,' she waved a hand around. 'Nigel was messier, but always knew where everything was.' She bit her lip, and Michael wondered if she was about to cry. But she didn't, just sniffed, before leading him into the main shop.

'It's bigger than it looks from the outside, isn't it? Where's the basement?' There was no sign of one as far as he could see.

'It's well hidden, let me show you.' She moved a small table and pulled back a rug. Marked in the flooring was a trap door. Fiona squatted down and pushed on a hidden catch, and the door opened. 'We replaced the old floor of original floorboards, and there was nothing to indicate a trap door. The other paintings belonging to Teresa are still there.'

She led the way, flicking a switch for the lights, and he joined her at the bottom. He saw rows of shelving, empty except for those nearest the steps. On these he saw neatly stacked, wrapped rectangular shapes He took in the dust-covered shelves, marked where other packages had once lain. 'There must have been a lot of stuff down here, once,' he said, softly.

'Yes. We assume Ernest sold it bit by bit over the years to fund his lifestyle.' She sounded sad, and Michael suggested she went back upstairs and he'd follow shortly. She agreed, and he stayed a few moments, wanting to make some connection with his grandfather. Daft, he knew, but there must be some essence left, surely? Apart from the paintings. After touching the old oilcloth wrappings, he went back upstairs, switched off the light and closed the trap door. After returning the rug and table to its rightful place, he joined her in the office. Fiona was sitting in the chair, staring into space.

'Is there anything here that could have been Leo's? The desk, perhaps? I'm trying to get an impression of him.'

Fiona stared at him as if she'd forgotten he was there. 'It could be, it's Victorian, and Ernest wasn't the sort to buy new if it wasn't necessary.' She stood, adding, 'Sit down and have a good look. Although we didn't find any secret drawers,' she said, with a slight smile.

'I just want to be somewhere he was and to touch something he touched if that makes sense.' He sat in the old chair and ran his fingers along the polished surface.

'Perfect sense. Feel free to open the drawers; there's nothing personal in them.'

It was beautifully made, befitting a gentleman, he thought. Mahogany, with a worn leather insert. He pulled on a drawer, and it ran smoothly towards him. 'Quality workmanship would be worth a pretty penny these days.'

'You'd be welcome to have it if you think it's Leo's.'

He was shocked. 'No, I wasn't trying to claim it...'

'I know you weren't. But I have no attachment to it. Why not take a photo and ask Teresa if she recognises it?'

'That's a good idea; I will.' He took a few shots and then idly opened another drawer, virtually empty except for a business card on top of some unused envelopes and stamps. His eye was caught by the address on the card. He picked it up. 'What's this? Didn't know you had an Australian connection.'

'I don't, that was on the floor...Oh! Oh, my God! We mustn't touch it. Here, put it in this envelope.' She pulled one from the drawer, and he dropped it in, wondering if she'd lost her mind.

'What's the matter?'

Fiona was taking deep breaths to calm herself, and he instinctively put his arms around her.

'I...I knew there was something about Australia that rang a bell! I found this caught under the desk after...after Nigel died and thought it might have been something to do with a customer. I shoved it in the drawer and forgot about it.' She stared at him, her eyes wide. 'You know what this means, don't you? Proof that Duncan was here!'

Chapter 31

Guernsey 2011

Before leaving the shop, Fiona phoned John and told him about the business card. He said to go to the police station, and he'd phone Inspector Woods and warn him they were on the way and would meet them there. Within minutes they arrived and were shown into the inspector's office.

He gave them a tired smile.

'Well, John tells me you may have some useful evidence for me. About our friend Duncan Domaille, right?'

Fiona handed over the envelope.

'I'm afraid we've both handled it, but we didn't know what it meant, so...'

Woods nodded, pulled on a plastic glove from a drawer and took out the card, dropping it into a bag before taking a closer look. Slowly, a grin spread across his face, and he looked up.

'I see what you mean. If this is Domaille's lawyer in Sydney, then it's a safe bet he must have dropped it in the office. No other way could it have got there. We can check for fingerprints and DNA. Well done!' He broke into a coughing fit just as John arrived and he waved him in.

John reached out for the bag and after a quick glance, let out a whistle, and sat next to Fiona grinning like a Cheshire cat.

'Will this be enough to convict him?' she asked.

Woods shook his head.

'Not on its own, but would count as strong circumstantial evidence if we can show he a) knew about the painting and b) tries to steal it again. It doesn't prove he was there on the night your brother died, only sometime before that.' Picking up the bag he walked to the door and called an officer, asking him to send it for testing. His expression was solemn as he returned and looked at Michael and Fiona. 'Are you both still up for trying to trap him? You know he might be armed? We could try and catch him another way.'

They exchanged glances.

'Yes, we're committed to seeing it through. Even more now we have some evidence against him,' Fiona said.

'Good, in that case, what we really need is for him to confess, or at least implicate himself in some way, on tape. Lead him on a bit if you have time. Ask him how he knew about the work of art etc. Would you be willing to do that?'

Fiona had seen enough TV detective dramas to know how it was supposed to happen, but would she have the time if he was threatening her with violence? Or worse? She gulped.

'I could try. Where would the police be?'

'We'll have a man in the back garden and others will be in the surveillance van in the street, which is being set up as we speak...'

John interrupted. 'Fiona, what you don't know is that I went to the house this morning and set the cameras to link to the equipment in the van, rather than my computer, so we can pick up Domaille on record, collecting audio as well as visual. You control them from your computer.' He added, shifting on his chair.

'Right, so you're saying from now on, everything we do is on camera? Every room?' Michael said, frowning.

'Not every room, no. There are no cameras in the cloakroom or bathrooms. And you only switch them on in the evening when alerted by the police. That's right, Ron?'

The inspector nodded.

'Yes, we have no wish to intrude on your privacy. We're monitoring Domaille's movements, and if he seems to be heading for your house, we'll ring and ask you to switch on the cameras at the same time as we send officers to the house.'

'Okay, that sounds fair enough. You happy with that, Fiona?'

She nodded. It all sounded more complicated than their original idea; dependent on both the police and technology to work. And there was no guarantee Duncan would do what they hoped he would.

It was hard to relax after returning home, and Fiona sensed Michael was also on edge. A furrowed forehead replaced his usual lazy smile. After unpacking her case and taking a long, hot shower, Fiona went to the kitchen where she'd left him drinking coffee and made herself a cup.

'We've still got three hours until sunset so how about sitting in the garden for a bit before supper? I might tackle the flower beds to keep me occupied.'

Michael glanced up from the newspaper.

'Are you sure you're not too tired? We've had quite a day so far.'

'I know, but since finding that business card I'm a bit hyper and need to do something physical or I'll never sleep.'

'I'll give you a hand if you show me which ones are weeds. You're right; we need to keep busy. I've always hated the waiting game, haven't you?'

'Yes, like waiting at the dentist's to have a filling, or going into the exam hall at uni.' She smiled faintly, and he grinned.

'Right, weeding it is! After you,' he said, standing.

Carrying her coffee, she led the way to the shed and dug out spades, trowels and secateurs. Michael carried them over to the flower beds while she finished her drink. Placing the empty cup on the table, she joined him and started pointing out what needed to be dug out. He agreed to use the spade for the more resistant weeds while she used the trowel on those small enough to work loose. Between them, they cleared one of the beds in an hour and made a start on another. Fiona checked her watch.

'Shall we stop now and cook supper? It's looking great, thanks. I can do some more tomorrow; there's no rush.' Silently she thought they might be glad of something to do another evening if Duncan hadn't turned up. As far as he was concerned, he had until Wednesday to make a move.

They replaced the tools in the shed and headed for the kitchen to check out the contents of the fridge and store cupboard.

'I could rustle up a chilli con carne,' offered Michael, holding a bag of rice and a packet of mince.

'Perfect. And there's ice cream for afters, so sorted. Do you need a hand?' Fiona said, lining up beans, cheese and sour cream on the counter.

'No, I'm good. Go and watch some TV and relax,' he said, smiling.

She pulled out two cans of lager from the fridge, handing one to him and taking hers and a glass to the sitting room. Being at the front of the house they'd decided Michael couldn't risk being seen there, but it was important that Fiona seemed to be behaving normally. She switched on the TV and stretched out on the sofa, trying to focus on the usual bank holiday drivel. By the time Michael shouted, 'Supper's ready!' she was on the verge of dozing off, bored by the repeat of a film she hadn't enjoyed the first time around.

Michael had set the table in the kitchen, at the back of the house and safe from prying eyes. A large dish of chilli and smaller dishes of cheese and cream were placed ready.

'Mmm, smells good! Is this your signature dish?' She grinned at him as she sat down.

'No, I can do better than this, given the right ingredients. This was potluck. When I'm planning to entertain guests, I might offer a roast with all the trimmings, or perhaps a paella. Depends on the time of year.' He smiled, taking two more cans of lager from the fridge before joining her at the table.

She piled food onto her plate and took a mouthful. 'That's good, Michael. Bodes well for your roast or paella,' she said, with a smile.

'Thank you for those kind words, Miss, you might get to try my other dishes sometime,' he said, in a little boy voice.

They both laughed.

Fiona filled her glass and took a sip, trying not to think of further intimate meals with Michael. Realistically, they would have no option but to spend a lot of time together while Duncan was at large. He hadn't said anything about when he'd leave, and she preferred not to ask. One day at a time…

They finished the meal as the sun was dipping in the sky and Fiona went around drawing curtains and blinds. After filling the dishwasher, they settled in the sitting room, now safe from prying eyes. It was just after nine, and it could be anytime from now on that Duncan made a move, and Fiona felt the muscles in her neck tighten. Michael, however, looked calm.

'TV's dire, but I've got some DVDs we could watch if you like.'

'Sure. Let's have a look.'

Fiona opened a drawer to display the collection, letting Michael choose.

'Hey, about this? *Life of Brian*, seen it loads of times but still makes me laugh. Okay with you?'

'Fine, I love it too.'

Fiona slipped the disc into the player and switched on the television, before plumping for an easy chair, leaving Michael the sofa. Within minutes they were giggling at the antics of the Monty Python crew. Fiona felt her neck muscles relax and let herself be carried away by the film. By the time it finished, they were both yawning and ready for bed. Upstairs, they arrived outside her room and Fiona hesitated. Michael gave her a quick hug.

'Don't worry, if he does come, remember we'll get ample warning, and I'm nearby. Try and get some sleep, okay?'

She nodded, the thought of Michael sleeping so close causing a mix of emotions. Not helped by the thought that a killer might turn up. He kissed her on the cheek before heading to his room. After brushing her teeth and cleaning her face, she slipped into bed, her mobile within reach. She must have fallen asleep as the next thing she knew her mobile was ringing loudly in her ear. Blearily, she saw it was John, and it was three in the morning.

'Hi, sorry to wake you, but Duncan's heading your way. Switch on the cameras.'

Chapter 32

Guernsey 1941

By early 1941 Leo had settled into the new forced routine of working for the Controlling Committee while enjoying an occasional meal with his friends Clem and Alice Le Page. He was unable to reciprocate the hospitality, not wanting to burden Elsie with the extra work and missed what he thought of as the 'old' life he had shared with Teresa.

As the months dragged by, he began to wonder if the old Guernsey would ever re-surface. German signs proliferated island-wide, and wherever Leo went, there were sure to be German soldiers in evidence. More and more arrived and empty properties belonging to those who had evacuated were commandeered for billeting, while some families were forced to share their homes with officers; not only feeding them but responsible for their laundry. Leo was thankful he'd been spared so far, putting it down to being off the beaten track.

The one bright spot was the arrival of Red Cross messages and Leo eagerly read the first one he received from Teresa. On the standard issue postcard, to be read by censors, she wrote, 'All well with Judith and me and we are enjoying good weather which will mean a good harvest. Judith is walking now and saying a few words. Please write soon. Love Teresa xx'.

Leo found his throat tighten as he read the meagre message. He had missed his daughter taking her first steps and saying her first words. He was both sad and angry, and for a moment a red mist descended, and he had to take deep breaths to calm down. This bloody war!

He looked at the date on the postcard. Two months ago. And his reply would likely take as long. Four months from sending to receiving a reply. Anything could happen in such a time, and neither of them would know. He sat down to write a reply, wanting to catch the next boat to France, from where the Red Cross would pass messages to England. He wrote, 'I'm well, working for the new Controlling Committee. Have closed the shop. Had to stop driving, no fuel. Elsie looking after me. My love to Judith and your parents. Love Leo x'.

Not long after sending this message, Leo had unwelcome visitors to his house. It was early autumn, and the trees had started shedding their golden leaves. Leo was at home, suffering from a heavy cold and not able to face the bike ride into work when a heavy knock sounded on the front door. He dragged himself out of bed, pulled on a dressing gown and opened the door to be faced by two German officers, who brushed past him without a word and began moving from room to room as if sizing them up. Leo's forehead was bathed in sweat, and he sat down, his legs giving way under him as he waited.

'So, Herr Bichard, is it not? I believe you live here alone, is that so?' The older officer, whose uniform declared him to be a major, stood with legs spread and hands behind his back as if he owned the place, Leo thought in disgust.

'Yes, that is true, Major.'

'You must leave, we need it for our troops. More of our men arrive today, and you have much unused space here.'

'But where am I supposed to go? I have no family–'

'That is no concern of mine, Herr Bichard. Please to make sure you have left by fifteen hundred hours.' He turned to leave but stopped. 'Ah, I saw a motor vehicle around the side. It is roadworthy, yes?' His eyes gleamed in anticipation.

Leo's heart sank. The Germans had 'bought' many vehicles since they arrived, paying well below the true value.

'It is, yes.'

'Good, we will require the keys, and you will receive a fair price for it later.' He held out his hand, and Leo shuffled to his study and retrieved the keys from a desk drawer, his mind whirling with how he was to find somewhere to stay in less than two hours. The officer took the keys and, with a brief salute, left. Leo sank back into a chair, his body drenched with sweat. He knew he had been lucky to hang onto his home this long, but it didn't make it any easier to bear. The only good thing was the lack of interest in him personally. As he was dwelling on his options, a voice called from the back door.

'Master Leo! Can I come in?'

'Of course.' He heaved himself upright and took slow steps to the kitchen. He found Elsie placing a covered bowl of soup on the table, looking warily around the room.

'Have they gone? I was about to bring the soup when I saw them arrive in a jeep and thought it best to stay away.'

He told her the reason for their visit and that he needed somewhere to live, and fast.

'Why, that's no problem! You must come and live with me and Bert. You know we have a spare room, and it means I can carry on cooking for you.' Her face creased into a smile and she bustled about, cutting slices of bread to go with the soup. Leo knew it made sense to accept, in fact, he had no other option, but his heart sank at the thought of sharing the tiny cottage with them. He loved Elsie like the mother he never had, but Bert wasn't a man he had any time for. And he'd be beholden to him. Stifling a groan, Leo thanked Elsie before forcing the soup down his throat. His appetite already poor, he could barely swallow thanks to the tightness of his throat.

'While you're eating your lunch, I'll start packing your clothes. And Bert can come and help shift stuff to ours.' She looked around the kitchen. 'Is it all right if I take some of your best pans and china? Don't want those Jerries spoiling Mrs Bichard's lovely things, do we?'

'Of course. Take as much as you want. And if Bert can help me pack a few boxes of our personal belongings, I'll arrange for them to go in storage, so as not to clutter your cottage.' Leo's febrile mind was racing with what he wanted to save from the clutches of the soldiers. For his part, the most valuable possessions were safe, but Teresa would be upset if he didn't manage to salvage as much as possible of her favourite items. Thinking of his wife made his stomach twist. He'd promised to defend their home and property and had failed miserably. But like everyone else in Guernsey, he had no choice but to obey. Gritting his teeth, he pushed back his chair and shuffled to the sitting room to telephone Clem with the news, and to ask about storing his goods.

The three of them had just carried the last items to Elsie's cottage when two jeeps full of soldiers arrived at the house. Leo was swaying on his feet, and sweat poured down his face as he watched the Germans swagger, laughing, into his beautiful home.

'Come on, Master Leo, best not to watch. Those devils will get their comeuppance one day, don't you fear. Let's get you to bed. Bert!'

Chapter 33

Guernsey 2011

For a moment Fiona was frozen, too panicked to move, her heart pounding in her chest. It wasn't until Michael called her name that she came to, jumped out of bed and rushed onto the landing to find Michael, his hair tousled, waiting for her, looking ready for action.

'I heard your phone. He's on the way?'

'Yes, I have to switch the cameras on.' She ran downstairs to the study and switched on her computer before activating the cameras. Michael followed her.

'You okay?' He squeezed her shoulder, and she was glad to be reminded of his presence – and his strength.

'I guess. Just a bit, um, nervous.' The truth was she was scared stiff, but couldn't admit it. If she did, then Michael might insist they cancelled the entrapment. And she owed it to Nigel to do her bit.

'Should we go back to bed? Pretend to be asleep?' She fought to control her body, starting to shake, feeling like the hapless Brian heading for his crucifixion.

'I guess. I assume he'll try and break in. But I'll station myself in your bathroom, to be close. All right?'

She nodded, not trusting herself to speak and they went upstairs to her room. They had just opened the door when her phone rang.

'False alarm. He's been here for a recce, walked up and down the street, presumably looking for signs of the police, went to the front of the house and checked the gate before going back to his car. The police are still tailing him, but I don't think he'll be back tonight as he's on his way home. You two all right?'

Phew! 'Yes. We're fine. A bit jangled from being woken up and...expecting him to turn up. Do you think he's given up completely?'

'No, I doubt it. I guess he wanted to see you were home and there was no sign of police or anyone with you. Remember he only discovered this morning about you finding the owner. My gut instinct is he'll be back tomorrow night. And we'll be waiting. Try and get some sleep. Bye.'

She relayed what John had said, and Michael sat down and grabbed her hands.

'Would you like a brandy? Your hands are shaking.' The concern in his voice nearly unnerved her.

'No, I'm fine. It's the adrenaline rush – fight or flight, and then, puff,' she clicked her fingers, 'nothing happens. Shall I warm up some milk for us? Help us sleep, perhaps?'

He nodded, and they went down to the kitchen, and she heated up two mugs of milk and splashed a tot of brandy in them.

'I'll go back to bed with mine, though I'm not sure I'll sleep. What about you?' She took a sip and began to leave.

'Yeh, I'll do the same. You know, the good thing is, he took the bait. So we know we'll get him when he tries for real. Right?' Michael smiled encouragingly.

'Right.'

Fiona had a restless night, full of weird dreams, waking on Tuesday morning full of foreboding. The memory of the previous night flooded in, and she groaned. Until the phone call from John warning her Duncan was on the way, she hadn't fully accepted the reality of the police trap and what it would be like coming face to face with a killer. It was surreal. Something that happened in police dramas on the telly, not real life. But in that split second, it was real, and it had frightened her. Now today, it was likely to become even more real, when he actually turned up at the house. Sitting up, hugging her knees, Fiona sent up a silent prayer to Nigel, asking him to keep her safe. She'd hoped, now she was home, he would have made contact again, but nothing. Squeezing her eyes shut, she willed him to appear, or give her a sign of his presence. Again, nothing. She dragged herself out of bed and into the shower, trying to wash away the heaviness in her mind and body. It wasn't helped by knowing the vicar was coming round later to finalise Nigel's funeral service. Not for the first time, Fiona wished she could disappear until it was all over.

'You look awful. Bad night?' Michael asked as she entered the kitchen. A pot of coffee was on the table, and he poured her a mug.

'Thanks. Not great, horrible dreams. How about you?'

'Didn't sleep much, but I'm okay.'

'It was some night! Still, as you said, it means Duncan's about to walk into our trap.' She took a swallow of coffee. 'Did I mention the vicar's coming at eleven?' She popped bread in the toaster and leaned against the counter waiting for it to brown.

'Yes, though I'd forgotten. Do you want me to disappear?' He gave her a keen look as if searching for signs of distress.

'No, I'll see him in my study. Do you have plans today?' The toaster disgorged the browned slices, and she carried them to the table.

'I don't think I can go anywhere.' He brushed his hair back, scratching the back of his head. 'Now Duncan's shown his hand; I can't risk leaving the house in case he's in the area. I know the police are tailing him, but they might not be able to alert us in time. But there's nothing to stop you going out.'

She had to agree; they didn't want Duncan catching sight of him.

'Sorry, it's going to be boring for you, stuck here all day. I've got to do a grocery shop, can I pick up anything for you? A magazine or a newspaper?' She ate her toast, slathered with butter and honey the way she liked it.

'A national newspaper would be good, thanks. Otherwise, I could do some weeding for you, now I know which plants are weeds,' he said, with a grin.

Fiona, her mouth full of toast, smiled. Her guest was proving to be pretty useful around the house, unlike some of the men she'd dated over the years. She assumed it was being an only child brought up by a single mother. He'd make someone a great husband one day. She nearly choked on the toast as the thought popped in, unbidden. Where did that come from? Although it was true, she acknowledged, she had no right dwelling on such things. Mind you, it was better than thinking about a possible tangle with a killer.

 Finishing her breakfast she took her dishes to the dishwasher, telling Michael she was off to the supermarket, hardly daring to meet his eyes. She grabbed the shopping bags and left, glad of the excuse to get away for a while.

Forty-five minutes later she was back and carried the bags inside. There was no sign of Michael and guessed he was in the garden. After unloading the groceries, she went outside and found him surrounded by a pile of straggly weeds from one of the beds. She hadn't the heart to tell him some were flowers, not weeds, and went to thank him.

He wiped the sweat from his brow and grinned.

'The exercise is doing me good, and I'm glad to help. It's quite a big garden for one person to keep tidy.'

'Yes, it was fine when Nigel was...around. We shared all the chores. I might think about moving soon, something smaller and with a sea view. And a low maintenance garden,' she added, with a smile. She glanced at her watch. 'The vicar's due any minute, I've left a paper for you in the kitchen if you want a break.' Feeling a bit guilty at leaving Michael working in her garden,

Fiona headed to her study for a quick tidy around before her visitor arrived. On her desk were the notes she'd made about the service. The familiar lump of lead settled in her stomach as she reread it. The doorbell jerked her out of a maudlin reverie and, taking a deep breath, she went through to welcome the vicar.

By the time he left an hour later, Fiona was emotionally drained. The man had been sympathy and kindness personified, and that was probably her undoing. At one time she had subsided into floods of tears, which he assured her was perfectly natural and to just 'let it all out', as he put it.

'People are not good at dealing with grief, I find. The stiff upper lip idea is a load of nonsense. Causes all sorts of problems to hold it in,' the vicar said, balancing a cup of tea on his knee. He was young but seemed wise beyond his years.

'Thank you, I know you're right, but crying can be so exhausting, and I have so much to do,' she replied, blowing her nose.

He nodded.

'When you're ready, tell me more about Nigel. I always say a few words about the deceased, even though I've usually not met them. Mourners like the personal touch, I find.'

They had gone on to discuss her choice of hymns and poems and between them agreed on an Order of Service. She could now have it printed with a recent photo of Nigel, laughing to the camera. It was a favourite of hers, taken last year before the effects of the MS had created lines on his face.

Fiona found Michael in the kitchen making a cup of coffee which he pushed towards her.

'Thought you might need that. You okay?' His eyes searched her face, and she knew it was obvious she'd been crying.

'Not too bad. At least it's another step completed. I have to go to the funeral home this afternoon to give them this,' she waved the sheets of paper, 'and to see Nigel.' She sat and took a sip of the coffee, her mind once more skidding back to her parents' funeral. She and Nigel had visited the Chapel of Rest together to see their parents lying side by side in their coffins, and it had been harrowing. She remembered how her knees trembled at the sight even from the doorway, and Nigel saying she didn't need to go in if she couldn't cope. But, to her, that would have been disrespectful to her parents, and she forced herself to walk forward.

Someone had worked hard to hide the injuries they had suffered in the crash, and their faces bore a healthy colour and looked so peaceful they could have been merely asleep. Fiona had clung onto Nigel's hand as they stood between the coffins and shed their tears. Too overcome to say more than 'Goodbye, I love you' she kissed their ice-cold foreheads and left. Nigel stayed a moment longer before joining her outside.

And now she had to go through it again, and she wasn't sure if she could do it. Now truly alone, this would be much harder. Would someone have worked a miracle on Nigel's poor face? He'd looked anything but peaceful when she found him...she took another swallow of coffee, willing herself to find the inner strength needed.

Michael came up to her, put the cup on the table and lifted her into a hug, not saying a word. Her initial reaction was to pull away, but it felt so good to be held in his strong arms that she allowed herself to relax and stood, semi-supported in his embrace. The deep rhythmic beat of his heart resonated in her ear pressed against his chest, and it was if his strength was flowing into her. Different to the experience with Paul, but equally positive.

'Hey, you were somewhere else, weren't you? Do you want to talk about it?' He released her gently, his arms grazing her shoulders as if he was afraid she would fall if he let go.

'I was remembering my parents lying in their coffins and how hard it was to deal with.' She looked up into his warm brown eyes; seeing compassion and something else she couldn't place. Sitting down, she finished her drink, barely warm.

Michael reclaimed his chair, saying, 'Can't a friend go with you today? I would, but it's not worth the risk of being seen.'

Fiona shook her head.

'It's better if I go alone and anyway, the staff are brilliant. I'm not due to go until two, so how about lunch now? I bought loads of salad stuff.' She rose to make a start, but Michael stopped her.

'Hey, I'll do it. You go outside and relax, and I'll bring the food out shortly. You can let me know if I've missed any particularly aggressive weeds.' He pushed her gently towards the door.

Secretly glad to escape outside, she went through to the garden and wandered around the newly dug flower bed. More poor flowers lay among the pile of weeds, but on the whole, he'd done a great job. A couple more hours and the garden would be weed free. Fiona slumped into a chair and closed her eyes, letting the sun caress her face with its gentle touch. The temperature was rising steadily with the longer days and with June arriving the next day, summer was truly beginning. Normally her favourite time of year, enjoying long, lazy days on the beach at weekends, this year would be different, and she couldn't imagine herself returning to her old routine anytime soon.

The thought of the business loomed large and although Ken's reports were encouraging on the sales front, she knew her heart wasn't in it enough to carry on. 'Sorry, Nigel,' she whispered out loud. 'It was your baby, not mine and I only came along for you. And now...'

A discreet cough from the doorway made her stop, flushing at the thought Michael might have overheard her talking to herself.

'Here we are, *salade niçoise* with crusty bread, washed down with a cold beer.' He began unloading everything onto the table.

'Looks yummy, thanks. Is there no end to your culinary talents?' she asked, a smile hovering around her mouth. She piled the salad on her plate and filled a glass with lager.

'Let's just say my repertoire might not last to the end of the week,' he said, his eyes crinkling.

'I am happy to cook, you know, so don't feel obliged to be Master Chef,' Fiona replied, spearing a piece of tuna.

'Your turn tonight then.'

'Fine by me.' She didn't mind cooking, particularly for someone else, but on her own, she tended to make simple meals with few ingredients. Nigel had loved his food, and she had made an effort to cook nutritious food to help him cope with his illness. It would be good to cook for Michael after being spoilt by Louisa, she thought.

After lunch, Fiona had time to make some calls before leaving for the funeral home. She phoned her closest friends about the funeral arrangements; a notice was to appear in the *Evening Press* the next day. While talking to Jeanne the question of what was to happen after the service arose.

'I hadn't given it any thought, but suppose close friends will come back here. There's no family so won't be many of us.'

'Would you like me to ask Colette to rustle up some refreshments? Her restaurant's closed on Mondays, and I'm sure she'd be willing to help out as well as attend the funeral.'

Colette was Nick's sister and a successful young restaurateur she and Nigel had met several times socially as well as at the restaurant. Fiona liked the idea and agreed Jeanne could ask. She certainly didn't want to do anything herself; they had employed caterers for their parents' funeral knowing they'd be in no state to organise food and drinks. Hoping that would work for Colette, she then phoned Ken to say he'd be welcome at the wake as well as the funeral and he seemed touched by this. The business was closed on Mondays anyway, so that wasn't a problem.

The drive to the funeral home passed in a blur. Fiona wondered afterwards how she'd managed to get there in one piece; her thoughts focused on the imminent sight of her brother. The woman supervising the arrangements, Angela, met her and led her to the Chapel of Rest before leaving her on her own.

Fiona took a deep, steadying breath, and walked over to the open coffin as soft music played in the background and a tall wax candle burned brightly at its head. Nigel's pale face looked unmarked and his brown hair, slightly curly like hers, lay neatly combed on his head. She had chosen his favourite pale grey suit and matched it with a blue shirt and red tie. He could have been asleep, waiting for her to come and wake him. Tears rolled silently down her face as she took her last look at her beloved twin, a pain like a knife twisting in her gut at the unbearable reality of losing part of herself.

'You weren't meant to leave me so soon,' she whispered, stroking his hair. 'You were beating your illness. Oh, if only you hadn't gone to the shop that night! We know who killed you, my darling, and we've set a trap for him. You'll have justice, I promise. Please help me be strong when I face him. I know you can't be by my side the way you used to be, but it would help if I knew you were around.'

She placed a hand on his and kissed the marble-cold forehead. The candle fluttered as if caught in a draught, and for a brief instant a smiling Nigel stood in front of her, his arms held out in an embrace. 'I'm here.' Uttering a cry, she moved towards him, her arms outstretched, but they met only air. He was gone.

Chapter 34

Guernsey 2011

Fiona didn't go straight home. Instead, she made the short journey to Bordeaux to sit in the car and weep. With her head balanced on the steering wheel, she may have looked as if she was taking a nap. Either way, no-one bothered her. She'd managed to stay in control while discussing the Order of Service, flowers and cars with Angela, but knew she couldn't face Michael yet. Or anyone else.

Anguish ripped through her, leaving her limp and exhausted. Slowly, the tears dried and she wiped her face and eyes, catching a glimpse of red, puffy eyes and a red nose in the mirror. She stared out over the sea towards Herm, remembering the time she spent there a week ago. A lifetime. So much had happened since, it was no wonder her emotions were all over the place, she thought. Grieving had taken second place to tracing and then meeting Leo's family and since then carrying out the scary plan to catch Duncan. And then there was Michael's effect on her.

Telling herself she'd go mad if she dwelt on it anymore, Fiona slid out of the car and ordered a large coffee from the kiosk. The barista stared at her as she handed over the drink. Fiona, her head down, almost ran back to the car, collapsing into the seat. As the hot double-strength liquid fizzled through her body, she felt more in control and stepped out of the car to take deep breaths of salty sea air. Ozone and caffeine, that's what she needed. Twenty minutes walking on the beach and she was ready to return home.

The rest of the afternoon dragged on, neither Fiona nor Michael finding it easy to settle. John phoned to check they were all right and to say Duncan had been into St Peter Port for a spot of shopping.

'The tail said he looked totally at ease and not like someone being watched, which is good. He did draw some cash from an ATM giving out UK notes so could be he's planning on leaving soon. My gut feeling still says he'll try tonight. Are you ready?'

Fiona had the mobile on speakerphone and Michael, after catching her eye, said they were.

'Good. Let's hope it's all over soon. Talk later.'

She began pacing around the kitchen, her nerves even more on edge after John's comments. The worst part was not knowing if Duncan would break in or boldly ring the doorbell. Either way, it wasn't easy to plan their response. Michael had to stay out of sight as long as possible, which meant she would be on her own for the crucial first minutes. Oh dear God, what had she let herself in for!

Michael put a hand out to stop her.

'Hey, take it easy. I know it's hard, and I'd gladly swap places with you, but we both know that's not going to work. Just remember, he needs you alive and conscious, so is likely to threaten rather than hurt you. I'll be seconds away if he starts anything, even if we don't get the admission we want, I'll step in. The police could still do him with breaking in or forced entry or whatever.' His gentle voice soothed her and, without thinking, she moved towards him and his arms folded around her. It was good to be held again, and they remained embraced for a couple of minutes before Fiona drew back.

'Thanks, you're right. I'm...I'm a bit emotional after...seeing Nigel and everything.' She forced a smile, moved to the sink and filled a glass of water. Propped against the worktop, she took a deep gulp. Michael, his arms folded across his chest, stood watching her with narrowed eyes.

'I'm not surprised. You're a remarkable woman, Fiona. You've had to deal with so much without any family to support you, and now you're involved in a real-life game of cops and robbers! You have my utmost admiration.' He smiled his warm, lazy smile and she felt the heat rise in her face and turned away, ostensibly to refill her glass but to want to hide the flush. Another gulp of water and she turned around.

'That's kind of you to say. But you just have to get on with it, don't you? And although I don't have a family, I do have wonderful friends, and that includes you. I'm grateful for what you're doing.' There, she'd said it. She did count him as a friend and hoped they'd remain so when he returned home.

'We seem to have formed a mutual admiration society,' he said, laughing. She joined in, glad to ease the serious mood.

'Are you still up for cooking, tonight? I'd be happy to take over if you're not in the mood.'

'No, I'll cook, I'd rather keep busy, and I bought some local beef steaks which are particularly tasty.' She glanced at the clock, surprised to see it was nearly seven. 'I'll start now if you want to have a drink in the garden.'

Michael nodded, taking a lager out of the fridge and went outside while she gathered the ingredients for the meal. It seemed ages since she'd cooked, the last time being a dinner with Nigel before she'd flown to London. Biting her lip, she concentrated on preparing and chopping mushrooms, tomatoes, green beans and new potatoes while allowing the steaks to marinate in red wine. She thought a glass with the meal wouldn't hurt and might help her nerves.

Fiona set the table in the dining room and called Michael to say it was ready. He helped her carry the food in and poured the wine.

'This looks and smells delicious,' he said, filling his plate. 'Fresh air and exercise does wonders for the appetite, doesn't it?' He grinned at her.

'Yes, and thanks for your hard work with the garden, it's looking loads better.' As she sat down and picked up her knife and fork, it suddenly hit her that in a few hours she might be facing a violent Duncan, at his mercy, for a few moments at least. And her hands shook.

'You okay?' Michael asked, reaching to grab one of her hands.

'Not really. Thinking about Duncan...' she trailed off and, removing her hand from his, took a swallow of wine.

'It's hard, I know. If you want to pull out–'

'No! I'll do it. Can't let everyone down. Just my nerves. Honestly.' Fiona forced herself to take a bite of the steak, taking her time to chew it, savour it. Focusing on the food would help take her mind off – later.

'As long as you're sure?'

She nodded.

'Right. We'll get through this, remember we're a team. You're not alone.' He patted her hand and started to eat. 'By the way, this is good. You're not a bad cook,' he said, with a smile.

'Thanks.' Fiona continued eating even though her throat was tight from fear. She'd be no good to anyone if she fainted from lack of food at a crucial moment. They both continued eating in silence, aware of the elephant in the room, by the name of Duncan and neither of them was able to dismiss it. Once they'd finished the main course, Fiona served a fresh fruit salad with a jug of thick Guernsey cream.

Michael emptied his bowl, saying, 'Thank you, that was a great meal. Shall I make us some coffee?'

'Please. You do that while I load the dishwasher.' She wouldn't normally be keen on coffee in the evening, but it could be a long night. They'd agreed to stay up as long as would be normal, about eleven, and would then go to their bedrooms but try and stay awake as long as possible. The coffee made, they headed for the sitting room to watch television. Fortunately, there was a good choice of programmes that evening to keep them entertained, although Fiona sensed the build-up of tension in her neck and shoulders as the sky darkened. Inspector Woods had emailed her a photo of Duncan taken the previous day and his face floated in and out of her mind. Square, close-cropped head, piggy eyes and leathery, lined skin and thin lips. Once seen, never forgotten kind of face. Glancing at Michael, sprawled on the sofa, he appeared absorbed, his eyes glued to the television, only the tapping of his fingers on his leg giving him away. With an inward sigh, she forced herself to focus on the programme, a sitcom she didn't normally watch but had some funny moments. Time dragged on, and it was nearly eleven when her phone rang. Immediately her heart leapt into her throat as she picked it up.

'Hi Fiona, he's on the move so best put on the cameras. I'll ring back in a few minutes to confirm if he's heading this way. Remember, I'll be outside in the van with a couple of officers.'

'Okay, thanks, John.'

Michael sat up, and she relayed John's message before leaving the room to switch on the cameras. She had to stay calm; she had to stay calm, the mantra ran through her head as she moved around, clutching her mobile. Minutes later, John called back.

'He's in Trinity Square, so we're on full alert. An officer's coming in now. You okay?'

'Yes. Just letting him in. Bye.'

She opened the door, and an armed policeman slipped in, nodding at her as she led the way to the door into the garden. Leaving him outside, she returned to find Michael clearing away any signs of his presence in the sitting room, and she quickly checked the kitchen. Nothing showed she had a visitor. He came in and gave her a hug.

'You'll be fine. We've got you covered as they say in the movies. I'll go to my hidey-hole when he arrives. Okay?' She nodded, unable to speak. The hidey-hole was the cupboard under the stairs, cleared to make space for him to stand in without too much discomfort. He had his mobile on silent so John could call him if necessary. Her mobile, also on silent, now vibrated in her hand.

'He's parked down the street and is walking towards the house. It looks as if he'll come to the front door, not carrying any tools. Good luck.'

Michael got ready to enter the cupboard while Fiona returned to the sitting room, where the television entertained an empty room. She just had time to take another gulp of wine when the doorbell rang. Taking deep breaths, she returned to the hall, noting Michael had disappeared under the stairs before opening the door.

She was faced with a large man in dark clothing, wearing a balaclava and pointing a gun at her chest.

Chapter 35

Guernsey 1941–1942

The first full year of the Occupation headed towards a close and no-one, except the Germans, appeared excited about Christmas. With fuel, food and other essential goods heavily rationed, there wasn't much to celebrate. Leo had to endure the humiliation of cycling past his house now filled with loudmouthed, uncouth soldiers, completely different to those who had arrived back in July 1940. From what he could see, these were the dregs of the German army, not deemed fit to be on the front line, but sent to the backwater of the Channel Islands to be in charge of POWs brought in for labouring. When they weren't working, they held drinking parties in the house and Leo dreaded to think what condition his once pristine home was in now.

Another Red Cross message from Teresa had cheered him, but he had hesitated about telling her about their home. In the end, he avoided the subject, not wanting her fretting. The postie knew he lived with Elsie and his mail was automatically delivered to the cottage, so Teresa didn't need to know. Or so he told himself.

The winter weather made the journey to Town on his bike both tiring and uncomfortable, even his heavy winter coat not offering complete protection from the elements. Leo had struggled to shake off his cold, and now the damp weather had led to a chest infection and a permanent cough. Probably not helped by Bert's insistence on smoking a pipe filled with cheap tobacco whenever he could get a supply. Wheezing, Leo left his bike in the rack and headed to the office, hoping someone had found some tea to make a pot.

'Morning, Leo. Grim out there today, isn't it? How are you getting on with the list of supplies needed from France?' Clem greeted him as he warmed his hands over the paraffin stove.

'Morning. I'll have it finished later today, just waiting on the latest figure for yeast. As most of the last consignment was mouldy, we need to make up the deficit, or we'll have no bread.' He threw up his hands. 'The old system worked so much better, with our representatives buying direct. Now, all we receive is the left-overs of the French rations. I dread to think what state the next supply will be in.'

Clem nodded.

'I agree, I can see shortages happening sooner than we planned.' He rubbed his own hands together over the stove, which gave off poor heat for the size of the room. 'Have you been able to dig the vegetables from your garden?'

'Elsie offered the soldiers a deal: we would dig up what was ready as long as we're allowed our share. And she would look after the weeding and planting. I'm not sure she'd be up to it, so I'll lend a hand and try and persuade old Bert to help. He needs a kick up the backside.' Leo frowned as he remembered Bert's pleas of ill health while poor Elsie ran around after him.

Clem made to return to his desk, but stopped, tapping his forehead.

'I nearly forgot, there's a chap waiting for you. Said his name's Ernest and it's about a job. Someone you know?'

Leo groaned.

'Yes, he worked for me and has been pestering me for months as I'd said I would put his name forward for work. But there's been nothing suitable as he has a bad leg.'

'I might be able to help. We're setting up a boot factory, and most of the work can be done sitting down. Ask him to come and see me tomorrow when I'll have more details. It won't be full-time, and the pay is basic but better than nothing, eh?'

Leo thanked him and went to the small waiting area where he found Ernest sitting on a bench twisting his cap in his hands, a sullen expression on his face. He passed on Clem's message, and if he was hoping for gratitude, he was disappointed.

'Part-time, eh? Not going to help much, is it? But I guess beggars can't be choosers, eh, Mr Bichard?' He threw him a surly look and limped out. Leo was left torn between guilt and exasperation and returned to his desk wishing death to all Germans for what they had brought on the Islanders.

In early January Leo was shocked to hear that the *Feldkommandantur* now wished to have a report of the financial affairs of the four registered Jews on the island. So far, they had been left to lead their lives as any other islanders, but this development worried him. Even though he had no reason to think his family history was likely to become known, he couldn't shake off a feeling of apprehension.

On a cold, breezy day in March, his fear was proved justified when Elsie, her eyes wide with fear, knocked on his bedroom door to say there were German soldiers at the door asking for him. Initially, Leo wasn't concerned, assuming it was to do with his house and smiled at the soldiers.

'Herr Bichard, you come with us now. *Bitte.*'

Leo felt the blood drain from his face but strived to remain calm as they escorted him to the parked jeep. When he asked where he was going, the soldier shrugged. The journey into Town seemed to take forever, and Leo's nerves were stretched to breaking point by the time they drew up at Grange Lodge, taken over by the Germans as their administrative offices. He was marched inside and motioned to wait in an anteroom, not a word said. It was thirty minutes later when a soldier came back and signalled Leo to follow him, opening the door to a spacious room holding a desk, filing cabinets and the Major who had commandeered both his house and car. Relief flooded through him. It must be something about the house.

'Sit, Herr Bichard.' The Major, pointed to a chair in front of the desk, his face stern.

Leo attempted a smile.

'Is there a problem with the house, Major?'

He shook his close-cropped head and fixed steely blue eyes on him.

'You have not been honest with us, Herr Bichard. It has come to our attention that you have Jewish blood. Why have you not registered this fact?' He banged his fist on the table.

Leo's mouth went dry, and he licked his lips.

'I am not a Jew, and you must have been misinformed, Major.'

'Is it not the case that your,' he glanced at the notes in front of him, 'French grandmother was Blanche Fournier whose parents were prominent Jews from Paris?'

His heart sank. How on earth had he learnt that? As far as he knew, only his father had known. It wasn't something he ever made public.

'You are right, Major, my grandmother was Blanche, but she renounced the Jewish faith and married a Christian, Jacques Fournier. Their daughter, Adele, married my father Henry Bichard, a Christian Guernseyman. Adele was brought up a Christian, as was I.' He kept his voice calm, but his insides twisted into knots.

The Major waved his hand dismissively.

'It makes no difference if the family has been Christian, the blood of Jews is passed through the female line, and in accordance with the law of the Third Reich, anyone with a Jewish grandmother is counted as a Jew.'

'I can only say, in my defence, I was not aware of such a ruling, and I have only ever considered myself a Christian. Under British and Guernsey Law, I am no Jew.'

The Major glared at him.

'You are now living under the Third Reich and must conform to our law. Your ignorance is no excuse, Herr Bichard, and you must now register as a Jew immediately. Your house will become our legal property.'

Leo's tongue stuck to the roof of his mouth.

'You need to sign these forms, and then you will be taken home.'

He thrust various documents across the desk, neatly typed in German.

'Do I not have the right of appeal? The advice of an advocate?'

The Major shook his head.

'Our decision is final. Now, sign please if you want to return home.'

Leo heard the underlying threat and obeyed, not knowing what he was signing, but wanting to get away from this repressive office.

'Good, you are now free to go. From now, you must obey any further orders concerning the Jews. Understood?'

Leo muttered, 'Yes,' and stood.

The Major gave a dismissive wave and Leo left, to be met by the soldier who had brought him. With a curt nod, the soldier led the way outside to the jeep, and he took a seat in the back. Leo's mind raced during the journey back to Elsie's cottage. Who had betrayed him – and why?

Chapter 36

Guernsey 2011

'What...' Fiona cried, as he pushed her back roughly into the hall, the gun close to her chest, her heart ready to burst out of her ribcage.

'Where's the painting?' His voice was rough, with an unmistakable Australian twang.

'What painting? I don't know...'

'Don't play the innocent with me, or I'll make you regret it.' He pushed her further back until they were in the sitting room. By now she was trembling violently, convinced he would shoot her before anyone could intervene. His eyes darted around the walls before swivelling back to her. Gripping her arm he growled, 'I saw the article in the paper. You and your brother found it, didn't you? In the shop? And it should be mine. So where is it?'

His fierce grip caused pain to run up and down her arm, and she let out a moan.

'How...how did you know it was in the shop?' She managed to twist her body around, so Duncan had his back to the door. Dear God, help me to do this.

'None of your business!' He tightened his grip on her arm, and she moaned again as the pain worsened.

'Did...did you kill my brother?'

'No, why would I? Heard he hung himself, didn't he? Nothing to do with me. Now tell me where it is, or I'll shoot you in your foot. And then the other foot until...'

Fiona barely registered Michael launch himself into the room, grabbing Duncan in a headlock and forcing him to drop the gun. Duncan twisted around, trying to throw him off balance but Michael kept one hand around his neck while reaching down to grab him between his legs, causing Duncan to scream in pain as he crashed to the floor. Just then the police rushed in, hauling a whimpering Duncan to his feet. Within seconds he was in cuffs, the balaclava whipped away, revealing his face. The one in the police photo.

Fiona, drained of adrenaline, felt her knees give, but before she could fall, Michael caught her and pushed her gently onto the sofa.

'Are you okay? Did he hurt you?' His concern took away the last vestiges of her resolve and her eyes watered. Pulling out a tissue from her jeans, she blew her nose and dabbed at her eyes, keeping her head down. She was conscious of Inspector Woods telling Duncan he was under arrest for the suspected murder of Nigel Torode and the armed assault on herself.

Lifting her head, she saw him marched away by a couple of officers. Woods and John, who'd now followed into the room, turned their attention towards her.

'Do you need a doctor? Are you hurt?' Michael asked, forcing her to look at him.

'No, my arm's bruised, that's all.'

Once satisfied she wasn't in need of medical help, Woods left, saying he'd send someone round to take their statements the following morning. Michael disappeared to pour a couple of brandies, and John sat beside her, pulling her into a comforting embrace. Now she could cry, and the tears soaked into John's sweater as he stroked her hair with a murmured, 'It's okay, it's over, let it out. You were so brave; we were all impressed. Well done.'

At that moment Fiona wasn't feeling brave. The whole surreal scene kept replaying in her mind like a broken record, the image of Duncan, hiding behind a balaclava and brandishing a gun, making her body shake. She could only imagine what he'd done to Nigel and how scared he must have been and this made her cry even more.

'Here, drink this, it'll steady you.' Michael thrust a glass of brandy into her hands, and she took a grateful sip, letting the fiery liquid do its work.

'Thanks,' she said, her voice little more than a whisper. John handed her his handkerchief, her tissue a sodden mass, and she blew her nose and wiped her face, conscious she must look a wreck.

John stood, saying he'd leave them to get some sleep and would be in touch in the morning. He patted her arm and Michael escorted him to the front door, locking and bolting it before coming back and sitting beside her.

'Is there anything else I can get you? Glass of water?'

'Yes, please.' Her mouth was so dry it came out in a whisper. He came back a moment later with a full glass, and she drank greedily while he sat beside her, one hand on her shoulder.

'Well, we've done it. The bastard's locked up and you're safe. You were bloody marvellous, Fiona.'

Draining the glass, she raised her eyes to his and managed a weak smile.

'Thanks. I've never been so scared in my life! Seeing him so close, pointing a gun at me, was far worse than I'd imagined. He's a brute,' she said, shivering.

'He is, but you kept going. I couldn't see you, but I heard every word, as I was listening by the door. John alerted me by phone when it was time for me to move in.'

'I've never been so relieved to see anyone in my life! I really thought he'd shoot my foot.' She picked up the brandy for a final sip, willing her body to relax.

'Wouldn't have put it past him. But hey, he didn't get the chance so best not to think about it.' He squeezed her shoulder.

'You were br...brilliant. Have you performed that move before? He was in agony,' she said, recalling Duncan's anguished cry.

'Well, actually, it's not one we practise on each other in case we, er, damage someone. But I've always wanted to try it out.' He grinned, and she found herself laughing. Might have been hysteria, but it felt good.

'Do you want to go to bed? I'm too hyped to sleep and think I'll stay up a while, listen to music or watch TV,' Michael said.

She shook her head.

'I'm not ready for sleep either. Shall we finish off that wine we opened earlier and put some music on?'

'Good idea. You stay there and choose some music while I fetch it.'

Pushing herself up, she was relieved to find her legs had regained their strength and rummaged through the CDs stacked by the player. By the time Michael returned, Adele was blasting from the speakers. They settled down with their wine, listening to the music and going over the events of the evening once more. Eventually, they succumbed to tiredness and went to bed. It was two in the morning.

Fiona woke the next morning after the deepest sleep she'd had for weeks. As consciousness filtered in she was aware of a change in herself, of lightness, of a letting go of a burden. That bastard Duncan had been caught! They'd done it, thanks to John, Michael and the police. It was heady stuff until the familiar ache for Nigel surfaced. Nothing would bring him back, but it was good to have trapped his killer. It was when she slipped into the shower, Fiona saw the deep purple bruises on her arms.

As she entered the kitchen, Michael looked up from filling the cafetiére, and his eyes searched her face. He must have been satisfied with what he saw as he smiled.

'Sleep well? Quite a night wasn't it?' he asked, stirring the coffee. Grabbing two mugs, he sat down, and she pulled up a chair, spreading her sore arms on the table.

'Slept like a log. And yes, it was quite a night.' Her fingers played with specks of food left from last night.

'Thanks again for what you did, Michael. It was pretty impressive stuff.' Fiona grinned at him.

'Glad to have been of service, Madam,' he said with a short bow, keeping a straight face.

She laughed, and he poured the coffee.

'Wish we could chill out this morning, but the police will be here for our statements soon. John's popping round, too. We have to decide what to tell the media.' She took the loaf out of the bread bin. 'Toast?' He nodded, and she placed four slices in the toaster before setting out plates, knives, butter, honey and marmalade. 'Does your family want to remain anonymous as the owners of the Renoir?' Collecting the toast, she returned to the table.

Michael frowned.

'I'd better talk to my grandmother, hadn't thought that far ahead. She's a very private person.'

'I gathered that, but it's going to make headlines.' She sighed. 'Nigel's death will be linked to Duncan's arrest, and the whole story will come out eventually, even if we don't want that. And the news will spread to the nationals...' She sat with her knife hovering over the butter, trying not to think about the likely media attention.

'Oh, Fiona!' Michael grabbed her hand. 'I hate to think of you and Nigel being fodder for the newspapers.'

'I don't like it either, but it's a price worth paying to bring justice for our families. We'll be the usual seven-day wonder, and at the end your family will be financially secure. Not a bad result, eh?' She raised a smile, enjoying the reassuring warmth of his fingers on hers. She would miss him when he left.

'I guess. Let's hope my grandmother agrees, although it doesn't sound as if she has much choice.' He let go of her hand, and they concentrated on finishing their breakfast before Michael disappeared to phone Teresa.

A sergeant arrived a little later and took their statements, saying the inspector would be in touch later.

No sooner had he left than John arrived, giving Fiona a warm hug before asking how she was. The three of them congregated in the kitchen to discuss the aftermath of the previous night's events.

'I don't suppose Duncan's confessed to killing Nigel, has he?' Michael asked.

'Not yet. I spoke to Ron earlier who said he's refusing to talk. But that could change, and anyway, he faces years inside for attacking Fiona last night.' He gave her a reassuring smile. 'Now, what do we tell the *Evening Press*? I think word got out about a major incident last night and Ron's being pressured to make a statement. If we make a joint one, I'd be happy to speak on your behalf and save you facing any intrusion at this time.'

'My grandmother would rather not have her name mentioned, suggesting I be her proxy, saying the painting belonged to my Guernsey grandfather before the war. We appreciate people would like to know more, but given her failing health...' Michael spread his hands.

'Of course, I think that's fair enough. Fiona?' John turned to her.

'Presumably, with Duncan charged with either the attack on me or my brother's death, my name will crop up anyway. So let's admit we found the Renoir in the hidden basement of our shop, and I was the one to have it verified and tracked down the rightful owner.'

John nodded.

'You're right, might as well tell the truth. I can say you hired me and that you wish your privacy to be respected while you grieve for your brother. Okay?'

'Yes. Sounds good.' Fiona twisted her hands together at the thought of the two hurdles ahead; the inquest on Friday and the funeral the following Monday. Only then would she be left in peace to grieve Nigel truly.

'What are your plans, Michael? Are you going home now?'

He looked from John to Fiona before replying. 'I thought I'd stay until after the funeral, to pay my respects to Nigel. I can move into a hotel now Duncan's under lock and key.'

Fiona's stomach flipped. She'd imagined him wanting to rush back to London and was touched and also pleased she didn't have to say goodbye yet.

'There's no need to move out, unless you want to, of course. The house is plenty big enough for two, and I'm not sure I'm ready to be on my own just yet.' She knew she sounded pathetic admitting to it, but it was true. Although a niggling voice in her head did query if it was the sole reason for wanting him to stay.

'Thanks, in that case, I'll stay.' Michael grinned at her, and she felt the heat rise in her face.

John, looking from one to the other, raised his eyebrows but only said that it was time he got going and would be in touch. He shook Michael's hand and went with Fiona to the door.

'I'm glad Michael's staying a bit longer; he's good for you.' He patted her hand, adding, 'I'll write a statement for the *Press* and email it to you for approval. Take care, now.'

Fiona phoned Louisa to bring her up to speed, knowing her friends would be relieved to know Duncan was under arrest. Louisa promised to let the others know and, like John, expressed her pleasure that Michael was staying on for a few days. She also suggested they came round for dinner on Friday and Fiona happily agreed. She'd no sooner put the phone down when it rang.

'Hello, Miss Torode, Inspector Woods. Thanks for your statements, by the way. Are you feeling okay after last night?'

'Yes, I'm fine, thanks. What's the latest on Duncan?'

'Well, he's proving uncooperative, but I'm not worried about it. We've sent both the business card you found and Nigel's belt for DNA testing. We've managed to lift fingerprints off the card and found a match for Duncan's...'

'Why are you checking the belt? I thought he wore gloves?'

'He did, otherwise we'd have found his prints on the alarm at least. We think the prong of the belt buckle caught on a glove, piercing a small hole and nicking a finger. Initially, forensics didn't examine the belt because we thought it was a suicide, but once you and John gave us reason to be unsure, forensics took a closer look. They spotted a piece of skin on the prong, but of course, it could have been your brother's.' A bout of coughing ensued, and Fiona's pulse raced at the possibility the skin was Duncan's. The inspector continued, 'Sorry about that. Where was I? Oh, the buckle, right. Well, forensics checked Duncan's gloves after his arrest, and there's a tiny hole in one of the fingers that matches the size of the prong on the buckle. So, there's a good chance the skin is his and why we're having it checked.'

'That's brilliant! So, assuming it is Duncan's, would that be sufficient proof for a conviction?'

'Yes, for sure. Combined with the fact we have him on tape saying your brother died by hanging, which has never been made public, then we have a good case. We have to wait a week for the DNA results to come back, I'm afraid, but as far as the inquest is concerned, we're likely to get a verdict of unlawful killing. I hope that will be some comfort for you.'

'It will, Inspector, thank you. And when will you and John make a joint statement to the *Press*?'

'Probably tomorrow gives us time to work out something we all agree on. It means it will appear on Friday, the day of the inquest and it's possible there'll be extra interest in the proceedings and you, as the victim's sister. So be warned. I'll keep you posted of any developments.'

Michael listened intently as Fiona told him what the inspector had said and agreed the signs were good for a conviction. Realising it was after one o'clock, Fiona opened the fridge. 'What do you fancy for lunch?'

He jumped up. 'Tell you what, why don't we go out? I noticed lots of cafés and restaurants in Town, and I've been stuck inside since Monday. You can choose.'

'Good idea, I think we both need to do something normal after the last few days.' She grabbed her bag, and they headed off towards George Road and the centre of Town. As they walked, the conversation turned to holidays and their favourite destinations. Fiona was surprised to learn they had similar tastes, both having enjoyed trips to Egypt and Greece. By the time they arrived at Dix Neuf in the Arcade, she was giggling at Michael's shared holiday misadventures. It was both a shock and a relief to find she could still laugh.

◆◆◆

Michael thought he'd better check in on his mother and grandmother and called them that evening from his room.

'Hi, Ma, how's things?'

'Same as usual. Nothing changes here, Michael. Mother's been struggling today, and I could do with more help A carer coming in once a day isn't enough.' A deep sigh echoed down the line. He bit his lip, knowing how hard it was for her, but at the same time wishing she wouldn't be so negative.

'Yes, I've been thinking about that. With the rest of the paintings up for sale, we should have some money coming in soon, enough to pay for a part-time carer. I can fund the cost until we get the proceeds. Give you a bit of a break.'

'That's very generous of you, but are you sure you can afford it?' Judith sounded both hopeful but uncertain. He wasn't surprised as his mother knew there were times when he struggled to make ends meet. But his last commission had paid well, and for once he had some money in the bank.

'Yes, Ma, or I wouldn't have offered. Let me know what it costs for a few hours a day, or whatever works best for you. And before I forget, I'm staying here until Tuesday, the day after Nigel's funeral.'

Judith did not comment other than to ask when he would be visiting them in Suffolk. He didn't commit himself and asked if his grandmother was free to talk to him. Judith took the phone up to Teresa's bedroom and said goodbye.

'Michael, good of you to call. Any news?' Teresa's voice was warm with a hint of excitement. If she was in pain, she hid it well.

He explained the imminent press release would not mention her name, but he couldn't guarantee the media wouldn't do some digging.

'Well, we'll deal with that if it happens. I'm sorrier for poor Fiona, having to face unwanted intrusion at such a time. Lovely girl. Do remind her she'd be very welcome to visit us whenever she's in England.'

'Of course, I've already said as much. She used to ride, and I thought she'd enjoy a hack over the fields. Did you ride when you lived in Guernsey?'

Teresa was always a keen horsewoman, riding until well into her sixties, even teaching him to ride on his fat little pony, Toby. He could picture it now, his grandmother elegant in her immaculate riding clothes, leading him in his less than tidy outfit, across the fields on an unwilling Toby. She had been so patient with him, and Michael had loved the time they spent together. A lump formed in his throat at the thought of her present frailty.

'Yes, a little. Leo wasn't as keen, preferring to drive around in his shiny new MG.' He heard her sigh. 'It was a beautiful car, though. Dark green with cream leather and he drove with the roof down whenever he could. I often wonder what happened to it. No doubt the Germans confiscated it, but it should have been on the island when the war ended. Perhaps that dreadful man Ernest got his sticky hands on it, like everything else.' Teresa's voice was bitter, and Michael wished he could do something to help.

'At least we found the Renoir, Grandmama,' he said gently.

He heard a deep intake of breath.

'You're right. I was being maudlin. It happens when you get as old as I am. And I'm truly grateful for its return. Not just for the money, which will make such a difference to us, I admit, but for Leo. I only wish I could afford to keep it, for his sake, but that's a foolish notion. I think he'd want us to be financially secure rather than poor with a valuable painting hanging on a crumbling wall.'

'I agree. And we can always have a print made as a memento. Now, I'd better leave you to rest. I'll call again in a day or two. Take care.'

The next morning Fiona showed him John's email of the media statement and having read and approved it, she sat down to email John with their agreement to publish.

Michael studied her as she tapped away on the keyboard. She looked more rested, he thought, and her eyes held more of a sparkle. With the inquest the following day, he decided she needed a distraction to keep the current mood alive.

'Shall we go out for the day? I'd love to see more of the island, and Paul told me there are some great bays and beaches in the north-west. We could take a picnic and swim.'

Fiona looked up and smiled.

'Sounds lovely. Give me a minute, and I'll check out the fridge.'

'I'll do it, you carry on.' Michael put together a decent mix of picnic food and included cans of lager and bottles of water and Fiona dug out a cool bag. They collected towels and swimwear, piling everything in the car and set off. Michael wasn't always keen on being driven by someone but had to admit Fiona was a good driver, and he sat back to relax and enjoy the ride. She kept up a running commentary as they headed out of St Peter Port and along what she called Les Banques towards something called The Bridge. He loved the names of places, part French and part parochial English and Fiona explained that the north of the island was initially split in two by a tidal channel, crossed at high tide by a bridge. The channel was drained in the early 1800s, but the name 'The Bridge' remained.

She drove around to L'Ancresse and parked. Out of the car, she stood still, looking out to sea, the wind tousling her hair. A look of sadness had replaced the earlier smiling face, and he joined her, holding her hand as his eyes swept admiringly over the curving expanse of golden sand.

'Are you all right?'

She turned to face him, her eyes troubled.

'This is where Nigel and I use to ride together, and it's reminded me of the inquest and...funeral.'

He drew her into his arms, wanting to comfort her, yes, but also wanting to breathe in her scent, to get close to her. Like they had on the night of Duncan's arrest, spending hours just talking, listening to music. There had been a bond between them, of a shared experience.

'I expect everywhere you go on the island brings back memories, doesn't it?' He continued to hold her, and she seemed happy to stay in his arms.

She sighed.

'You're right. I'll have to get used to it. Hopefully, it will be easier once...it's over.'

He rested his chin on her head and breathed in the smell of her hair, the fruity smell of shampoo mingling with the salt of the air. He dropped a kiss on the top of her head. Fiona pulled back, her eyes locked onto his.

Her face was flushed from the breeze, and he could no longer hold back, lightly kissing her parted lips.

Her eyes opened in surprise.

'Sorry, I hope I haven't upset you.'

She shook her head.

'No, it's fine. Shall we drive on to another bay, sheltered from the wind?'

'Sure.'

They returned to the car, and Fiona carried on driving around the coast, an odd look on her face. Not upset, exactly, more puzzled, he thought. He hoped he hadn't blown it by kissing her so soon, but only time would tell.

Chapter 37

Guernsey 2011

Fiona dressed with care. She hated black so chose a midi-length navy skirt and pale grey blouse with a linen navy jacket. It was the kind of outfit she wore when working at the V&A, but not needed as a partner in an antiques business, more used to organising collections and deliveries of goods. Her face had gained colour from spending time on the beach, and she applied the minimum of make-up; a touch of eyeshadow, mascara and pink lipstick. Her freshly washed hair settled in curls around her head as she checked her reflection.

Sunglasses. Inspector Woods had phoned earlier to say there might be more spectators than usual thanks to the piece in the newspaper that morning and he expected the media to be present. She picked up her sunglasses, large enough to hide behind even though the day was cloudy.

'This might not be the most appropriate thing to say under the circumstances, but I think you look lovely,' Michael greeted her as she arrived downstairs. He was dressed more casually in black jeans and a crisp white cotton shirt.

'Thanks, I thought I'd better make an effort even though I'm not expected to be called as a witness. Oh, is that today's *Press*?' she pointed to the paper on the worktop.

'Yes, John dropped it in while you were changing. Thought we'd like to see it before we left for the inquest. He had to shoot off, but sent his regards.'

Fiona's hands trembled as she picked up the paper. The headline screamed, '*Man arrested for the murder of local antiques shop owner*' and underneath was a picture of the shop with her and Nigel standing in front, smiling at the camera, taken for the article published when they took over the business. Her heart squeezed at the sight of her brother's smiling face, unaware of the horror that lay ahead. Further down the page, after the police statement was a picture of a Renoir painting similar to the one found, accompanied by John's account. The story flowed onto the inside page. Looking up, she saw Michael watching her.

'You okay?'

She pushed the paper away as if it were dirty.

'Fine. It's just a shock seeing it in print. Silly, I know, but until now only a few people knew what happened and now...' she shrugged, aware she couldn't stay under the radar anymore.

Michael eyed the clock.

'The taxi will be here in a minute, are you ready? Remember I'll be sticking to you like glue, and you don't have to talk to anyone if you don't want to. Except the Magistrate.' He grinned encouragingly, and she managed a half-smile. She could do this. She wasn't alone.

In the back of the taxi next to Michael, she thought about the time they had spent together yesterday. His kiss had surprised her but in a good way. The touch of his lips had sparked a frisson of desire in her, leaving her confused. Did he fancy her, or was he just sorry for her? He hadn't kissed her again, seemed a bit quiet, but then so was she. The afternoon had been pleasant enough, but something had changed, and they both knew it.

As anticipated there was a small crowd of people hovering on the steps of The Royal Court and Fiona spotted a woman with a microphone standing by a man with a television camera. Fixing her sunglasses firmly on her nose, she waited for Michael to open the door of the taxi and, holding onto her arm, escort her towards the entrance. Keeping her head down, she let him brush away the questions fired at them as they headed for the door.

Inside she found Inspector Woods waiting with a couple of officers.

'We're through here,' he said, pointing to a door along from the reception. 'No more questions!' he called to the insistent reporters. 'We're here for an inquest, remember. Please wait until afterwards when Mr Collins,' he indicated Michael, 'and I will answer a few questions.' The reporters drew back, and the trio continued down the corridor, the police officers watching for any further nuisance. Fiona found herself pushed gently through the door by the inspector, who pointed out where she was to sit. Michael joined her, grabbing her hand.

'Okay?'

'Yes,' she murmured, glancing around the courtroom. Nearby were seats for the public, and many were filled. The inspector sat to one side with a large folder in front of him. The magistrate arrived, and the proceedings began. Fiona listened as the purpose of the inquest was confirmed to all those present, and the magistrate asked the inspector to offer his report. He stood to read it out, presenting Fiona's witness statement as part of the evidence, followed by the toxicology report and the autopsy report.

The magistrate asked him further questions before summing up. It then took a matter of minutes for him to utter the words, 'Unlawful killing,' and to offer her the court's condolences. It was over. She felt numb and didn't move until Michael pulled at her arm, whispering, 'Let's get out of here.'

The inspector directed them to a back exit while he went out to answer questions from the reporters. Michael escorted her to the entrance of the St James Assembly Hall where they were meeting later in the café. He then returned the short distance to the court to face the reporters.

Fiona took the stairs to the top floor and found a seat by the window to catch the spectacular views over the harbour and islands. She ordered a coffee and finally allowed herself to reflect on what had happened. She wasn't unused to media attention, having held interviews on behalf of the V&A in the past, and the more recent promotion for their business, but this was different. It was as if people wanted to know her innermost thoughts and feelings, to tear away her carefully prepared carapace and see the grief underneath. How dare they! It was her grief, not theirs. Her pain and she'd be damned if she let them try to make capital of it. Anger bubbled up inside until it began to dawn on her the anger was misdirected. It wasn't the prurient curiosity of the public or the media that fuelled her anger; it was the man who had killed her brother. Duncan Domaille. Her hands gripped the cup as she imagined what she wished could be his fate. In her mind, he deserved to hang the way he had killed Nigel, but she knew that wouldn't happen. And she knew she would never forgive him. Slowly, the anger drained away, leaving her empty, as if the air had been sucked out of her body. She jumped as a hand touched her arm.

'Hey, it's only me. You looked miles away. Everything okay?' Michael's eyes were wary, and she felt guilty. After all, he'd borne the brunt of the reporters. He sat next to her.

'I...I realised how angry I am and I have to let it go. It's not going to be easy.' She pulled out a tissue and blew her nose.

'No, it won't, and I understand. I've been there, but not for the same reason. Don't let it destroy you, Fiona, or the bastard will have won.' A waitress hovered into view, and he ordered a coffee. 'We've managed to satisfy the reporters for the moment, although it's clear they'd like to know more than we're saying. I get the impression violent crime is a rarity here.'

'It is, hence the headlines when it does happen.'

Michael's coffee arrived, and he waited until they were alone again before saying, 'They loved the story about the

Renoir and were disappointed neither of us wants to give many details, but they were very polite, saying if in the future we changed our minds, blah di blah.'

Fiona nodded, shocked by her earlier anger at the reporters who were only doing their job.

'What do you want to do this afternoon? Go home and chill out or...?'

'Home, I think. I need to make some calls and then chill before we go to Louisa's for dinner. You don't have to stay with me; you can borrow the car and go for a drive.' Secretly, she wanted to be on her own for a while, to try and get her head sorted.

'Are you sure? Only if you don't mind, I'd quite like to explore a bit more.'

'Fine by me.' She smiled inwardly; sure he couldn't wait to get behind the wheel. It was a man thing.

Monday morning dawned cloudy, but dry and warm and Fiona was glad about the lack of sun. Somehow, it wouldn't have seemed right to bury Nigel on a bright, sunny day, the kind that called people to the beach. Apart from going through the house with the vac and duster, aided by Michael, and some paperwork, she had spent a relaxing weekend. She had sent a cheque to John, with some cash for Andre Bichard, feeling grateful to the man who'd led them to Teresa. There was still loads to do, like sorting out Nigel's clothes and possessions, but she decided to wait until after Michael had left, anticipating the emotional maelstrom that might be unleashed. Today Fiona wanted, needed, to be brave. Much had happened in the weeks since her brother's death and what she craved most were peace and calm. Friends had suggested she take a holiday and the idea was appealing. But not immediately.

After showering Fiona pulled on jeans and a T-shirt. She would change later for the funeral at twelve-thirty. Padding downstairs she found Michael was not yet up so went into the garden with a cup of coffee. The early morning dew moistened the grass and shrubs, and she had to wipe the chair with a tissue before sitting. Birds sang to each other as they did every morning, the avian equivalent to switching on the radio for a mix of news and music, Nigel had said, laughing, one morning a lifetime ago.

'Can you hear the birds, Nigel? I wonder if they're singing a special song for you. You were always the one to make sure they had food in the winter when we were children. And they'd even eat out of your hands.' She sighed, the memory so clear in her head it was painful. Taking a sip of coffee, she tried to close her mind to the memories pushing into her consciousness. One day, she would welcome them, even be able to laugh at the humorous memories which surfaced. But not today. Fiona envied people like the Irish who held riotous wakes for their deceased loved ones, but it wasn't her style. She would honour her brother in her own way and knew he would understand and approve.

As she continued to listen to the birdsong, a single feather fell nearby, landing on a rose bush. She walked over to pick it up. Large and white, like a seagull's, but she couldn't see any in the sky. Something popped into her head, 'A feather is a sign from an angel, watching over you'.

'Is this from you, Nigel? Thank you.' She held it gently in her hand and felt tears prick her eyes. Sniffing, she rubbed her hand roughly across her face, and her nostrils filled with the intense perfume from the rose bush. Fiona bent to support a flower in her hand. Her mother had planted the bush, and it had continued to thrive over the years. A red hybrid tea rose of an unknown variety, it had long been a favourite of Fiona's, and she knew it was the perfect flower to place on Nigel's coffin as it was lowered into the ground.

She went inside for the secateurs and cut a stem with a newly-opened flower head, popping it in a glass of water for later. The feather she placed by Nigel's photo in her study. Coming out, she met Michael at the bottom of the stairs, dressed, like her, in jeans and T-shirt.

'Morning. You're up early, everything okay?'

'Yes, I happened to wake earlier than usual, and I've been in the garden. The birds were in full song, and it was lovely just sitting there listening.' She kept her head averted, not wanting to share what else had occurred.

'I bet. We don't have many birds where I live, lack of trees. I'd noticed how plentiful they are here.' He moved towards the kitchen, asking, 'Have you eaten?'

'No, but I'm ready for something now.'

'You sit down, and I'll do it.'

She was happy to sit and watch him make the toast, pour juice and brew the coffee. His movements were quick and assured, and she could imagine him in the studio, crafting a sculpture. Soon, toast, juice and coffee were placed on the table, and she helped herself.

'I was just thinking; I'd be interested to see that sculpture you sketched out at Moulin Huet when you've finished it. And bronze or marble would be ideal mediums.'

He laughed.

'They would, but bloody expensive! I'll have to see how much the Renoir sells for.' He must have seen her raise her eyebrows. 'Oh, Grandmama has promised me a generous portion of the proceeds, so...' he shrugged his shoulders.

'I'm pleased for you, and you deserve it. Have you had any feedback from Christie's yet?'

'They've contacted a couple of potential buyers who have expressed an interest and will have a viewing when they're in London. Roger did point out it could be weeks or even months, but he remains upbeat about a sale before too long.'

Michael had the tact not to mention the commission she would receive after a sale, for which she was grateful. It seemed like blood money to her but knew she'd be foolish to refuse it. Who could predict the future and when she might be glad of a financial cushion? The thought brought her back to the present and the impending funeral. Finishing the toast, she stood.

'Colette will be here soon with the refreshments for the…wake. I'd better clear the dining table and ensure everything's ready.'

'Hey, don't worry, it'll take a minute to clear, and we did a check last night, remember? The rooms are fine, and anyway, people are likely to go outside if it stays dry. All we have to do is tidy away the breakfast things and then change. I think I told you Colette's bringing a spare suit of Nick's?' She nodded. Michael had only brought casual clothes with him, and Nick had kindly offered to lend him a grey suit, both being of a similar size. Together with Paul and Andy, they had volunteered to be pallbearers and Fiona was pleased to accept.

'Are you still up for giving the eulogy?' Michael asked.

'I…I think so. Paul's offered to take over if I make an idiot of myself, but I'd like to try. It's not that long, anyway.' Fiona bit her lip, remembering how brave Nigel had been reading the eulogy for her parents. She had been a tearful mess, but dear, wonderful Nigel had given the performance of his life, holding back his grief until after the last mourner had left. They had collapsed into each other's arms and cried until they could cry no more. And she was determined not to let him down now.

The doorbell announced Colette's arrival and Fiona went to let her in while Michael tidied the kitchen. Colette, usually a bubbly, chatty girl, was subdued but still gave Fiona a warm hug before bringing in her supplies and setting out the items that wouldn't spoil. The rest went into the fridge until the mourners arrived. Between them, they set out glasses and bottles of wine and spirits, together with cups and saucers for tea and coffee drinkers.

'There, that's all done. I'll shoot off from the chapel as soon as I can, so will be here when you get back. Oh, Michael, I nearly forgot the suit. It's in the car.' Colette rushed outside, followed by Michael, who came back carrying a suit in a dry-cleaning bag. They looked at each other for a moment, and he said, softly, 'Time to get changed.'

She nodded and went upstairs to her room. After slipping out of her clothes, she pulled on the outfit she'd worn for the inquest before carefully applying her make-up. Her hand shook as she put on the lipstick and had to steady herself. Standing back from the mirror, she picked up her handbag and popped in tissues and the typed eulogy. There was no hat.

Michael was waiting for her in the kitchen. She hardly recognised him in a suit and tie, thinking he looked quite dashing.

'The car's due in five minutes. Would you like a little Dutch courage?' He held up a bottle of brandy.

'Yes, please.' She smiled in spite of herself. It was if he could read her mind. The brandy coursed through her, bringing a fiery boost to her nerves.

'Good, it's brought some colour to your cheeks. And I think that's the cars arriving. Ready?'

Putting his hand under her elbow, he steered her to the front door. Fiona caught her breath at the sight of the sleek black hearse carrying the coffin, topped with her wreath of red, white and gold flowers forming the Guernsey flag. She had asked for no flowers from other mourners, asking for donations to the MS Society instead. Clutching the single rose, she walked past the coffin, and with moist eyes, took a seat in the second car. Michael sat beside her, gripping her hand. The hearse moved off, and they followed behind, driving at a sombre, stately pace.

The journey was not long; taking them up Prince Albert Road, along Mount Row and then right into King's Road, leading to Route Isabelle and Le Foulon. Fiona noted the courtesy shown by other drivers and saw the few men wearing hats doff them as they passed. She had to dab at her eyes occasionally, drawing on all her strength to stay calm.

'You're doing very well,' Michael whispered, with an encouraging smile.

The hearse approached the stone arch at the entrance to the cemetery, slowing down even further. Angela, the funeral director, stepped out of the hearse, taking up her position in front of it carrying a long black cane. She set a slow walking pace for the cars to follow, looking dignified in a dark grey skirt, tall black boots, black coat and a black silk top hat. As they neared the chapel entrance, Fiona spotted a crowd of people outside, none of whom she recognised, along with the group of her friends and acquaintances. Then she saw the vicar standing next to Nick, Paul and Andy waiting for the coffin. Their driver stopped and opened her door, and she walked towards the vicar with Michael by her side.

'Good afternoon, Fiona. We have quite a crowd here, I believe not only those who knew Nigel, but others who had heard of his tragic death and wanted to pay their respects,' the vicar nodded towards the crowd waiting quietly to the side. 'It will be a tight fit, but I pray we can seat everyone.' He shook her hand and smiled.

'Thank you.' She nodded towards the waiting pallbearers before her friends gathered around her, ready to enter the chapel. They exchanged quick, muted greetings before Angela gently ushered her inside, her friends forming a tight-knit group around her.

She took a seat in the front row, and as there were no other family members present, friends filled the rest of the seats, flowing over to the other rows. Empty seats at the front were reserved for the pallbearers. On all the seats had been placed the Order of Service and Fiona gripped her copy as Louisa sat on one side of her and Jeanne on the other, with Charlotte further along.

'What a super photo of Nigel,' said Jeanne, breaking the ice.

'Yes, isn't it? Hope he'd approve of my choice and...everything.' Fiona managed to reply, as a lump formed in her throat. How on earth was she going to be able to give the eulogy if she struggled to talk to her friend? Wishing she had a flask of that wonderful brandy to hand, she tried taking deep breaths instead.

'He'd be very proud of you, Fiona, just as we all are. And look at how full the chapel is now. They're not just paying their respects to Nigel, you know, but to you as well.' Louisa tilted her head, and Fiona followed her, seeing the chapel was full. She was both awed and scared. Even more faces focusing on her. Her face must have registered her fear, as Louisa said, 'Don't worry about how many are here. Just talk to us, your friends, as if we were the only ones present.'

She had no more time to think about it as the organ started up, indicating the arrival of the coffin, preceded by the vicar. Everyone stood as the service began.

Forty minutes later, Fiona followed the coffin as it was borne away in preparation for the internment. She was strangely calm and had read the eulogy without mishap, although tears had threatened more than once. As she had paused, towards the middle, she knew with absolute certainty that Nigel was standing beside her in the pulpit. Turning her head slightly, she saw him, as clear and as solid as the congregation. He was smiling and looked happy. Her heart skipped a beat, and she wanted to say something, but couldn't. Nigel whispered, 'Thanks, Sis, you did me proud. Mum and Dad are waiting. Time to say goodbye.' She felt a light touch on her cheek, like a kiss, and he was gone.

It took her a moment to compose herself before continuing her speech, experiencing a calmness which stayed with her as she took her seat to a spontaneous round of applause. Even the vicar joined in before leading them in the final hymn.

As Fiona stood at the chapel door, the mourners filed past, offering their condolences one by one. She thanked them for coming, the sea of strangers surging past. Then the friends and acquaintances staying for the internment came out, offering hugs, handshakes and kisses as appropriate. Together they followed the coffin, led by the vicar to the grave. Fiona remained calm, hugging to herself the last image of her brother and his words. It wasn't until the vicar had intoned the final prayers that her composure cracked and as she threw the rose onto the lowered coffin tears seeped out of her eyes. Michael, on her left, must have noticed and gave her arm a squeeze.

'You're doing brilliantly, but it's okay to cry.'

She nodded, reaching into her bag for a tissue. It was time to leave her beloved twin in his new resting place.

Chapter 38

Guernsey 2011

By the time Fiona and Michael arrived back at the house, Colette had let herself in with the spare key and finished setting out the food. A young woman, Jess, joined her, who worked in her restaurant and between them would serve as waitresses, leaving Fiona free to concentrate on her guests. Colette hugged her.

'Lovely service and I think most of us were in tears after your beautiful eulogy. You must be shattered; do you want tea or something stronger? Or I could pour a drop of whisky in a cup of tea?'

'Think I'll go for the last one, thanks.' Fiona smiled, not sure how it would taste but past caring, just wanting to get through this last ordeal. She was soon handed a cup by Colette while Jess served Michael with whisky. Fiona took a sip and gasped. Catching Colette's grinning face, she guessed there was more than a mere drop of whisky in the tea. But did it matter? Desperate for something to stop her stomach rumbling, she went to check the wonderful array of food in the dining room, Michael at her heels. Spoilt for choice, she settled on a couple of blinis topped with smoked salmon, soured cream and a sprig of dill, followed by a mini pizza.

'I needed that. Help yourself, Michael, it's delicious. I might not get much time to eat once everyone arrives.'

The sound of cars pulling in the drive made her swallow the last bite.

'Here, you've some cream on your lip.' He grabbed a napkin and gently wiped her mouth.

Fiona, feeling self-conscious, nodded her thanks, before walking to the front door. Colette was already in place with a tray of drinks to offer mourners. She gave

Fiona a thumbs-up as Jess opened the door and stood back. At least, Fiona told herself, she knew everyone coming, and most were close friends. Fiona greeted everyone as they arrived, encouraging them to take a drink and help themselves to food. It wasn't long before the house began to fill and some moved outside. The day remained dry, and a watery sun poked through the clouds. She stood for a moment to take a breath of fresh air and noticed John and Inspector Woods huddled together.

'Thanks again for coming, Inspector. I'm sure you must be a busy man.'

'It was the least I could do and a very moving service, if I may say so.' He balanced a cup of tea in one hand while sharing a plate with John.

Looking around to make sure they were not overheard, she said, 'May I ask if there's any news? Has Duncan said anything yet?'

He grimaced.

'Fraid not. That bas...Domaille still refuses to say anything. Even his advocate's losing patience with him. He's not doing himself any favours by keeping shtum. But we're expecting the DNA results back in a day or two, which will push the case forward.' He gulped his tea.

'Good.' She turned to John, with a smile. 'Looks like your job's finished. I'm so grateful for everything, John. You went above and beyond your remit.' She leaned forward and kissed him on the cheek.

He cleared his throat.

'It was a team effort, and you more than played your part, Fiona. I shall miss working for and with you. I – oh, someone wants to talk to you.' He nodded to someone behind her, and she turned to see Ken hovering nearby.

'Fiona, may I have a word?' Ken, dressed in sombre black, looked uncomfortable.

'Of course, let's move over there, where it's quiet.' She pointed towards the bottom of the garden, for the moment empty of people.

'I have to leave soon, but I wanted to express my condolences properly and ask if our arrangement is to continue.'

'Thank you, and I'm happy for you to run the shop. I...I don't know what my plans are yet, but I do know I couldn't come back yet.'

His face cleared.

'Oh, that is good news. Or rather, I'm sorry you aren't feeling ready yet, but I am so enjoying the work, and I have quite got my feet under the table, as it were. It's a pleasure to go in every day, and my wife seems much happier with me no longer under her feet.' He gave an awkward laugh.

Fiona could understand the wife's feelings.

'I'm sorry I haven't kept in touch much lately, but life has been...complicated. How are the sales? And have you notified local collectors about the Naftel and Toplis paintings?'

Ken rubbed his hands.

'Sales have been extremely good, far better than when I helped out Mr Domaille. And we're selling to visitors, not just locals. And I've already heard from one collector keen to purchase several of the paintings.'

'That's good. Look, I want us to have a proper chat when I'm feeling less stressed. Can I give you a ring to arrange a time? Probably sometime next week?'

'Certainly, I do appreciate this is not the right time for business.' He shook her hand with some vigour before making his way back to the house. Fiona let out a sigh. Ken was hard work, but his enthusiasm for the business had given her an idea. She was in thoughtful mood as she returned to mingle with her friends. Louisa and Paul were talking to Louisa's father Malcolm and his wife Gillian, and she joined them. She had spoken only briefly to

Malcolm earlier and wanted to catch up properly. A tall bear of a man, he exuded an ease that belied his wealth and business success. Catching sight of her, he threw an arm around her shoulders, squeezing them.

'How are you doing, my dear? I was just asking Louisa what your plans are, but she didn't know.' Three pairs of eyes swivelled towards her.

'That's because I don't have any, yet. And isn't it true that you shouldn't make big decisions when you're grieving?'

'Absolutely! I can certainly vouch for that,' Malcolm said, glancing at Louisa who nodded her agreement. 'What you need is to do nothing for a while, and we all thought it would be a good idea if you spent a week with us at La Folie. On the house, naturally,' he grinned.

She was taken aback. La Folie was the epitome of luxury, with prices to match.

'I...I don't know what to say, Malcolm. You're very kind...'

'Nonsense, you know darn well I can afford it, and I won't take no for an answer. Our friend John's been telling me what you've been going through and we don't want you cracking up, do we, Gillian?' He turned to his wife, a semi-retired doctor who oversaw treatment at the centre, and had been involved in Nigel's therapy.

Gillian winked at her.

'You may as well say yes, Fiona, my husband tends to get his own way.'

Paul and Louisa both chipped in with a 'yes, he does!'

'It seems I'm outnumbered. Thank you, I'd be delighted to come and stay.'

'Good, that's fixed. Paul will sort out the details with you later.' Malcolm patted her arm before excusing himself to talk to another guest. Just then Michael appeared at her side, thrusting a glass of wine in her hand.

'I noticed you hadn't had a drink for ages and thought you'd probably need one by now.'

'Thanks, I do.' She took a grateful swallow as Louisa told him about Malcolm's offer.

'What a great idea. To be honest, I was worried how you'd be on your own, and now I know you'll be in good hands, I can relax,' he said, smiling.

She was touched. More and more he showed what a caring man he was. Before she could reply, another guest came up to take their farewell and Fiona spent the next twenty minutes saying goodbye to various people. Only a handful of her closest friends remained, and she found it hard to maintain any meaningful conversations. A wash of tiredness swept over her, and it must have shown on her face as Paul suggested they all leave and let her rest.

'It's been hard, I know, but you've done marvellously, and now it's time to look after yourself. There's a room available from Thursday for a week, and I'll personally ensure you receive full-on pampering,' Paul grinned as he gave her a goodbye hug.

Within minutes she was alone with Michael, while Colette and Jess cleared up in the kitchen.

'Go on up to bed; I'll supervise here.' He gave her a gentle push towards the stairs, and she was glad to go. By the time she reached her room, not only was her body telling her how tired it was, but her heart was silently screaming in pain. She wanted oblivion.

It was still light when she finally woke and for a moment wondered why she was in bed during the day. As memories rushed in, Fiona curled into a ball, eyes tight shut, wanting to reclaim her deep sleep. But her brain wouldn't allow it, and she gave in, swinging her legs over the side of the bed and stood, stretching her arms over her head. Glancing at the clock, she was shocked to see it was after seven. Thinking Michael would be wanting dinner, she slipped into jeans and a loose top, pushed her feet into sandals and dragged a brush through her hair. By the time she was on the stairs, the aroma of something cooking had drifted up to meet her. Pushing open the kitchen door, she saw Michael standing at the hob, stirring what she now recognised as a bolognese sauce, next to a pot of simmering pasta.

'Good sleep? I wasn't sure whether or not to wake you, so was going to leave you some to heat up later.' His eyes locked onto hers, but he continued stirring the sauce.

'I slept well, thanks. Absolutely shattered. That smells amazing, so I'll happily join you.' She looked around the kitchen, immaculate apart from the area around him. 'Colette get off okay?'

'Yep, those two worked hard before they left. Anything worth keeping's in the fridge, and she left us a special dessert, apparently one of your favourites from her restaurant. A kind of syllabub, Colette said.'

'Ah! *Du Lait Cailli Êputhé*! Yes, it's gorgeous and full of booze, a local concoction which I'm sure you'll love. It was very kind of her.' Fiona chewed her lip as she filled a glass of water. It was humbling to receive so much kindness, even from people she hardly knew. But tragedy seemed to bring out the best in people, as she had found when her parents died. She stood drinking the water, watching but not entirely seeing Michael as he added herbs and wine to the sauce.

'You okay? You look miles away.'

'Just thinking.' She gave him a half smile. Although physically different, in some ways he reminded her of Nigel: caring and intelligent; happy to help in the kitchen; keen on art in all its myriad forms; rising above past loss. She knew they would have got on like a house on fire and wished they'd had the chance to meet. If only...she had to stop herself from going there. That way lay madness. Painful as it was, she had to accept what had happened and get on with her life. And at this moment in time an attractive, intelligent man was making her a delicious dinner, for which she was suitably grateful.

'May as well eat in here, I think, and I'd love a glass of that wine, please.'

Michael obliged by pouring her a large glass as she set the table, ready for what would be their last supper together in her house. A dispiriting thought, which she brushed away. Enjoy the moment, girl, she told herself.

Michael's flight was late morning, giving them time for a leisurely breakfast, which they shared outside. The sun had returned in a cloudless sky, and Fiona could already sense it would be a hot, beach-ready day. Not that she was in the mood for the beach, or much else if it came to it. Acknowledging it wasn't an entirely healthy comparison, she saw herself as a wounded animal, hiding away to lick their wounds. And with Michael about to leave, she was free to do just that.

Glancing across at him as they drank their coffee, he looked almost as miserable as she felt. His usual lazy smile had disappeared, and his brows were drawn together in a frown. They had hardly exchanged a word that morning, and Fiona knew it was just as much her fault as his. Over dinner last night, Michael had played the perfect host, even though that should have been her role. His attempts to take her mind off the events of the day by telling her stories of his student days raised only the odd half-hearted smile. Now she wondered if he regretted staying so long and she felt a pang of guilt for not telling him how much of a difference it had made having him there. She cleared her throat.

'Michael, I know I haven't said much, and I'm a poor host at the moment, but I'd like to say how much I appreciate all you've done over the past ten days. You've been a super guest and...and great company. I...I'm not sure I would have coped as well without you.' She looked down and took a gulp of coffee, hoping the heat rising in her neck didn't show. As he didn't immediately respond, she risked a glance at him. The frown had cleared, and he was staring at her.

'I, oh well, it was nothing. I only did what anyone else would have done under the difficult circumstances. And you've been a lovely host. To be honest, I'm sorry to be leaving, and I shall miss both you and this beautiful island of yours. I hope to return one day, in happier times.' His smile lit up his face, and her stomach flipped.

'You should; there's a lot of Guernsey you haven't explored, as well as the other islands.' She waved her arm roughly in the direction of Herm and Sark. 'Once the Renoir's sold you'd more than be able to afford to stay at one of the premier hotels or even La Folie if you're looking for serious pampering,' Fiona said, a smile tugging at her lips.

Michael laughed.

'Sounds like you've had enough of me staying here!'

She tried to say that wasn't what she meant, but he put his hand up, saying, 'Only kidding! And you're right; it might be fun to enjoy some luxury for a while. I'll be interested in hearing how you fare at Malcolm's place. I know a lot of wealthy people I would recommend it to if it's good.'

'Take my word for it; it's excellent. Charlotte swears it saved her sanity the couple of times she was a guest.' Fiona finished her coffee, glad she had opened up and grateful for the change in their mood. She so wanted them to part friends.

Michael stood, saying, 'I'd better get my stuff, we need to leave soon, I think.'

Fiona nodded and began clearing the table, piling the pots onto a large tray. She'd loaded the dishwasher and tidied the kitchen before Michael arrived in the doorway. Grabbing her bag, she headed outside to the car. The drive to the airport took less than fifteen minutes, and it passed in silence as if neither knew what to say as they approached the inevitable goodbye. Michael stared out of the window, barely glancing in her direction while she concentrated on the road, not particularly busy at this time of day. A leaden weight began to take root in her belly as she turned in at the airport entrance and drove to the terminal. She parked the car and Michael grabbed his bag. They stood awkwardly on the pavement.

'I can only stop here to drop you off, so…' she faltered.

'This is it then. Goodbye, Fiona, we're staying in touch right?' She nodded as he dropped his bag before putting his arms around her. 'Good, I'll ring you later.' Moving back, he lifted her chin and planted a lingering kiss on her lips. Before she could say anything, he turned and was gone, swallowed by the revolving door. She stood rooted to the spot, the taste of his lips on hers leaving her shaken. It was only the approach of a security man which goaded her to move. Once in the car, she touched her lips briefly, before starting the engine. The kiss had again stirred something buried deep inside her, and she was afraid of what it meant. And what, if anything, it meant to Michael.

Chapter 39

Guernsey April 1942

During the next few weeks Leo watched for any further public announcements regarding Jews, but none came. Clem had approached him at work to say the Germans had advised the Controlling Committee of Leo's new status and expressed his shock and dismay.

'Your father never mentioned his wife's background, except to say she was a wealthy young French woman. And she was delightful; it was clear to all Henry married for love, not money. Even if we'd known of her heritage, none of us would have cared. It's only in the twisted minds of the Nazis that Jews are considered second-rate people.'

'Will I be able to continue working for the Committee? I'd be lost without something to do.'

'Of course! The Jerries did try to have you removed, but we pointed out how invaluable your work was, for both the Germans as well as islanders and they backed down. We only wish we could help more, but our hands are tied while we live under martial law.'

Leo appreciated his friend's support, but still felt vulnerable and began to lose his appetite due to the stress of his situation. Elsie did her best to tempt him with her cooking, made harder with the reduction of rations for islanders. The Occupation forces continued to receive more generous rations and as all their food was paid for by Guernsey, this only added to the building unrest. The puzzle of who had betrayed him continued to haunt Leo. Initially, he had even wondered if it had been Elsie or Bert. But when he had confided in Elsie about what the Germans had found out, she had been genuinely shocked.

'Oh, my lord! I had no idea. Your father never said a word, and why should he? It was his business, no-one else's. And you've no idea of who could have done such a thing?' Leo shook his head, relieved it wasn't her. 'Well, Master Leo, whoever it is should be strung up. And when this war's over, and them buggers leave, that'll happen to anyone who was a traitor.'

As time passed Leo lost weight, and his persistent cough worsened. By the time the final blow fell, he had also lost heart.

On 17th April a soldier handed him a letter from the *Feldkommandatur*. In English, it commanded him to report at St Peter Port Harbour on 21st April prior to deportation to France. The words leapt out of the page, and he dropped the letter as if it had scorched his hand. Deported! He'd heard of others who had been sent to France and not heard of again. Rumours circulated of concentration camps filled with Jews from conquered countries and Leo guessed that would be his fate. He took the letter to the President of the Controlling Committee who promised to protest in the strongest possible terms, telling him not to worry, they couldn't treat a Guernseyman in this way.

The next day he heard the Germans had refused to change their ruling and he was to be deported with three other Jews and an American lady. His last few days on Guernsey were painful, Leo convincing himself he'd never return. Would never see his beloved wife and daughter again. His friends rallied around, telling him not to give up hope, but he could only shake his head in sorrow. He continued to work, in spite of his now poor health, not able to face being stuck in the cottage all day with Elsie and Bert. She was inconsolable, and her tears made him feel wretched.

When the day arrived, Clem had arranged for a car belonging to a doctor to pick him up and take him to the harbour, where Clem and Alice and a few other friends from work were waiting to see him off. It was a subdued farewell, and his fellow deportees looked as miserable as himself. They were ushered aboard the ship by armed soldiers and quickly bundled below decks. Leo managed to take one last look and spotted a familiar face in the small crowd gathered on the dock. His eyes widened in shock. Ernest's broad smile told him everything. Before he could shout out, he was pushed down the steps, wondering again if he would ever return to his beloved homeland.

Chapter 40

Guernsey 2011

For the rest of the morning, Fiona moped around, feeling deflated and weepy. She knew it was natural after the heightened emotions of the funeral and the excitement of Duncan's arrest, but it didn't help her mood one jot. After lunch, she forced herself to clean the house, and it kept her fully engaged until she walked into Nigel's bedroom.

His presence was still there, in his pictures, the photos on his desk, his laptop and other paraphernalia. She opened his wardrobe and smelt the scent of him lingering on his clothes. It wasn't his aftershave so much as the smell of his skin. Fiona pulled out a jacket, burying her face in it and the tears fell. Falling onto the bed, she pulled the jacket around her and curled into a ball.

'I miss you so much, darling brother, it hurts,' she said to the empty room, half-hoping Nigel would appear with words of comfort. But the room remained silent and in her heart, she knew he was gone. Gone to whatever place dead people went to. Brushing away her tears she hung the jacket on its hanger and left the room. It was too soon to think about clearing out his clothes. It could wait until after her stay at La Folie. If she was still going. A big part of her wanted to hide away and not be among other people. She would phone Louisa later and tell her.

Dragging the vacuum cleaner behind her, Fiona entered the guest bedroom, hit by a blast of Michael's aftershave. Going into the en suite, she saw a broken bottle of *Chanel Pour Monsieur* in the waste bin. He must have forgotten to tell her. Not that it mattered, she thought, leaving the bin on the landing to take downstairs. She went back and opened the window before stripping the bed, trying not to imagine Michael lying between the sheets still impregnated with his smell. Different to Nigel's but, she realised with a shock, just as evocative. She was in love with him! The realisation hit her like a physical blow and Fiona crumpled to the floor, her back resting against the bed. Of course, she'd known she fancied him, but in love? The kiss – both kisses – had stirred something she couldn't ignore. Her emotions were all over the place, and it seemed almost obscene to fall in love when Nigel had died so horribly. Was she confusing love with grief? The thoughts circled her head making her dizzy. With an exasperated sigh, she stood and, grabbing the dirty bedlinen and the bin went downstairs to the utility room. Once the washing machine was on and the broken bottle safely wrapped in newspaper, Fiona poured herself a glass of wine before going outside. Flopping onto a lounger, she had taken a large swallow when her phone rang.

'Hi, it's me. Just calling to say I'm back home. How are you?'

Fiona took another sip before replying, trying to calm the thumping in her chest. How could she talk to him now? After what she'd just discovered?'

'Oh, okay, thanks.'

'You don't sound okay, what's the matter?'

If only he knew! Her hands shook, and she had to put the glass down.

'Nothing, just, you know, it's been a bit odd.'

'I see. Have you been out? Done anything?'

'Been busy cleaning the house–'

'Oh, sorry, I forgot to tell you about the bottle I dropped. Did you find it?'

'I smelt it first, but no worries, it's now safely in the bin.' She could still smell his aftershave, pervading the house as if to remind her of him. Clearing her throat, she asked, 'Have you spoken to your family?'

'Yes, they're fine. Ma has taken on a part-time carer to help with Grandmama, and they both said to remind you to come and visit when you feel up to it.'

'Thank them for me, please. Are you working on the commission again?'

Michael told her he was and chatted for another minute before signing off. Fiona was left unsettled and picked up her wine and took a large swallow. It had been difficult to be at ease with him, even on the phone. And she couldn't contemplate spending time with him at the family home in Suffolk, much as she'd like to see Teresa again. Deciding the best course of action was to forget it all and get hammered, she topped up her glass.

Fiona must have nodded off because the strident melody of her phone woke her. As she pulled herself upright, her head pounded in protest.

'Hello.'

'Fiona, it's Louisa. Are you okay? You sound a bit odd.'

She cleared her throat. 'I...I fell asleep in the garden after a glass of wine.' Looking at the bottle, it was more like four or five glasses, and she stifled a groan.

'Right. We've all done it!' Louisa chuckled. 'I wanted to check how you were. Assume Michael got off okay?'

'Yes, he rang me a while ago to say he was home.' Fiona hesitated. 'Actually, I'm glad you rang as I was thinking of maybe not coming to La Folie. I'm not sure I could cope with being around people.'

She heard Louisa sigh.

'I was afraid you'd say that, but are you sure you can cope on your own? To be honest, girl, you don't sound as if you are. How much did you really drink?' Louisa's voice was soft.

''Bout half a bottle or so. Just wanted to blot it all out. I'll be fine.' Fiona didn't believe it but didn't want her friend worrying.

'Eventually, sure, but what about over the next week or so? I went completely to pieces after Mum's funeral, and that's why we thought being cared for at the centre would do you good. You don't have to mix with the other guests if you don't want to. Simply enjoy good food, uplifting therapies and no need to lift a finger. Come on, what's not to like?'

She had to agree; it did sound more inviting than sitting around wallowing in misery with a permanent hangover.

'Okay, you win. Sorry, I'm being such a pain.'

'Don't be silly. You're grieving, which is horrid, especially on your own. Now, promise me you'll keep it together until Thursday? Easy on the ol' vino?'

'I promise. Thanks, Louisa, you're a star.'

'No problem. I'll ring tomorrow for an update, and we'll expect you at La Folie about ten on Thursday. Bye.'

Fiona weaved her way into the kitchen and drank a large glass of water. Time to get a grip and make some supper.

Fiona was in the middle of catching up on her emails on Wednesday morning when the phone rang.

'Good morning, Miss Torode, Inspector Woods. At last, I have some good news...' he broke off overtaken by a coughing fit. Fiona tapped her fingers on the desk, impatient to hear more. Recovered, he continued, 'Sorry about that. Yes, we've got the DNA results back, and Domaille's DNA matches that found on the belt and the business card. We've got him by the...I mean, the evidence is conclusive, and I've charged him with the murder of your brother as well as the assault on yourself.' His voice rose in triumph.

She punched the air, silently crying, 'Yes!'

'Brilliant, Inspector. Thank you for believing me against the odds.'

'It's me who should be thanking you. After all, if it hadn't been for you and John's detective work, we'd never have nailed him, and that would have been a gross injustice. The trial's set for two months' time, and as yet Domaille hasn't entered a plea. Faced with the evidence, I'm hopeful he'll plead guilty and save everyone a load of trouble. His advocate's meeting with him later to tell him the good news.' He chuckled, and Fiona smiled.

'Will I need to be a witness?'

'Only if he pleads not guilty, so don't worry for the moment. Your friend Mr Collins will be needed, too. Will keep you posted. Bye for now.'

'I've got you justice, Nigel,' she whispered to the empty room. 'Now you can truly rest in peace.'

◆◆◆

Michael frowned. There was something not quite right about the bit he was working on. He stood back to gain a better perspective and eyed the contorted twists of metal critically. What was it? His phone rang, disturbing his concentration and he swore. Tempted to ignore it, he glanced at the screen and saw her name.

'Hi, Fiona. How're you doing? Sleep well last night?' All worries about the sculpture dissolved, replaced by the pleasure of hearing her voice, even though they'd only spoken the previous evening.

'I'm fine, thanks and had a good night. And I've heard from the inspector...' She told him about the DNA results, and he heard the relief in her voice.

'Great news, I'm pleased. So now you can go off on your retreat and forget about it, and come back a new woman.'

'Don't know about that, but I am looking forward to switching off. Which reminds me, mobiles are frowned on, as are laptops, so I'll be under the radar for the week.'

'Right, let's catch up when you're back. Look forward to hearing all about it.'

After switching off his phone, he propped himself on the edge of his desk, gazing unseeingly at the sculpture of the giant sunflower. Fiona. She'd hardly been off his mind since he left Guernsey. No-one had had this effect on him since...and that was years ago. Which meant he must be falling for her – in a big way. It was madness; he'd only met her two weeks ago. But they'd shared so much in such a short time, including the potentially life-threatening encounter with that thug Duncan. Had that heightened his feelings towards her? Running his hands through his hair, he didn't know the answer. Although he'd miss talking to her for the next week, it might give him a chance to stand back, get a clearer take on what he felt. His eyes finally registered the sculpture, and he saw what was wrong. Two strips of metal needed moving down a bit. Smiling, he took up his tools and began work.

◆◆◆

By Thursday morning Fiona was looking forward to getting away from the house and felt almost cheerful as she loaded her case in the car before setting off to Torteval. Soft white clouds dotted the sky and the day promised to be warm. She'd packed her bathers ready to use the indoor pool which also had a sliding roof for fine days. Louisa had shown her around soon after they met and Fiona had been envious of the guests strolling around looking relaxed and carefree. And now it was her turn.

Half an hour later Fiona stood in the beautiful room which was to be hers for the week, gazing at a sublime view of the gardens leading to the cliffs and beyond the sea. Breathtaking. All the rooms had names rather than numbers, and hers was *Serenity*. She could certainly do with some of that, she thought, admiring the golden maple wood furniture and soft-toned polished plaster walls. A room as serene as its name. The silk-draped four-poster looked deeply inviting, and the en suite oozed

Anne Allen

luxury, complete with a walk-in power shower. Fiona sighed. She would have been mad to turn this week down.

She met Paul in his office later to discuss treatments, including an aromatherapy massage each day as well as sessions of yoga or Pilates, all aimed at ultimate relaxation. He also suggested counselling by their therapist Molly, and she agreed to try it.

The days slid by in a sybaritic haze and by the end of the week, Fiona felt lighter; mentally, emotionally and physically. She had found the counselling painful at first, but Molly had drawn her gently through the grieving process, allowing her to know it was okay to cry at times but not to let it take over completely.

In the last few days, Fiona managed to join with other guests in the dining room, enjoying normal conversations about work and partners, or, in her case, the lack of them. She couldn't help think about Michael, but was he a possible partner? Or simply a kind, caring man who wanted to help her cope with grief. The thoughts unsettled her, and she had to push them away, or she'd go mad.

It was good to laugh again, and Fiona promised to stay in touch with a couple of the women she met based in London. The city had figured large in their chats, and it brought home to her how much she missed it. On her last full day, Fiona wrote a list of changes she wanted to make in her life and resolved to make a start once she was home.

'It's been wonderful! I can't thank you and the staff enough, Paul. I'm almost reluctant to leave,' she said, smiling. They were in the entrance hall, her case by her side.

'That's what I like to hear. You're looking so much better, Fiona, and I think you're on the right path now. But you know you can talk to Louisa or me anytime, right?' He gripped her shoulders; his amazing eyes focused on hers.

'Yes. I'd like to thank Malcolm for his generosity, but what do you give a multi-millionaire?' She laughed.

'Did you know he's set up a charity for children in India, to help with their education? I'm sure a donation would be much appreciated. Here's the web address if you want to go ahead.' He grabbed a piece of paper from the desk and wrote it down.

'Perfect, I'll do that. Would you two like to come for supper at the weekend? I owe you both big time.'

'Love to. I'll check with the boss lady and get back to you.' He gave her a goodbye hug, and she left, finally ready to face living on her own again.

Chapter 41

Guernsey 2011

The first change Fiona planned concerned the business, and she arranged to meet Ken after hours on Thursday evening in the shop. She hadn't been in since the day they found the Australian business card and was a little apprehensive about how she'd feel. The Closed sign was up, and she used her key to open the door, setting off the bell. A quick look around allayed her fears, and she smiled as Ken came out of the office. After an exchange of pleasantries, she suggested they adjourn to a nearby pub. Once settled with their drinks she came straight to the point.

'How would you feel about becoming a partner in the business, Ken?'

His eyes opened wide.

'Well, this is a surprise! In fact, I was afraid you'd changed your mind about taking over again.' He sipped his beer. 'I'm honoured to be asked, but my savings are not likely to be sufficient for me to become an equal partner. What were you thinking?'

'My thought was a split to suit us both. I don't wish to pry, but do you have any money you could invest, even a relatively small amount?

She could see him performing a mental calculation and hid a smile. He was interested, for sure.

'I'd have to confer with my lady wife, of course, but I do have money tied up in other investments which I could release.' He tapped his glass, looking thoughtful. 'Would somewhere around forty thousand be considered sufficient?'

'Yes. I'd rather have you as a partner than sell the business, which could take ages. I want to have minimum involvement in the day to day running of it as I have other priorities. And of course, you'd still receive a salary plus a share of profits, which, judging by recent figures, are looking pretty healthy. We can draw up a contract through our advocates to ensure it's fair to us both. What do you think?'

The gleam in Ken's eyes was her answer.

'I would be pleased to go ahead, assuming my wife agrees. As she seems happy with my working again, I don't anticipate much of an issue.' He frowned. 'What happens if you do decide to sell in the future? Where would that leave me?'

'I don't think it's likely, as I can afford to keep it as an investment. There's more chance you will want to retire, and then we could sell the business and share the profit. Okay?'

He nodded and raised his glass.

'I'll drink to that!'

Fiona raised hers, breathing a sigh of relief. First step accomplished.

The next on her list was to devote more time writing the book for the V&A, which would also mean spending time at the museum for research. Now her reason for being in Guernsey had gone, Fiona was rethinking her priorities. On Friday she phoned her old boss at the museum to say she was back on board with the book and what would be the chances of her taking up her old post. Told they would be delighted to consider her return in some capacity but would need to discuss it further, face to face, she said she'd be over shortly.

Deciding it was time to talk it over with someone, she phoned Charlotte, who invited her round for coffee. Fiona's stomach fluttered with excitement at the thought of taking back control of her life, aware of how much she had sacrificed for her brother. Willingly, and if he were still alive, would continue to do so, but now...now it was time to do what was best for her.

'My, you look well! La Folie's worked its magic again, I see,' Charlotte greeted her at the door, smiling broadly as they hugged.

'Now I understand why you keep singing its praises. It was fab, and I even spotted a couple of celebs.'

'Oooh, do tell. Let's have coffee in the garden, and you can tell me more. James is having a nap so we won't be disturbed.'

Fiona filled her in on the details of her stay and Charlotte listened with rapt attention, nodding and making occasional comments. When she finished, Charlotte sighed, saying, 'I know it's selfish of me, but there are times when I'd like to retreat there for a few days. James is teething, and we're all having sleepless nights. The thought of all that pampering!' She took a sip of coffee and looked at Fiona, her head tilted.

'You've something more to talk about than La Folie. Come on, tell Aunty Charlotte.'

'Yep. While I was there, I came to the conclusion I need to make changes in my life. Big changes. Like selling my house and buying something smaller with a sea view and buying or renting a flat in London as I might be working at the V&A again.'

Charlotte's elegant eyebrows arched.

'Wow, that is a big change, and I can understand why you want to do it. I always felt you were not totally happy about leaving London. You seemed so passionate about your work. Have you spoken to the museum?'

Fiona told her about her phone call and what she'd arranged with Ken.

'Sounds like it's all happening.' Her eyes narrowed. 'Does this decision have anything to do with a certain sculptor based in London?'

She felt the heat rise to her cheeks and quickly took a swallow of coffee.

'No... I mean we're good friends and everything, but nothing happened between us unless you count a couple of kisses.'

'Come on; it's as clear as day you two fancy each other. If you hadn't been grieving, I think Michael would have been happy to more than kiss you,' she said, grinning. 'I'm right, aren't I?'

'I guess. His, er, kiss, was pretty incredible.' Even thinking about it made her pulse race.

'So, has he said anything about meeting up again?'

She told her about the open invite to stay in Suffolk and that they'd agreed to stay in touch.

'I think he's taking it slowly, because of Nigel. I noticed at the wake how his eyes kept following you around. Spending more time in London would make it easy for you two to get together.'

'It would, but that wasn't my reason for wanting to go back.' Fiona heard a voice in her head say 'you sure?' and shifted on the chair.

'Well, for whatever reason, or reasons,' Charlotte said, grinning, 'I think it's the right decision, much as I'd miss you. But don't buy or rent in London yet, you're welcome to stay at my house for as long as you need. Mrs T doesn't have much to do these days; my mother only makes an occasional foray into town, and we only go over once a month or so. Give yourself time to see how it pans out.'

Fiona was taken aback.

'It's very generous of you, Charlotte, but I don't want to impose...'

Her friend waved her hand dismissively.

'Nonsense. You've stayed several times in the past, and Mrs T thinks you're a pleasure to have around. I won't take no for an answer. At least your friends will know you're safe and well looked after. And as your publisher, I have a vested interest in your welfare.'

Fiona reached over and hugged Charlotte, feeling blessed to have such a friend.

'Thank you.'

'Right, that's settled. Now, you said something about buying a smaller place here. Does this mean you'll come back regularly?'

'Absolutely. I might be able to work three weeks out of four in London and come back here for a week. I'm not giving up Guernsey entirely; it's in my blood.'

Charlotte clapped her hands.

'Good, then we'll still see you. So, what's the next step?'

'I plan to have an agent value my house and take it from there. Whatever happens, I know I have to move. It holds too many memories and is too big for one person. My dream is a small cottage or apartment either by the sea or with a view like yours.' She swept her arm, encompassing Cobo Bay spread out below them.

'When you're ready, I'd love to go house-hunting with you. I adore nosing into people's homes. Such fun!'

Fiona was happy to agree. All she had to do now was talk to an agent. And arrange a trip to London to discuss her job.

It was amazing, she thought, fastening the seat belt on the plane, how quickly things happened once you'd set the ball rolling. In one of his lectures at La Folie, Paul had told his audience that once you'd made your intentions clear about what you wanted or needed, then the universe would work with you to achieve it. This had had a powerful effect on Fiona and prompted her to write the list of new goals. A mere week later, she was on the way to London to see her boss at the V&A, had put her house on the market and left Charlotte to draw up a list of possible new homes. And she was to have dinner with Michael that evening. Her toes curled in pleasure at the memory of their phone conversation two days before.

'You're planning to work in London again? That's great! We'll be able to catch up with each other, if you'd like to, that is.' He sounded genuinely pleased.

'Yes, I'd love to. I'm flying over on Thursday and will be staying at Charlotte's in Bloomsbury for a few days. There are loads to tell you, so much has happened this past week.'

'I'm intrigued, and I have my own news to share. How about dinner on Thursday night? I'll book somewhere local to you if you give me the address.'

Fiona told him, and Michael promised to call once he'd booked, which he did on Wednesday. Now she was on the way and wasn't sure which was exciting her the most – taking up her old job or seeing Michael again. Tough call.

Chapter 42

Guernsey April 1942

Ernest caught Leo's look of shock just before he was bundled below deck and laughed. Even if Leo suspected him of being the informer, he'd never be able to prove it, assuming he came back alive. As he limped away from the harbour, Ernest congratulated himself on his sweet revenge against the man he considered responsible for his ill-fortune. No job for over eighteen months and then only a scrappy, horrible job in a boot factory! When he'd been as good as the manager of the premium antiques business in Guernsey. Even now, the anger ate away at him and he clenched his fists wishing he could have punched Leo's face before he left, hopefully never to return.

Ernest stopped to allow a troop of soldiers to pass, nodding at one who he'd befriended. Fritz grinned, making a sign of drinking. Ernest smiled. They were due to meet that evening for a drink, and he looked forward to it, mainly because the German paid. He was also good company, speaking decent English, unlike many of the Jerries. Ernest didn't have many local friends, and for some reason, he and Fritz had hit it off from the start. In fact, it was him who had, unwittingly, given Ernest the idea of betraying Leo.

Fritz got drunk one night and told him about what was happening to the Jews on Hitler's orders. They were sent to concentration camps where most of them were killed in gas chambers, even the kids, Fritz had said, laughing. A die-hard Nazi, he agreed with Herr Hitler the Jews had to be exterminated. Ernest had listened in horrified fascination. He had nothing against Jews himself, had hardly met any in Guernsey and those he had seemed the

291

same as everyone else. But listening to his friend reminded Ernest of a conversation he'd overheard years before, between Leo and his father, Henry.

They were in the office at the back of the shop and Ernest, a young lad not long out of school had just started work there and had been upstairs in the attic checking stock. As he came down, he heard the men talking and, being nosy, took up a position within hearing distance but out of sight.

'I wish I'd met Mother's family, Father. They sound so interesting. Fancy living in Paris rather than a tiny island like Guernsey.'

'Well, I only met Adele's parents, not her Jewish grandparents, who had died a year or two before and left Blanche, your grandmother, their fortune. Blanche had rejected Judaism and converted to Christianity when she married Jacques Fournier. Great patrons of the arts they were, which is why they had Renoir paint that picture of your mother, Adele with her brother and sister. Hang on to that, my lad, it's a piece of family history. Not many can say Renoir painted their mother.'

'I will, I promise.' There was a pause. 'You've never said how you met Mother. Was it here?'

Ernest heard Henry light up a cigar and take a deep draw on it.

'No, I'd gone to Paris to look for stock. French style was all the rage and customers wanted more. I was talking to the owner of an antiques business when Adele walked in with a friend. The owner introduced us, and we ended up going to a café for a drink. We became friends, and I met her parents, the Fourniers. Lovely couple, I had no idea how wealthy they were. It was only later I learnt about Blanche's parents having been wealthy Jews.'

'I–'

The shop bell tinkled, and Ernest quickly retraced his steps and made as if he was just coming down when Leo came out of the office to welcome the customer.

Ernest had always prided himself on his memory, and he'd never forgotten what he heard that day, even though it hadn't seemed important. It was just something else to squirrel away in his brain with all kinds of titbits gathered over the years. When he heard that the Germans were targeting Jews in Guernsey, he saw his chance and arranged through Fritz to meet an officer. After spilling out what he knew, he was dismissed without any reward, and he had to content himself with providing his own. If Leo were to return, Ernest planned to steal some of the smaller paintings or ornaments they had hidden in the safe place; not much, but enough to bring him a decent sum of money. If he didn't return, but Teresa did, he planned to tell her Leo had sold him the business before he was deported and would show her a forged sale document to prove it. Whatever happened, Ernest meant to give that snooty Leo Bichard a metaphorical bloody nose. And make himself some money in the process.

Chapter 43

London June 2011

Michael arrived at the Bloomsbury address in a state of near panic. Normally unfazed by anything, for some reason he was nervous about seeing Fiona again after the two weeks break. He knew his feelings for her were strong and their kiss at the airport had melted his insides. By the look on her face, she had felt something too. And now she planned to move back to London; they could have a proper relationship. Which was what he wanted, but also slightly scared him. He didn't want to be hurt again. As he stood on the doorstep of the imposing Georgian town house, he took a deep breath before pushing the bell.

The impressive mahogany door opened and Fiona stood there, smiling and looking gorgeous in a silk purple blouse and a short black skirt.

'Hi, good to see you. Come in.'

He stepped inside, barely registering the beauty of the entrance hall, his eyes on Fiona. Taking a step forward, he kissed her mouth, gently holding her arms. He felt her respond and they stood, lips pressed together for several seconds before he pulled back with a smile.

'Hi, it's good to see you, too. And you look fantastic. That week at the retreat seems to have done you good.'

'It was amazing. I'll tell you more over dinner, and you can tell me your news. Let me grab my bag and a jacket.'

He watched as she collected her things from a large, antique table in the middle of the spacious hall, at the same time taking in the exquisite proportions of the hall and staircase.

'This is some place Charlotte has. Beats my tiny flat in Battersea,' he grinned.

'It's been in the family for yonks, probably like your farmhouse.' Slipping on her jacket before he could help her, she added, 'Shall we go?'

The restaurant, a bustling Greek bistro, was in a neighbouring street, and they arrived five minutes later. As they were shown to their corner table, Fiona remarked how she loved Greek food, giving him a dazzling smile. Michael felt the previous nervousness dissolve and began to relax. While they perused the menu, he ordered two glasses of champagne. Fiona's eyebrows rose.

'Are we celebrating something?'

'Sort of. We've had a nibble from a buyer for the Renoir, and we'll have a definite answer in a week, but Christie's are pretty confident it'll be a yes. So, three and a half million pounds is worth celebrating, don't you think?'

'Definitely, I'm so pleased for you all. And I've been offered a contract with the V&A, so we both have cause to celebrate.'

'That's great, we...' The waiter arrived with their champagne, and they touched glasses before taking a sip.

'Lovely. I'm so pleased you asked me to dinner, it's a perfect way to celebrate my return to the big smoke.' She smiled at him over the rim of her flute.

He cleared his throat.

'It's my pleasure. Now, I want to hear all about your plans. What about the business and your house?'

His eyes never left her face as she explained about the changes she was making. Not only was he mesmerised by her animated expression, but he was also impressed with what she'd already accomplished and how clear-headed she was compared to a couple of weeks ago. She was to start her job mid-July, a little over two weeks away, so not long to wait, he thought, pleased. Occasionally, he caught sight of the sadness at the back of her eyes, particularly when she mentioned Nigel, and she would become quiet as if her mind was elsewhere. But she soon rallied, and he managed to make her laugh at a joke he'd heard recently.

They talked about his family and their plans once the sale of the painting went through and the evening sped by. All too soon it was time to escort Fiona back home, and he kept his hand on her elbow as they walked the few yards to Charlotte's house. The evening was warm, with a cloudless sky, and Michael wanted so much for it not to end. They stood on the steps to say goodnight, and he pulled her towards him, before lifting her chin for a kiss. As she opened her mouth, he let his tongue probe hers, and the kiss lasted until Fiona drew back, laughing, saying she needed air.

Pushing her hair back from her face, he said, 'That was nice. I wouldn't mind more of that.'

Fiona looked wistful.

'Me too, but I can't ask you in...'

'Hey, I understand. But when you're back next month, can we go out together? As a couple? I'd love for us to get to know each other better if it's okay with you.'

'It's very okay with me. In the meantime there's the phone, we can keep in touch.' She smiled, tracing her finger down his cheek.

'We will, I promise.'

Epilogue

Guernsey – late September 2011

'Well, what do you think?'

'I think it's stunning and you're lucky to have bought it. What a view!' Michael said as they stood on the balcony of the brand new apartment at Cobo, admiring the bay spread out before them.

'It ticks both boxes, great sea view and only yards to the beach, and you're right, I am lucky. If my house hadn't sold so quickly, I might have missed it. I owe Charlotte for telling me it had come back on the market.' Fiona swung round to take in the open plan living area inside, waiting for her to fill with furniture and the items she'd kept from the family home. She bit her lips, thinking how painful it'd been to clear out, particularly Nigel's possessions. Many tears were shed that day. But the good news was Duncan pleading guilty and sentenced to life imprisonment. Now, she had a clean slate, ready for a new life.

'You okay?' Michael's warm voice in her ear brought her back to the present as he threw his arms around her.

'A bit maudlin. Letting go...'

'I understand. You've done brilliantly, darling. You've achieved so much these past few months, that you take my breath away.' He smiled, the lovely lazy smile she'd come to love.

'Flatterer! It's not been easy, but I'm pleased. I'm in a good space now.' She meant it. Her job at the museum was rewarding, and she was happy with the progress on the book. But the best thing in her life was the man by her side. No question. They'd become closer over the weeks, and she spent most weekends at his flat if they weren't in Suffolk. Michael had first taken her there in early July, and it was a complete contrast to her initial visit with John.

The Renoir had been sold, and everyone was in celebratory mood.

'Welcome, Fiona. It's good to see you again,' said Teresa, vivacious in spite of the wheelchair. Judith smiled, and they all shook hands.

'I'm glad to be back to help you celebrate. It's brilliant news.' She looked around, a mischievous smile on her lips. 'Have you booked the builders yet?'

Teresa laughed.

'Yes! The list's been drawn up, and we can't wait to get started. Although it will mean much noise and mess and Judith and I will need to move out for a while, more's the pity. Now, sit down and tell us how things are with you, my dear.'

Michael disappeared while she chatted with them, reappearing a few minutes later to hand her an envelope. On opening it, she found a cheque for £350,000.

'Oh! Thank you, Mrs Bichard. It's very generous of you. I'd have been happy just to see you reunited with your painting.' It was true, it had been a pleasure to help the family, and through the painting, she had met Michael.

'We owe you so much more than money, my dear. As you probably noticed,' she pointed to the wall, where a painting glowed with vivid colour, 'we have had a fine art print made, and Michael promises to pass it down to his children one day. Not quite the same as having the original, but we don't have to worry about insuring it,' she smiled.

'Hey! You've wandered off somewhere again.' Michael tapped her arm playfully.

'Sorry, I was thinking about Suffolk and your family. The building work must be finishing soon, and I can't wait to see the transformation.'

'Nor I. In the meantime, it looks as if you'll be busy furnishing this place so you can move in. Excited?' He held her tight.

'You bet. It'll be great to have my own space again after staying in other people's homes for weeks. I was beginning to feel like a displaced person,' she said, half seriously.

Michael frowned.

'I hadn't thought of it like that, but you're right. You'll be able to come here every month now. Lucky you,' he said, his eyes on the view.

'You can come, too. If you can take time out from your work, it would do you good to chill. Time off to plan your sculptures.'

He looked thoughtful, and she wondered if she'd presumed too much. Their relationship was still young, and they didn't live together, so perhaps...

'I've been thinking; it seems silly you staying at Charlotte's when I've got my flat. And Grandmama has given me a share of the sale proceeds, and I want to buy something bigger, perhaps a house with a studio in the garden.' He cleared his throat. 'What I'm trying to say is, would you like to move in with me, my darling? If it works out, we could, you know, one day consider a permanent arrangement.' His smile was tentative, and her stomach flip-flopped. Not quite a proposal, far too soon, but a first step.

'Yes, of course, I'd like to. Will next week be too soon?'

THE END

COMING NEXT
The Inheritance

The story begins in 1860s Guernsey, when a young widow, Eugenie, starts working for the famous writer, Victor Hugo, as a copyist, forming a close friendship with him and his mistress, Juliette Drouet. She later remarries, and her house is passed down the generations until, in 2012, it is inherited by Tess, a young doctor living in Devon.

Looking for a fresh start, Tess decides to move back to Guernsey and live in the house bequeathed to her by her Great-Aunt. The house has not been touched for sixty years, and in the course of renovation, Tess discovers Eugenie's journal and various items once belonging to Monsieur Hugo. The story of Eugenie's friendship with the great man had been part of the family history, embellished over time. Tess now uncovers the truth behind the rumours as she faces her own struggles.

Made in the USA
Middletown, DE
10 August 2022